TAKEN, NOT DESTROYED

Armas Locas Series

Book 1

S VON

Copyright © 2024 by S Von

All rights reserved.

No part of this book may be reproduced in any form or by any electronic or mechanical means, including information storage and retrieval systems, without written permission from the author, except for the use of brief quotations in a book review.

This is a work of fiction. Unless otherwise indicated, all the names, characters, businesses, places, events and incidents in this book are either the product of the author's imagination or used in a fictitious manner. Any resemblance to actual persons, living or dead, or actual events is purely coincidental.

No AI Training: Without in any way citing the author's exclusive rights under copyright, any use of this publication to "train" generative artificial intelligence (AI) technologies to generate text is expressly prohibited. The author reserves all rights to license use of this work for generative AI training and development of machine learning language models.

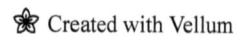

❦ Created with Vellum

- Editor
  - By the by Editing Services
- Page edge design
  - Painted Wings Publishing Services
- Cover design
  - Miblart

Triggers And Tropes

This novel may contain scenes and descriptive adult content that might be triggering for some readers. Please proceed with caution. Visit my website for further details.

For my husband.... Thank you for being my rock. For listening, giving advice, tolerating my moods and just loving me.
For Sarah... thank you for being the best editor a first time author could've been blessed with meeting. This book is as much mine as it is yours. I was blessed to have found you and we have a great many words in our future.
And to all those in the dark romance community - good girl!

Contents

Untitled	iii
Triggers And Tropes	1
Prologue	7
1. Raella	11
2. Raella	18
3. Raella	25
4. Raella	33
5. Raella	42
6. Segundo	50
7. Raella	56
8. Raella	63
9. Raella	71
10. Segundo	79
11. Tulipán	88
12. Segundo	95
13. Tulipán	102
14. Tulipán	109
15. Tulipán	115
16. Tulipán	120
17. Tulipán	126
18. Segundo	131
19. Segundo	136
20. Tulipán	141
21. Segundo	147
22. Tulipán	153
23. Tulipán	159
24. Segundo	165
25. Tulipán	171
26. Segundo	178
27. Tulipán	185
28. Tulipán	192
29. Tulipán	198
30. Tulipán	205
31. Segundo	210
Epilogue	216

Afterword	222
Author note	225

Prologue

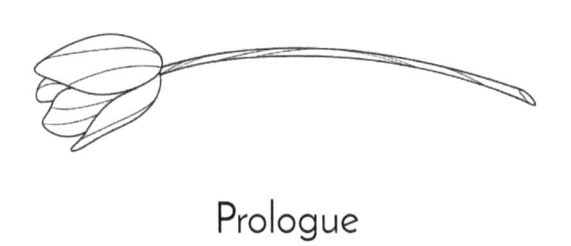

I closed my eyes and took a deep breath, praying that when I opened them again, I wouldn't see my reflection. I wanted to wake from the nightmare and be back in my bed. Even though my life wasn't perfect, it was better than where I'd been for the past few weeks. Where they'd taken me against my will. I blew that breath out and opened my eyes, slowly, with that prayer still in my heart.

A wall of mirrors stretched out across the entire wall in front of me. A pair of blue eyes gazed back at me, filled with anguish, bordering on defeat. It was the face of a woman I almost didn't recognize anymore. I'd never considered myself a go-getter or a fighter, but when I believed in something, I could be stubborn. *She's stubborn as a mule*, was what my mom used to mutter behind my back.

A dark form moved behind me, and my gaze shifted until it landed on him. On the man who was responsible for me being there. I shifted and pulled at my arms, which were secured to a cage-like device that held them extended out to my sides in the form of a T. The movement pulled at my shoulders, sending tingling pains down to my right thumb. I moaned and relaxed my arms.

The dark-haired, dark-skinned man met my gaze in the mirror. His ebony eyes were like black pits that led straight to the gates of Hell.

Evil radiated off him. I still had no idea what he wanted from me or why I was here.

"Wh—" I started to say, but before I could get one word out the man growled, reached behind him, and whipped out a gold-plated handgun.

He pointed it at me, curling his lip up into a sneer. The skull and gun tattoo on his neck writhed as his muscles flexed.

My whole body began to shake. I knew this man was dangerous from the moment I saw him. I tried to shrink, to make myself smaller, less of a target, but the leather cuffs strapped to my ankles and arms made it impossible. I whimpered and lowered my gaze.

I have to survive this!

I heard movement behind me, then two male voices, the words too quiet to make out.

All the small muscles in my arms shook; there was nothing I could to do stop it. It took everything inside me to not look in the mirror, to see what he was doing behind me. A trail of sweat made its way down my back despite the cool air in the large warehouse-like room.

This evening had started out bad, gotten worse, and now the potential for my death was real. This couldn't happen. I couldn't die like this, not without speaking to my family just one last time. A single tear escaped from the corner of my eye and made a path down my cheek.

"You disobeyed me." His low growl came from directly behind me.

I jolted at his nearness, then lifted my gaze and found him standing just to my left with a black, stick-like instrument in his right hand. I tried to look around him in the mirror to see who the other voice belonged to, but his presence dominated the space around me. I couldn't take a proper breath.

His dark blue, button-up shirt hung open, exposing the toned muscle of his heavily tattooed chest. He kept my gaze prisoner in the mirror as he prowled around me. Sweat beaded on my forehead and ran down the side of my face. The tear I'd shed earlier forgotten, along with my family and any thoughts beyond surviving this asshole.

When he stepped in front of me, his gaze dropped, assessing every

Taken, not Destroyed

inch of my scantily clad body. The outfit he'd chosen for me to wear consisted of straps of cloth that connected to cover my nipples and genitals, but nothing else. My cheeks heated as I dropped my gaze to his bare feet, noticing the small hairs on his big toes, hoping he couldn't read my emotions.

Suddenly, his strong, tattooed fingers gripped my chin and tipped my head up, forcing me to meet his soulless gaze. His touch sent my stomach crashing to the ground. Nothing good came from his touch.

"Who do you belong to?" He'd asked me this before.

"Y-you," I choked out, knowing the answer that would satisfy him, even if I didn't believe it.

The edge of his thin lip twitched up slightly, then he released my chin and pulled a switchblade out of his pocket. I tried to pull away, but it was no use. My captor took the cool blade, slid it along my shoulder, cutting the straps of my outfit. One at a time, the fabric dropped away, exposing my ample breasts. My nipples peaked in the cool air. I gritted my teeth.

His gaze dropped to my chest briefly, his eyes narrowed. A moment passed and the silence in the room grew deafening. He took a step back and lifted the black stick, which looked to have some kind of pad at the end, and ran it across my chest with a gentleness that sent shivers straight down my front to my belly.

My lips parted on a quick inhale.

The man ran the pad across my breasts again, then flicked both nipples.

I let out a soft moan and curled my shoulders inward. The sensations were new. Soft and ticklish, then spicy and stinging. My nipples tightened more and warmth spread from them down toward my belly. I struggled to pull my thighs together.

How could I like anything he did?

I pressed my heels into the ground. Did he want to sexually torture me? Was he a sadist? Before I could go down that rabbit hole, he used the leather tip to trace a line between my breasts all the way down to my belly button, wiping all thoughts from my brain. I couldn't help my body's reaction as I arced into the movement. He snapped the leather tip against my fabric-covered sex and tingles of pleasure shot through my body. I dropped my head back on a moan I absolutely couldn't stop.

What the fuck?

Then his hand was on my bare belly, moving down, dipping beneath the small triangle of fabric between my legs. His fingers slid into the wetness that'd gathered there. In one swift move I brought my head straight up and tried to pull my hips away from his touch.

"So wet," he said just as my forehead connected with his. "Fuck!"

His finger left my moistened folds. In the next beat his open palm landed on my right cheek. When my eyes refocused, he stood directly in front of me, seething. His white-flecked dark hair was rumpled and at some point he'd lost his button up.

My forehead throbbed and my cheek stung. My heart was pounding so hard I was sure he could hear it. His breaths came out like a beast ready to charge. Leaning closer, he gripped my neck in his strong hand, almost cutting off my ability to breathe.

"You. Will. Obey." A small amount of spittle landed on my face, then he stormed off into the room.

I couldn't take my eyes off him in the mirror. I had no idea what he'd do next. I'd just managed to royally piss off a man who'd just pointed a gun at me. *Was I a complete idiot?* I could see him talking to a rotund white man with a goatee, who sat in a grouping of chairs not far from where I was chained up.

They spoke louder than before, but I still couldn't make out their words. My captor slammed his fist against his palm, then pointed at me.

Fuck. This was worse than last time, and last time was bad.

My lower jaw began to shake. Unable to wait and watch the fury, I focused my gaze on myself in the mirror. This wouldn't be like last time.

No crying. No dying either.

I'm not just going to live. I'm going to survive.

Not just for me. For them.

1

Raella
JANUARY

As I drove home from the last of three overnight, twelve-hour shifts, daybreak stained the sky with its yellowish-orange hues. For the past four years I'd worked full-time nights as a nurse in the ICU, even though it set my husband's hair on fire. Before, he'd insisted I stay home and raise our children, and to avoid a no-holds barred argument, I did. I stayed home with our two kids when they were young, only picking up shifts here and there. Once they reached high school age, though, I increased my hours. Of course, then his argument changed. He decided we didn't need the extra money. He made enough as an attorney, and as his father had recently died, leaving us with plenty, there was no need for me to go to work. But I couldn't sit at home and center my life around him, no matter how much he wanted me to. I went to nursing school to help people, and I couldn't give up that dream just because he felt I needed to be at his beck and call twenty-four seven.

Blowing out a cloud of breath, I leaned forward and turned up the heat. January in Kansas brought blowing winds that chilled the bones. My phone rang. I knew it was Brian without looking. The warmth from the car's heater couldn't warm my insides at that knowledge. I'd ignored the twenty or so text messages that'd come through since I'd left the hospital. I didn't want to fight with him about my plans, it was my birthday tomorrow, and I just needed to have a good day, a good week actually. I clicked the button, so the call came through the car's speakers.

"Yes, Brian? I'm driving," I said through my teeth.

"I need my suits." He jumped right in, no greeting as usual. "I have a business meeting at ten."

I forced a smile, even though he couldn't see it. "I'm already outside the city."

"Go back," he snapped.

Rolling my eyes, I sighed. This was just like him. To let me get over halfway to our ranch in the country, then send me back into the city, where we both worked, to pick up his suits, that he didn't necessarily need right now. "Why can't you pick them up? Leave early or something?"

"My meeting's at ten." I heard the distinct click of metal against metal.

"Are you working out?" My hands fisted the steering wheel as I slowed down and pulled into a gas station. I could fight him on this, but he always won. Unless it was really important to me, it wasn't worth the fight. He could be a real asshole about things.

"Raella, just help me out. I need those suits for my meeting. It's important." The metal slammed together, as if he'd dropped the weights, wanting to make a point. "And don't be late."

I leaned against the seat, resting my head back and closing my eyes. "Fine. I'll go back and get your suits."

"Oh, before you go," his voice came through the speakers, completely changed, sounding like he was trying to make nice with me or seduce me. I shivered as I remembered what it'd been like to have that be his goal, back when we first met and I wanted nothing to do with him. Back then, he'd chased me until I finally agreed to marry him.

While waiting in silence for him to continue with whatever else he had to say, I started my trip back toward the city, my jaw clenched.

Taken, not Destroyed

"I have a surprise for you, so do hurry." Then the line cut off.

Our marriage had been like this for a while, ever since I refused to give up my nursing career completely. So, basically the whole marriage. My best friend Paige asked me constantly why I put up with him, but my parents raised me with good Christian values; I couldn't just divorce him because we didn't get along. I suggested counseling a couple times, when we had fought, but he'd acted like I was insane. He said we didn't have marital problems. He didn't see anything wrong because he always won; I always gave in. Just like now.

My foot pressed down against the gas as I passed beyond the speed limit, not really in a hurry to meet his deadline, just ready to get off the road and rest after a long night at work.

I pulled up outside the dry cleaners and yawned, then got out of the car. I pulled my coat tight and ducked my head against the freezing wind as it whipped my long, white-blond hair in every direction. I opened the glass door, stepped into the warmth of the store, and into a mile long line. I held back the groan and pulled out my phone.

The man in front of me shifted on his feet, crossing and uncrossing his arms multiple times over the next ten minutes. Finally, he called out, "What's taking so long? I have places to be."

The skinny boy behind the counter looked at the man with wide eyes, opening and closing his mouth like a fish out of water. The customer at the counter looked back at us, then picked up her items and scurried away, seemingly happy to have just gotten away before the shit hit the fan.

"I'm sorry, sir. It's just me." He focused on the next lady in line and held out a shaky hand. "Do you have your pick-up ticket?"

I groaned and glanced at the clock. It had been thirty minutes since Brian had called. If I left now, I'd be on time, but without the suits. If I waited, I'd be an hour or more late, but I'd have the suits. Either way, I'd lose. I fingered the delicate, silver cross I'd worn since high school graduation and decided to wait it out. My sister Misti had given it to me as a graduation present and it had been my good luck charm ever since.

Maybe he'd go easy on me?

I pulled into the garage an hour later. I stood in the garage with my hand on the door handle to the house, Brian's dry cleaning slung over my other arm, a tightness gathering in my throat. Even though the two of us danced this dance often, it still didn't make it any easier. He couldn't just be grateful, he always had to criticize. *God be with me.* I twisted the handle and opened the door.

The moment my foot touched the wood-paneled floor, Brian appeared in the doorway to the mudroom, sock-footed and dressed only in his snug black underwear.

"It's about time," he boomed. "What the fuck have you been doing?"

My eyes widened. Of course, he knew when I arrived home; he'd probably tracked my progress the whole way on that GPS app he thought I didn't know about. Brian narrowed his moss-green eyes and crossed his arms over the muscular chest he spent an hour on every morning.

I rolled my shoulders, then held out his suits. "I'm sorry."

He studied my face for a beat, then grabbed the suits out of my hand, spun on his heel, and stalked off into the house. Despite his propensity to be an asshole 90 percent of the time, the man had a nice body, even at the ripe age of fifty. I moved into the kitchen and bit my bottom lip as I watched the muscles in his ass flex.

Abruptly, he stopped and turned, revealing that sculpted chest and washboard abs. My eyes traveled down. I preferred when he walked away, but I was female and could enjoy a man with a nice body. I crossed my arms and kicked out my hip.

His lips pressed into a thin line. "Your surprise is on the table. It's ruined, but—" He lifted his shoulder, then left me standing in the kitchen staring after him.

Once he'd disappeared into our bedroom, I turned toward the kitchen table. I didn't know what to think about this sudden surprise of his. The last time he'd tried to convince me to give up my career and be a stay-at-home mom was the last true gift the man gave me. Probably fifteen years ago, when we'd moved to Manhattan from Kansas City. At the time, I wanted a more rural life, like what I'd grown up with, but Brian wanted to work at a larger law firm. We compromised and bought a large ranch about thirty minutes outside the city. It was one of the few times we managed to make a decision that made us both happy. Even though it meant I was farther from my family.

I took tentative steps around the kitchen island and stopped at the head of our rectangular glass kitchen table. The table was capable of seating eight people since Brian insisted we be ready to seat an army, even though we rarely seated our immediate family all at once. Either he, or one of our two kids, were always missing, especially after the kids reached high school.

In front of the chair where I usually sat, someone had set out a plate filled with French toast piled with strawberries and whipped cream. A champagne glass filled with orange juice, likely a mimosa, sat nearby. There was also a glass vase with a single rose and a candle that looked like it'd burned for a while and been blown out recently.

I stuck my finger in the whipped cream and tasted it. This was my absolute favorite breakfast. I didn't even think he knew that, let alone how to cook it. I ran my hands down my front, then over my hips, feeling the extra weight he constantly reminded me I needed to lose.

Maybe the food's poisoned?

"What do you think?" Brian asked from behind me.

I ran my tongue along the bottom of my teeth. "Who made it?"

Brian stepped into my line of sight at the head of the table. Mostly naked Brian was sexy, but dressed in a suit, he was drop-dead gorgeous. His sandy, blond hair styled perfectly and his million-dollar smile, which he flashed at me, didn't hurt either. He came closer, enveloping me in his sandalwood scent. "So?"

I couldn't figure out what he wanted from me. *So?* He made me breakfast, or more likely someone else made it, and he was taking the credit. What did he want? I took a small step back and forced a smile on my face. "Thank you. This is very thoughtful," I said.

"I know." He sounded all proud of himself, then reached around me and picked up an envelope. "This is the real surprise."

Glancing quickly between his mossy eyes and the plain white envelope, I wasn't sure if this was a joke, or if I'd find divorce papers in there. He never did anything without a reason. First, the fancy breakfast with too many calories, and now he handed me a plain white envelope. With a slightly shaky hand, I reached up and took the offered envelope, keeping my gaze trained on his face, which gave nothing away. Like any good attorney, he had the best poker face around; I rarely knew what he was thinking unless he opened his mouth and told me.

Brian glanced at his watch and pursed his lips as I slid my finger under the seal and pulled out a few sheets of paper. After unfolding them, I tried to skim the documents, but Brian started talking before I could get very far.

"Ten days," he said.

I glanced up, my brows drawn together, then looked back at the paper in my hands. "Ten days?"

"In Mexico," he explained. "For your birthday."

My hand with the papers fell to my side, and I looked up at him again. "What? Mexico? You bought a trip to Mexico?" I blinked several times, trying to make sense of what he was telling me.

"So relaxing." He exhaled and rolled his head, cracking his neck.

My heart rate picked up. I looked at the sheet he'd given me, checking the details. Maybe he really was filing for divorce? "Tomorrow," I gasped. "We're leaving tomorrow?"

His nostrils flared. "Yes, Raella. Tomorrow."

"Brian." I opened and closed my mouth, trying to come up with a response. My sister and Paige had a birthday party planned for me tomorrow. I changed my schedule at work, so we could have this party. People were coming in from out of town. Brian had known about it for months. This wasn't a small thing. My chest constricted. "My . . . my birthday party. It's tomorrow. You've known about this."

"Reschedule it." He waved his hand. "I have to go. I'm already running late. You best pack." He leaned over and lightly brushed his lips across my cheek, then left.

I stood rigidly, staring out the back window of our house, not seeing anything as I let the bomb that was Brian's "gift" sink in.

2

Raella

Hours later, after a short nap, because I couldn't sleep, I sat on the living room couch with my third glass of champagne. I'd called Misti and broke the news, which resulted in an hour-long lecture where she demanded I divorce Brian and come live with her until I could get the money that I deserved from the divorce settlement. This wasn't the first time she and I had had this conversation and it likely wouldn't be the last.

I took a long sip of the bubbly drink, letting the flavor of tart apple burst on my tongue. I closed my eyes and swallowed the cool liquid. My sister and I had a special relationship, since I practically raised her. My twin brothers were ten years older than me, and my parents hadn't been interested in having more kids. So, when I was born, then her, we were like a second family. One that wasn't wanted.

I was eight when Misti was born, and I ended up taking care of her, doing most of the cooking and cleaning, helping her with her homework, until I left the house to go to college and got married. Maybe that was why she resented Brian so much. She went through her teenage years without me. I'd had my husband and my own children to raise.

I sighed, glancing at the clock. Paige was due in thirty minutes.

Taken, not Destroyed

We'd planned to have a late lunch, initially to finalize party plans, but now I had to break the news about Brian's disastrous plan. I pulled open the delivery service app on my phone, ordered her favorite Thai, and scheduled it to be delivered in thirty-five minutes. The best way to win Paige over was through her stomach.

Once Paige and the Thai food arrived, the two of us settled around the kitchen table. I passed over her favorite spicy chicken pad thai and scooped out some pineapple chicken onto my plate. I watched my friend as she dug into the long, thick noodles.

I pushed the rice and chunks of chicken around my plate and considered how to start. She'd wanted the party to be something small and intimate. It'd been Misti who inflated it into an all-out bash filled with people I'd met in nursing school, who I barely talked to anymore, and colleagues from work, who I never talked to beyond those walls. Paige would be upset regardless, especially since she'd agreed to attend something that was way outside her normal comfort zone.

I cleared my throat, and she glanced up from her dish. Her round cheeks caved in as she pushed her lips forward. "What's going on, Rae?"

I set my fork down. "I have something to tell you." I dropped my gaze, focusing on her almost transparent noodles. "You're not going to be happy."

"Okay." She set her hands in her lap.

Meeting her wide, tree-bark brown eyes, I straightened my shoulders. "Brian gave me a gift this morning."

"That's . . . great?" She cocked her head.

"Well, not entirely." I ran my fingers over my cross. "It's a ten-day trip to Mexico."

She nodded, her eyes trained on my face, obviously waiting for the bad news.

"We leave tomorrow morning." I stiffened, unsure exactly how she'd take this.

She rubbed the heart tattoo on her right forearm, the symbol for her parents who died in a car accident during our freshmen year of college. Her gaze seemed to go off over my head, while the rosiness of her cheeks appeared to get a deeper shade of red. The silence grew and pressed against my ears.

"Paige?" I reached across the table, but didn't touch her.

"Why?" She shook her head. "Why tomorrow?" She shoved her chair back with a loud screech, almost toppling the chair as she stood.

I reached for her again. "Paige."

She put up her hand. "No, Rae. Give me a minute." Her curvy form disappeared around the corner, then bathroom door slammed shut.

"Fucking Brian," I said, then decided to pack up our lunch. My stomach had twisted into a hundred knots, so there was no way I could put food into it right now. I doubted Paige felt like finishing hers either.

After about ten minutes, Paige emerged from the bathroom. Her eyes were red-rimmed but dry. My arms ached to hug her, but I knew better than to do that without an invitation. She stood against the counter with her eyes downcast.

"Misti said she'd call everyone." I ducked my head. I knew she'd appreciate not having to talk to all those people, especially since she didn't even want to invite them.

At my statement, Paige glanced up. "That's good," she said while rubbing her hands together.

"I'm sorry." I stepped forward, reaching for her but again stopped short. "Truly."

She took my hand in hers. "Don't apologize for him. He did this for a reason."

"I know." Brian always had his reasons. I just didn't always know what they were.

She dropped my hand and pushed her hair behind her ear. "Why? Why did he give you this trip?" Her dark brows pulled together. "He hasn't taken you on a trip like this before, has he?"

I rubbed my chin. "No. We didn't even go on a honeymoon because I had school. We promised we'd go later. Then Landon came. And Shannon." I sighed. "Then we couldn't see eye to eye about my career and the kids." I shrugged. "I guess we just never found time or couldn't stomach the thought of spending so much time alone together." My gut wrenched. How could two people who didn't want to spend time together stay married? It didn't seem right, but we had.

Paige harrumphed. "Why the surprise trip now?"

"What do you think?" It was easier to find out what she thought first, since she usually thought her ideas were better than mine. I never could get a read on whether Paige liked or hated Brian. Maybe that was why Paige had never married, she couldn't decide what she wanted in a man. Or if she even liked them.

She shrugged one shoulder. "I'm not sure." She tapped her lips and looked at me. "You know his mom gave him advice in the past, maybe this is her doing? Would she suggest such a thing?"

I played with my wedding ring. While Joan Calgary was a nosy, lonely housewife, especially since her husband died, I couldn't see her suggesting something like this. She knew about the birthday party. I didn't think she would purposefully ruin it, especially if the goal was to make things better in my marriage. Which was always her goal when she tried to butt in.

"Maybe. But she knew about the party," I said.

Paige shook her head. "It would be nice to know why, after almost twenty years, Brian bought a trip to Mexico."

I scoffed. "Does it really matter though? I still have to go." I ran my fingers through my thin, straight hair, working through the massive amounts of tangles. I watched my friend as she rubbed her face and realized that I hadn't spent much time with her in the past month, especially since I'd changed my usual three-night weekend schedule to accommodate my Saturday night party tomorrow. "Hey, do you mind if I run and take a quick shower? Will you stay and help me pack? We haven't spent much time together." I shrugged and smiled at her. "I miss you."

Sometimes we'd go weeks without seeing each other, and with my boss making me agree to work right away when I got back—it was the only way she wouldn't fire me on the spot for the last-minute change in my schedule—I needed to take this opportunity to enjoy my friend.

Paige's full lips tipped up. "Sure. I took the day off anyway."

After a steamy shower, I found myself staring at Brian's side of the closet. He had a long line of suits arranged by color, light to dark, blues, grays, and black, jackets on top, matching pants on bottom. They filled one whole side of the closet. The colors began to blend in with one another.

Why did he need to send me back to pick up his suits this morning?

"What're you doing?"

I jolted at Paige's voice behind me and put my hand to my chest. "Shit." I turned to find her standing behind me holding two wine glasses filled with a golden liquid. I raised my brows.

She shrugged. "It's five o'clock somewhere." She handed me a glass, then took a sip of hers.

I took a sip of the cool liquid, tasting hints of pear. "What is this?" I asked.

"A bottle of sauvignon blanc I found downstairs." She winked.

I laughed. "One of Brian's special bottles?"

Paige made a noise deep in her throat, then turned and walked to my side of the closet. The damage was already done. I never understood why he kept so many bottles without drinking them anyway. Taking another sip, I followed her.

"Okay," I said, reaching for a luggage bag on the top shelf. "One swimsuit. I'm not spending my days lazing on the beach." I pointed at my face. "Or I'll come back looking like a lobster."

"Oh." She reached into her back pocket. "I forgot to tell you. Your phone went off a few times." She handed it over.

I glanced at the screen. A missed call, three texts, and an email all from Brian. "Geez. If only I had a life." Paige chuckled and I could see her roaming through my closet while I read through the texts and email. Brian had sent a document attached to the email from his secretary Mrs. Peabody that contained information about activities in and around Puerto Vallarta. I clutched my phone to my chest.

"Oh, she's a wonderful woman," I exclaimed.

"Who?"

"Mrs. Peabody."

Paige cocked her head.

"Brian's secretary. She put together a list of activities we can do

Taken, not Destroyed

besides sit around at the hotel's beach." I scrolled through the list for a second time, zeroing in on some of the things that sounded fun.

"Will Brian go for that?"

I glanced up. Paige traced a line up and down her jaw line with her finger, her eyes trained on me. "He bought the trip for me."

"Did he?" she asked, widening her eyes.

I opened my mouth, then closed it. We'd established earlier that there was no clear reason for this trip. If he was truly trying to fix our marriage after close to twenty years of shit, then he'd go for the excursions. But if he was true to his usual self, I'd end up either burning to a crisp on the beach or going alone.

Picking a few shirts from the hangers, I pulled them down and folded them against my chest. "I could just go alone," I announced with fake confidence. "On the adventures, I mean."

Paige pulled open a drawer, grabbed some material and tossed it, striking my side. "No. That's not a good idea, Rae."

I grabbed the soft items from the floor and saw she'd tossed a couple bikinis. I stuck my tongue in my cheek. "But, ten days," I whined. "What can I do at the beach for that long?"

She glared at me. "Anything's better than Kansas during the winter."

We stared at each other for a few minutes, neither breaking the silence. I didn't want to argue with her over this. She was right, it'd help if I at least knew Brian's motivation, but he'd never openly admit anything. And I couldn't come out and ask, he'd act like I was ungrateful just for thinking he needed a reason besides what he'd said. When Paige glanced away to pick up her wine, my insides melted into a puddle of goo.

Maybe I should apologize?

We continued to pack, Paige focusing on beach appropriate wear and me on clothes for adventures like touring ruins and hikes. Neither mentioned the fact that we had different packing goals. Once my suitcase was overflowing, I closed the lid and sat on top while she yanked on the zipper around the three sides.

We both exhaled at the same time and our eyes met. She offered me her hand, which I took, and she pulled me to a stand.

"Thanks for helping, Paige. Really." I picked up the empty wine glasses and bottle. I stopped briefly and gave her a genuine smile, appreciating the fact that even though she'd been mad about the party and disagreed with what I wanted to do, she still stayed to help me.

"Sure." She smiled back, then followed me out of the closet.

After I arrived in the kitchen and set down the glasses and bottle, she touched my arm. Her hand was warm and sweaty. I turned and raised my brows.

Her brown eyes were glossy. "I don't think you should do the tours without him."

It was an interesting thing for her to say. I frowned. "Why? Because it'll piss him off?"

Her shoulder raised. "Yeah, maybe."

These were the times when I needed her to support me instead of him. This was supposed to be my trip. If Brian didn't want to do what I wanted so I had fun, then for once, I should be able to defy him. It wasn't like I planned to cheat on him or something nefarious. I shook my head.

"Okay. Thanks again for helping me." I opened my arms, inviting her in for a hug, which surprisingly she stepped in to. I wrapped my arms around her and pulled her close, basking in the rare moment when she'd allow me this type of connection.

She stepped back and rubbed at her eye. "No problem, Rae. I hope you guys can have some fun."

I watched her walk out the front door. Maybe Brian would surprise me and do something I liked for a change. The fact that Paige had hugged me, and my sister hadn't jumped through the phone to kill me, gave me a little hope that this trip wouldn't be a complete disaster.

3

Raella

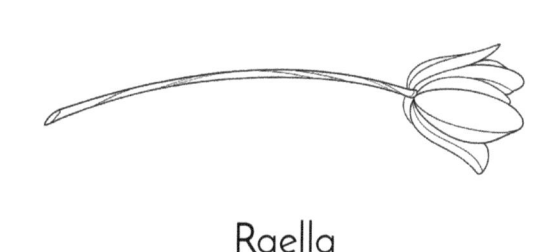

Early the next morning, I sat, bundled in a sweater, beside Brian in first class on the plane that was destined for Puerta Vallarta, Mexico and our ten-day vacation. After Paige left the previous day, I'd printed off the information Mrs. Peabody had put together for me and highlighted all the adventures that looked interesting. Brian had been uninterested in talking about it when he arrived home from work. Instead, he'd picked a fight over the fact that I hadn't packed his suitcase. Telling him he was a grown man that could pack his own hadn't gone over well.

I glanced up from my tray table, where the pages lay, stacked in a neat pile, ready for me to discuss with Brian. Every time I opened my mouth to broach the subject, I'd look at the sharp cut of his jaw or tension in his shoulders and change my mind. He hadn't said two words to me yet this morning. How could someone be so childish about something so small? I had no idea he wanted me to pack his luggage.

"Would you like a beverage?" A cultured, female voice interrupted my thoughts.

A flight attendant stood in the aisle next to Brian. "Yes," he replied as his eyes traveled down her shapely body. "I'd like a rum and Coke, one cube of ice." He leaned on his aisle seat arm rest and flashed his winning smile, the one that used to make me melt in my panties.

I stifled a groan as one side of the blonde's bright red lips curved up in a way that almost made her seem more desirable, even to me. "Of course, sir." Then her blue-eyed gaze shifted to me. "And you miss?"

Hugging my middle, I dropped my eyes. "I'll have a diet . . . whatever, please." I still had about fifteen pounds to lose.

"Coke or Sprite?"

"Coke," I said, shrugging one shoulder.

After the flight attendant had delivered our drinks, and Brian had flirted with her some more, I spread the colorful papers describing multiple fun adventures out. I needed to find a way to discuss this with him in a calm manner. He insisted this was a trip for my birthday. Though he'd yet to acknowledge it.

I straightened my shoulders and pulled out the flier on a day trip to some ruins in the mountains. "Brian?"

"Huh?" He took a sip of his drink, then swirled the caramel-colored beverage around in the plastic cup.

"Mrs. Peabody sent me some information." I rested my fingers on the paper and held onto my cross with my other hand. "I'd like to go on a few of these adventures. Would—"

"Fine," he grumbled. "You can go." His eyes stayed fixed on some distant spot in front of him.

"Don't you want to come too?" My voice sounded whinier than I'd intended.

His jaw flexed. The whirring of the plane engine pressed in on my senses while Brian took another sip of his drink. "Stop fidgeting, Raella."

I froze. I'd been running my cross charm back and forth along the chain. "You might enjoy one of them." His secretary had sent this file to me through him. He couldn't have planned on us spending ten days in Mexico doing our own thing. That would be ridiculous. Even if our relationship wasn't top notch, he had to have thought of that before booking this trip. Right?

Brian shifted, then downed his drink. He leaned out and caught the

Taken, not Destroyed

eye of the blond flight attendant. She swayed her hips as she walked over.

"Another drink, sir?" she asked, inclining her head.

"Absolutely." He handed her the empty cup.

I stared daggers at the side of his face. He had his attorney mask on. When the flight attendant brought his drink, he slammed back half of it in one gulp. I knew better than to force him to answer me, especially in public. What did he expect us to do in Mexico if he didn't want to do things together? Exhaling loudly, I sat heavily back into my seat and crossed my arms.

We spent the rest of the plane trip in silence with only one thing on my mind, *Why had he bought this trip for me?* I couldn't come up with anything good. He didn't want to participate in making plans, and he'd had three rum and Cokes as if he was trying to drink away the fact that he didn't want to be here.

Once the plane landed, we disembarked into a typical airport hallway with large windows and a sign directing everyone to turn right toward Customs. I followed Brian in his baby-blue polo and khaki shorts down the long hall. He insisted on dressing appropriately for Mexico rather than the freezing weather at home. On the other hand, I looked ready for freezing winds in my long sleeves, sweater, and jeans. I'd told him that smart people layered, and I had a tank top and shorts underneath.

"You're too slow, Raella," Brian barked over his shoulder as some of the passengers began to pass us.

I bit my lip, glancing up and down the hall. "I need to use the bathroom." I wasn't sure my words even reached him. I raised my arm. "Brian!"

His head twitched, but he didn't stop. It almost seemed like he picked up speed as his sandy-blond head disappeared farther into the crowd. I gritted my teeth and shifted as my bladder screamed to be emptied. *Fuck him.* Spotting a bathroom, I turned and redirected, bumping into several people along the way.

"Excuse me. Sorry." I said the appropriate words without true remorse as I pushed my way through the crowd to stand in a line at least six deep. I glanced down the hall but couldn't spot Brian anywhere. My shoulders slumped as I turned to stare at the top of the old lady's head in front of me.

The second my bottom hit the toilet seat, my phone started dinging with incoming text messages. I ignored it as my whole body unwound while I sat there waiting for my bladder to drain. I couldn't even think what Brian was harassing me about right now. I knew it was him. No one else would badger me with texts without giving me a second to respond.

After I finished up, I washed my hands and face, then took off my long-sleeved shirt, tied it around my waist and shoved the jeans and sweater in my carry-on. When I looked halfway presentable, I dug in my pocket for my phone.

Ten missed texts from Brian, the first four gave me the gist of his issue.

> Where are you?
>
> Why aren't you answering me?
>
> WHAT THE FUCK RAELLA?
>
> This isn't the best way to start a vacation.

No shit, asshole.

Once I made it back out into the hallway, I was relieved to see the crowd had thinned substantially. I typed out a quick response, letting Brian know I got held up in the bathroom and had just reached the line at Customs. I chose the shortest one and stood, my leg bouncing as I imagined the flames shooting out of his ears. It was his own fault for taking off without me, but he'd never see it that way.

After ten minutes, I made it to the counter and handed a handsome Hispanic man my passport and entry form. He glanced up at me, then studied my passport photo. His dark eyes met mine once again and his thin lips tipped up slightly. The agent sat there, staring at me for what seemed like an inappropriate amount of time.

I pushed some hair off my sticky forehead. "Is everything okay, sir?" My voice sounded strained.

"*Sí, señorita.*" He dropped his gaze, then placed a stamp in my passport. Just then, text messages started to ding on my phone again. The agent narrowed his eyes at me, then slowly passed my documents back through the hole in the glass barrier. "Enjoy your vacation."

"*Gracias*," I said, taking the items and rushing down the hall toward baggage claim.

I stepped off the escalator near the baggage claim and craned my head every direction searching for Brian. The baby-blue shirt should've made him easy to spot, but at the moment I was struggling. People seemed to jump into my path everywhere I turned. Tall people. Short people. Elderly people with walkers. Mom's pushing strollers. Every step I took someone, or something, tried to slow me down.

When I finally broke through the crowd, I found Brian standing, fisted hands on hips, next to the exit with our luggage piled at his feet. For once his impatience was written all over his face. When his moss-green eyes met mine, sweat began to pour down my back.

"I'm coming," I shouted and stumbled as I tried to pick up speed.

When I reached him, Brian looked down at me, his face red, jaw flexing. He pushed over my bag without a word, spun on his heel, then walked out the sliding door into the sun. It made his sandy-blond hair look brighter, like a Ken doll headed to the beach. And honestly that's what he would be soon, a Ken doll on his way to the beach for rest and relaxation.

Nothing about this vacation felt relaxing.

In the van, the driver had some kind of upbeat music playing over the radio. The AC was on full blast. Goosebumps lined my arms, so I rubbed my hands up and down to bring some heat to them. I needed to straighten some things out. We couldn't spend ten days in Mexico at each other's throats. One of us wouldn't make it home. But this tension felt worse than normal.

"Look, Brian." My leg bounced. When he shot me a look out the side of his eyes, I pressed my knees together. I hadn't really thought this through. "We're here now, so . . ."

"What're you trying to say?" He popped his knuckles.

I cringed. "This is supposed to be a fun vacation."

He tipped his head toward me and raised one eyebrow. "Your point?"

He never made anything easy. I really needed to figure out what he was thinking when he planned this vacation. "What did you plan on doing here? Did you want to do anything fun together?" I bit my lip.

Brian turned in his seat to face me. His eyes roamed over my face and body, stopping frequently on my breasts that were more exposed in the tank top. "What everyone does in Mexico," he responded as if I'd asked the dumbest question in the world.

My shoulders curled forward as the van pulled to a stop and the driver exited, followed quickly by Brian. I sat in my seat staring at the space my husband had just vacated wondering if he'd ever give me a straight answer.

The van dropped us off at a breathtaking resort. There was so much to see, I couldn't take it all in at once. While Brian checked us in, I looked around the lobby. There were no doors in sight. The entire level was open to the outdoors from the front entrance all the way through to the back patio that looked out over the ocean. I stood in the middle of the lobby watching the ocean waters drift up onto the shore, then fall back. Even from this distance, I imagined I could hear the waves as they crashed against the shore.

"Let's go." Brian tapped my shoulder and held up two keycards in front of my face.

Nodding, I took one from him, then tucked it in the pocket of my shorts. I followed him to a bank of elevators. He pressed the button for the tenth floor, but before the doors closed, another couple joined us. They continued to whisper in each other's ears and laugh during the whole ride. Brian stood like a statue with his arms crossed, eyes pinned on the changing numbers above the elevator's doors. I swallowed and leaned away from him.

This was going to be a long ten days.

When the elevator stopped at ten, the four of us walked off. Brian and I trailed quietly behind the flirty couple until Brian suddenly stopped at a door and inserted his keycard in the lock. I couldn't help but watch the happy couple as they fell all over each other trying to get into their room down the hall. Once they'd disappeared into their room, I stepped into mine.

Something inside me ached to have that. How did I get stuck with a husband who had no desire to spend time with me, let alone look at me? My gut twisted as I took in the nice, but standard, hotel room. It had white tile floors and a king-size bed with white linens. On the wall opposite the door was a large, four-paneled sliding glass door that opened onto a balcony. The view was endless blue. Only changing hues where the ocean met the sky. It was beautiful beyond anything I'd ever seen before. I stood at the open glass door and took a deep breath of the warm salty air.

"Unpack," Brian said from behind me. "I want you to keep your ring in the safe."

I straightened and turned. He was sitting on the edge of the bed. "Why?"

He pursed his lips. "After you're unpacked, we should get something to eat," he continued as if I hadn't even spoken.

"Brian." I put my fists on my hips. "Don't ignore me. Why do I need to put my ring in the safe?" On some level I understood why he was getting annoyed. I rarely asked him to explain himself, but at home I understood most of his demands. I deserved to understand.

He worked his jaw back and forth, then stood. "There are thieves in this country. I think—"

"There are thieves everywhere. I—"

He slammed his fist down on the dresser. "Just do as I say."

My breath caught and I blinked several times before I saw him clearly again. *What the fuck was that?* We stared at each other for a minute. His face was flushed red. I'd seen him angry before, but there was something beneath the anger. Something I couldn't explain. His nostrils flared as the tension between us grew. I needed whatever this shit between us was to calm down.

I put my hands up. "Okay. I'll put my ring in the safe. Whatever you say." I slid past him into the room to find the safe. I locked up my wedding ring and the diamond earrings I'd worn as well.

When I found Brian again, he was sitting out on the balcony with a glass filled with honey-colored liquid. I saw an empty Captain Morgan shot bottle sitting on the dresser next to the TV. Brian found more alcohol. I stepped out onto the balcony and took the chair next to him.

The sun was just coming over the top of the building and would soon bathe our balcony in its heat. But for the moment we mostly sat in shade. I bit at the skin on my lower lip, while Brian sipped on his drink looking like nothing in the world bothered him.

I blew out a breath. "I would really like to go on a couple of these trips together. It would be a great birthday present."

He closed his eyes and pinched the bridge of his nose. "Your birthday present *is* this trip." His voice sent chills down my spine. "A five-star, all-inclusive resort. Do whatever you want."

Bile churned in my stomach. This wasn't the response I'd expected. Or maybe I hadn't let myself admit that he'd brought me here with no intention of spending time with me because it didn't make any sense. I pressed my fingers against my forehead, against the headache that had formed over the last ten minutes.

"Get cleaned up. Put on a dress or something." He stood and hovered behind me. I could feel him like a weight on my shoulder. "Meet me for dinner at five. I'll text you which restaurant."

Without waiting for a response, I heard him walk away, shuffle some things around in the room, then leave. The full weight of the fact that I was on a ten-day vacation with a husband who didn't truly want to be here with me settled on my back like a five-hundred-pound pack. Not to mention, he'd made me miss a party with people who wanted to spend time with me and celebrate my birthday.

4

Raella

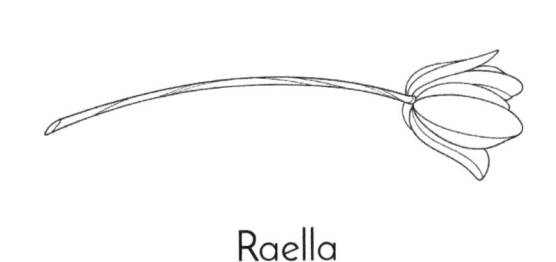

The next morning, I stood in the bathroom of our hotel room in front of the full-length mirror admiring a red sundress with large white flowers that I'd found after dinner at the hotel's boutique. The material felt like feathers against my skin and cost Brian more than I wanted to admit out loud. The strapless design was outside my usual box, but I had to keep busy last night. So, I bought a sundress I'd likely never wear again.

After I rubbed sunscreen onto every visible slice of skin, I pinned one side of my hair back in a barrette, then stepped out into the main room. Brian laid curled on one side, snoring, with his back to me. I hadn't heard him come in last night, but the smell of alcohol and cigarette smoke was hard to miss.

I leaned against the wall and watched his chest rise and fall a few times. What possessed him to book a ten-day trip for us to Mexico? He hadn't acted happy about the trip beyond the fact that he'd gotten me a surprise. I couldn't let it go. It seemed so out of character for him.

Sighing, I picked up my backpack purse, checked to make sure I had the essentials, then left the room, making sure to close the door without waking him.

In the lobby, I quickly made my way to the counter where I could book off-property excursions. One of the front desk clerks pointed it out last night when I'd asked, but had told me it closed at six, twenty minutes prior. A dark-skinned, handsome man stood behind the counter. Currently, he was speaking with a tall, thin brunette, who had a large-brimmed, white beach hat on.

I stood back and watched their exchange. The woman had a long, narrow face with bright red lips that matched her manicured nails. She talked with her hands and seemed to have a lot to say. When the two were finished, she thanked him and almost ran me over on her way to leave.

"Oh, excuse me," she said, then looked me up and down with an air of posh indifference.

I stepped to the side to give her space. "I'm sorry."

She watched with a pair of emerald eyes as I moved toward the counter. "David's the best. He'll take good care of you," she offered, then walked away with an exaggerated sway to her narrow hips.

The guy behind the counter, David, met my gaze and gave me a wide, toothy smile. "*Buenos días, señorita,*" he said in a voice that ran over my skin like silk. "*¿Cómo puedo ser de utilidad hoy?*"

I understood some Spanish, so I knew he'd asked if he could help me, but I didn't know how to respond. "*Buenos días, señor. ¿Hablas inglés?*"

"But of course, beautiful lady." He smiled again, then winked. "How may I help one as fine as you today?"

My cheeks heated. It was his job to flatter, but no one really talked to me like that. Brian had stopped flirting after we'd married and just demanded whatever he wanted, whenever he wanted it, in or out of the bedroom. I couldn't remember the last time a man looked at me as if I were desirable.

"Um." I swallowed against my suddenly dry mouth.

Ducking my head, I licked my lips and played with my cross. I had to pull myself together. I was a grown woman for Pete's sake. It was ridiculous that this young man could give me such a simple compliment and turn me into an imbecile. I glanced around, then spotted a

Taken, not Destroyed

brochure sitting on the counter for the tour I wanted to book. I grabbed it and pushed it toward him. "I'm interested in this tour."

David's chocolate-brown eyes sparkled, and a dimple formed in his right cheek when he smiled. "Absolutely. We have a tour leaving in an hour." He leaned forward, resting his forearms on the counter. "The ruins are beautiful in the evening, much like señorita."

Butterflies flew around in my stomach. My face was so hot, I bet it was beet-red. I looked away from his intense gaze and resisted the urge to fan my face. "I-I . . . Sure." I nodded rapidly. "Today works."

David gestured toward the hotel's entrance. "Mrs. Hamilton will join you."

Frowning, I glanced in the direction he indicated and saw the woman with the hat sitting in a lounge chair, her attention pinned to her phone. My eyes popped open, and I turned back to David. "She's on today's trip?"

"*Sí,*" he replied, excitement evident in his voice.

My stomach turned over and I tapped my nails on the countertop. Brian would flip his shit when he found out, but he'd made it clear that he didn't want to go on one of these excursions with me. He could do what he wanted, and so could I. We'd both be happy. I nodded and clapped my hands. "Okay. Let's do it."

"Excellent, *señorita*." David exclaimed, his eyes shone bright, then he focused on his computer screen. "What room are you in?"

"1015." I glanced at my watch. "What time did you say the tour leaves?"

"Ah, Mrs. . . . " He paused and glanced up at me, his eyes roving over my face, chest, and hands before he responded. "Ten. There is time." He cleared his throat. "Will you be alone today, Mrs. Calgary?"

This was my chance to ask Brian one last time to come, but he was passed out. He hadn't even had the decency to spend time with me last night. Nope. If that other lady was going on this trip alone, I could too. Plus, it had to be legit, since Mrs. Peabody gave me the information and I was booking it directly through the hotel. *It had to be safe. Right?*

"Yes." I squared my shoulders. "Just me. Raella."

David gave me a curt nod, then returned his gaze to the screen while his fingers hovered over the keys. His eyes darted across the screen as if reading something, then he continued to type.

Gooseflesh rose on my arms. "Is that a problem?" I asked.

"No." David smiled but it didn't reach his eyes this time. "Of course not. I am almost finished. One moment." He disappeared into the back room.

I gripped my cross as my throat tightened up. I watched the brunette as she sat on the lounge chair typing away on her phone. She appeared relaxed with no concerns over the upcoming trip. I set my hand on my heart and took a few deep breaths. It didn't matter what Paige had said. Brian had insisted I do what I want . . . alone. Everything would be fine.

David reappeared and handed me a sheet of paper. "This is the itinerary. Your trip includes lunch and dinner. You will visit two different ruins today. Expect to be back at the hotel around eight this evening."

I raised my brows. "Wow. Really?"

"*Sí*. The second location has a local market for you to shop. You will have dinner there and can go inside the temple. There is much to do." He sounded excited.

My heart rate picked up. I wanted to get there now. Even though I'd chosen to be a nurse, history was a secret passion of mine. I loved to learn about the past and see how people used to live. This was such a rare opportunity for me to actually visit a place like this. "I'm so excited."

"Your driver is Hilago," David continued. "The van is marked MiniTours." He glanced at his watch. "He should be here in twenty minutes. Please wait with Mrs. Hamilton."

I skipped a little bit on my way to the lounge chairs near the front entrance. Once there, I sat across from Mrs. Hamilton. I sent Brian a text to let him know my plans, on the off chance he was up and wanted to join me. I wasn't surprised when Hilago appeared before I'd heard back from my husband.

"Good morning, ladies." Hilago spoke English with hardly any accent. "Are you Mrs. Hamilton and Mrs. Calgary?" We glanced at each other and nodded our heads. "Then, follow me, please."

Hilago stood about four inches shorter than me and walked with a slight limp. He had a full head of graying black hair, a two-day old beard the same color, and was missing most of his teeth. He wore a pair of beat-up jeans that threatened to fall down and a T-shirt that had probably been white at one point, but not anymore.

I stood and followed the man to a blue minivan with letters on the side. Half the M was missing and the R was completely gone, but I could tell at one point the sign said MiniTours. Hilago opened the sliding door and gestured for us to get inside. I climbed in and took the seat behind the driver, while Mrs. Hamilton took the seat next to the door.

"We will be picking up one more." Hilago shot us a closed-mouth smile, then slid the door closed with a pop.

Mrs. Hamilton pressed her red lips into a thin line, then crawled into the back. She took off her hat and began to fan herself with it. "I hope he turns on the air conditioning." She had a slight accent I couldn't place.

"Me too." It really wasn't so bad that I couldn't sit for a few minutes, but I didn't want to start out on the wrong foot. She seemed so much more put together than me with her fancy hat and blue jacquard Fendi tote. I wondered if she'd ever had any of her fancy jewels stolen.

When the silence became uncomfortable in the warm van, I decided to pull out my phone. I didn't do small talk with strangers well if they weren't the ones directing it. I needed a distraction. I pulled open solitaire and started a game.

Mrs. Hamilton settled on the bench seat behind me and continued to fan herself, making tutting sounds every so often. If I had to listen to that the whole drive, I was going to lose my shit. But before I could turn and ask her to stop, Hilago opened the door and hopped inside.

"Are you ready to go?" His gravelly voice suggested years of cigarette smoking. The older man started the van without waiting for a response and a rush of hot air came from vents above my head. Before long, the air cooled and my body melted into the seat as we made our way into the streets of Puerta Vallarta.

The view out the window was similar to any city, except for the signs were in Spanish and there were palm trees everywhere. There was soft music coming from the speakers. I pulled out my phone and called Paige. After her warnings yesterday, it only felt right to let her know I'd decided to go on this trip and let her know it seemed like I was going to be okay.

"Hey, birthday girl. How's Mexico?" She pronounced it the Spanish way. Her voice sounded happier than I expected after we'd parted yesterday.

"It's good. Hot, but not terrible." I bit my lip and glanced at Hilago. I hadn't really considered the fact that I wasn't alone in the van.

"That's good. What're you two doing?" She jumped straight to it.

I sunk down in my seat. "I'm headed on a trip." I swallowed against the lump in my throat. "Now."

There was dead silence. I pulled the phone away from my ear. It was still connected to the call. "Hello?" I asked.

When she responded her voice was so quiet, I barely heard it. "And Brian was up for that?"

Cringing, I replied, "It was his idea."

"He booked you guys one of those trips?" She almost sounded excited.

I pressed my hand against my forehead and questioned my decision-making skills. Why had I called her? I could've called her after the trip was over. "No. It's just me." I glanced back at Mrs. Hamilton, who was once again engrossed in her phone.

"The trip? You going alone, was his idea?" Her voice was shrill. "I can't believe it, Rae. I told you—"

"I know." I turned to face the window, hunching to hide my voice. "He said he didn't care. I told you I didn't want to sit around the hotel."

"Fuck," she spat.

"It's fine. It's going to be fun. I'm not the only female going alone." I glanced out the side of my eyes and met Hilago's dark gaze in the rearview mirror. I saw a flash of something, which might have been humor, there. It was gone as quick as it came, then he looked back at the road. My head throbbed. I needed to get off this phone call. "I'll send you tons of pics. Okay?"

Without waiting for a response, I ended the call and stared down at the phone in my lap. I was a big girl, and this was my choice. Why did she feel the need to lecture me over it again?

"Sister or best friend?" Mrs. Hamilton asked with humor in her voice.

I rolled my eyes, glad everyone in the van found my situation funny. "Best friend," I answered, then turned to meet her emerald gaze.

"My sister gave me shit before I left home," she continued without prompting. "She couldn't believe I wanted to vacation in Mexico alone. She swore I was going to get kidnapped or killed, but look at me after a whole week by myself. I'm just fine. This is my third excursion from the hotel." She flashed me a beautiful, straight-toothed smile. "I'm Arielle, by the way."

I twisted farther in my seat, so our knees almost touched. "I'm Rae. It's nice to meet you." Just having someone who understood made some of the tension leak out of my neck.

The tour van slowed to a stop. "One more woman will join the group, then we will make our way to lunch." Hilago slipped out of the van and disappeared into the front doors of the hotel.

I turned back to Arielle. I couldn't believe she didn't have anyone to travel with her. "Where's your husband?"

She blinked her thick, mascaraed lashes and clasped her hands on her lap. "He's probably enjoying one of his many mistresses, while I enjoy his money."

Just then, the sliding door across from me opened and a young woman stood on her tiptoes. She couldn't have been older than twenty-five, had a shock of bright red, spiked hair and deeply tanned skin like she'd spent more time in the sun than was healthy. Still a little floored over Arielle's statement, I wasn't sure I was ready for the new ball of energy who stood ready to hop into the van.

"Hi, ya'll. This is going to be so much fun," the girl said with a thick Southern accent. She hopped into her seat, then turned sideways with a bright smile. "I'm Darla."

Arielle and I introduced ourselves while Hilago walked around to the driver's seat. Darla bounced in her seat. Her energy was intoxicating, and I got more excited for this trip as Hilago started driving without a word.

As we drove on, Darla talked nonstop. She battered each of us, including Hilago, with questions. She told stories about herself and just plain talked about nothing. I learned more about my travel companions during that time than I knew about Paige.

Surprisingly, Brian hadn't called or texted, and I was beginning to worry he hadn't woken up yet. Not that I wanted to fight with him about this, it was just strange behavior, and he was nothing but predictable. Even though those thoughts flitted through the back of my mind, I refused to let them bring me down. I wanted to stay happy and enjoy this adventure and my new companions.

"We are coming up to the lunch restaurant, ladies," Hilago announced, cutting off one of Darla's stories.

Simultaneously, we all looked out the front window as he drove up to a free-standing, wooden building that could only be described as a shack. There were no signs labeling it as a restaurant. There were three cars in various conditions, from slightly new to run-down, possibly barely running, parked out front.

"Is it a good restaurant?" Arielle asked, her voice sounded hesitant.

I was inclined to agree with Arielle on this one.

Hilago laughed. "Yes, *señoritas*. It is my sister's restaurant. The food is fabulous, but times are hard, and it is not easy to fix a building." With that he exited the van and walked around to open the door next to Darla.

The three of us exchanged looks. Darla shrugged her shoulders and exclaimed, "This whole thing's an adventure. Let's go."

The second she was out of the van my phone rang. I glanced at the front and saw Brian's picture. My heart stopped and bile rose in my throat. I had to answer. My gaze met Arielle's.

"I'll catch up inside. I just need a minute." My chest constricted as my thumb hovered over the green connect button. She shrugged, then followed Darla. I closed my eyes, took a deep breath, and steeled myself to deal with my exhausting husband.

5

Raella

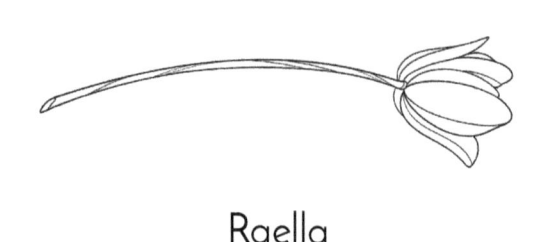

"Hello?" I answered the phone, hoping I hadn't let it ring so long the call was sent to voicemail. Brian really would've thrown a fit over that.

"Where are you?" His voice was quiet and controlled. He was wearing his attorney mask. He could even do it over the phone.

I pursed my lips. "What? Now?"

"No, Raella, twenty minutes ago," he snapped.

I rolled my eyes. I'd already told him where I'd gone. "At this moment, I'm outside a restaurant."

"Vague." I could almost see him pinching his brow through the phone.

"What do you want me to say? I don't know *exactly* where I am." A headache started to form behind my eyes, I pressed two fingers against the center of my forehead. Hard.

The man could track me. Why did he ask such inane questions?

"You didn't check with me before leaving the hotel."

I opened my mouth and glanced around at the empty van. With the A/C off, the temperature was beginning to become almost too hot to handle. Even though a soft breeze came in through the door, sweat ran down my back and beneath my arms. I had no response to him. I didn't want to fight over this. I shouldn't have to check with him first, especially after he'd basically told me to do what I wanted yesterday, and because I was a fucking adult. But I knew this was just Brian.

"This is where Shannon gets it," he continued, like he wanted to fight. Our daughter graduated from high school last spring. She was currently on a tour of Europe with her high school boyfriend. Against Brian's orders. "She should be in college, like Landon. He's on the right path."

Of course he thought Landon was on the right path. He was following in Brian's footsteps and headed to law school. "What do you want, Brian?" I closed my eyes and exhaled. I was tired of this already and we hadn't been here a whole twenty-four hours. How were we going to last ten whole days?

"Whatever." I heard a sound like glass breaking. "You do you, Raella." The call cut off.

I glanced at the blank screen with my stomach tied in knots. *What just happened?* Brian's behavior made no sense whatsoever. One minute he wanted me to do my own thing, the next he wanted to pick a fight with me because I'd done just what he'd told me to do. I buried my sweat-coated face in my hands and swallowed the scream that'd been building since I'd answered.

Just then I heard the scuffling of feet and Darla's perky voice busted through my melancholy. "Hey girl!" The van bounced beneath me, and I glanced up to see Arielle climbing in the open door. "We brought you food." Darla held up a Styrofoam container and fork.

Once everyone had taken their seats, I opened the lid and picked at the chicken and rice dish. It smelled delicious but tasted like ash on my tongue. I downed half the water bottle I'd packed just to choke down the small amount of food I ate. Logic dictated I needed to eat something, since I'd skipped breakfast.

The second Hilago's foot pressed on the accelerator, Darla started in on one of her stories, but I wasn't listening. Yesterday was my birthday and no one had even acknowledged it. Brian had ruined my party with this little vacation, so this excursion needed to be my special time. I couldn't let him destroy this vacation completely.

I turned in my seat to face the two girls I'd come to know pretty well and even considered friends. "I turned forty yesterday," I blurted. Two sets of eyes landed on me. "My husband ruined my party by bringing me to Mexico. And he's making this trip miserable by . . . well, by just being him." My face heated, then Darla sliced through the silence with her high-pitched, Southern accent.

"Whoop-de-doo. That's awesome!" She bounced in her seat and looked to Arielle, who nodded her head. "How old are you? Twenty?"

I rolled my eyes. "Ha. I just said forty."

Darla bent over and dug in her bag. When she sat back up, she held up a glass bottle filled with clear liquid. "Nope. Twenty." She winked. "We should celebrate."

"I agree," Arielle chimed in, clapping her hands together.

Warmth spread through my chest. These two women who'd been strangers only a few hours ago, now wanted to celebrate my birthday. Easy. All I had to do was tell them. Even though it probably wasn't smart to drink a bunch of alcohol, then spend time out in the sun, I wasn't going to say no. I reached for the bottle, which Darla easily gave up.

"Tell us one thing," Darla said, her hazel eyes shining with mischief. I cocked my head, holding the cool bottle to my lips. "What was the best birthday you've ever had?"

I bit my lower lip. That was hard since my parents hadn't really wanted us two girls, and obviously hadn't read the book on how to prevent pregnancy. I rested the bottle on my leg.

"I guess my best birthday was when I turned sixteen." I glanced up at the roof, as if I could see the day replaying there. "My brother Rick came home to visit. He rarely came home once he went off to college. He's ten years older than me and was married by then." I took a drink of the liquor and savored the burn as it went down my throat. Both women stared at me with wide eyes, their mouths pressed tightly closed.

My next few breaths came in quick succession before I could

Taken, not Destroyed

continue. "Rick picked me up early that morning. He took me into the city, bought me a fancy breakfast, then set me up at a spa for a facial and massage. He took me to a museum." My gaze dropped to the bottle in my lap. "It doesn't seem special to others, but to me . . . to me it was everything. No one had ever done anything for me like that."

Both women clapped and I took another swig of the burning liquid. "Fabulous," Darla exclaimed, then held out her hand for the bottle. She passed it to Arielle. "Your turn."

We continued like that until Hilago took a turn that flung me backward into the side of the van. I flung my arms around until my hand found purchase on the cool glass. I looked back and met the gazes of my two companions. We broke out in fits of laughter. I held my stomach until I managed to quiet.

The van slowed to a stop. "We're finally here," Hilago announced. He opened the lid of a cooler and pulled out three bottles of water. "You should drink, *señoritas*."

Darla took the bottles and passed them around. We quickly finished them, so Hilago handed out more. I frowned. "What about you, Hilago?"

"Yes, me too." He reached inside and pulled out a bottle, then exited the van to open our sliding door.

The three of us filed into a large field surrounded by about ten other vehicles. In the distance, I made out the tip of a triangular temple at the base of a mountain range. There was a long gravel path lined with palm trees and other short bushes that showed the way to a wall that seemed to surround and hide the full temple from view.

Once my feet made contact with the ground, my knees wobbled and head spun. I put my hand on the nearest body and realized it was Darla. She turned toward me and grinned. "Yeah, me too," she whispered.

Managing to find stable footing, I slipped my sunglasses on, then turned toward the path Hilago had already started to walk toward. I hurried to catch up, trailing behind the others. "Wow, this is all so gorgeous," I blurted into their conversation when I was close enough to be heard.

"It is," Arielle agreed, then hooked her arm in mine.

Hilago glanced back, then took a sip of his water. "It's all very old."

Darla and Arielle drank more too. My mouth felt suddenly dry, so I downed more also. The sun was high in the wide, cloudless sky. The heat pressed against my shoulders like an iron on a white shirt. I rubbed the dew-covered water bottle against my heated neck and face as I followed Hilago toward the wall that surrounded the temple.

Hilago stopped at the edge of the wall, just inside the path we'd walked up to the temple on and began to explain about the glyphs and pictures painted on it. I heard his words, but they began to fade until they sounded something like Charlie Brown's teacher. I knew I was supposed to follow the group, but my legs were tired. My gaze fixed on a picture of a two-headed dog, my feet rooted to the ground, while Hilago's voice drifted farther away. As I stood, staring, I sipped on the water. My eyes would drift closed, then my head would bob forward until I snapped my eyes open again.

I felt a hand on my arm. I turned to meet Arielle's green eyes, her brows drawn together. "Are you okay?" she asked.

I rubbed a hand down my face. My immediate response would've been yes, but if I answered truthfully, I would say not entirely. My head spun more now that it had before. The air around me felt cool against my skin, but the sun felt like a ball of fire.

"I think I need to rest a bit." I blinked until her face came back into focus.

She nodded and gripped my arm. "Let's find some shade." She glanced up. "Maybe we overdid the vodka?" She covered her lips and chuckled as if we shared in a little secret.

I nodded in agreement. Arielle slung her arm around my shoulders as we made our way back to the start of the tree-lined path and sat in some shade. We leaned against a palm tree and watched the people who walked around the temple courtyard.

"That girl's nonstop," Arielle said, inclining her head toward Darla as she flailed her hands in the air while talking to Hilago. "I don't know how she keeps going after all the vodka, in the sun." Arielle had taken her hat off. Sweat lined her brow. She began to run her fingers through her brown locks, fluffing it out.

"She's young and full of energy," I agreed. "She reminds me of my daughter." I dropped my gaze and began to trace a circle in the dirt.

"How old is she?" Arielle asked. "Your daughter."

I looked up at my new friend. "Eighteen and free-spirited."

Arielle's gaze drifted from me to Darla, then back. Her lips tipped up slightly.

Just then Hilago's gaze landed on Arielle and I sitting under the tree. He directed Darla to walk our way. She continued to talk and swing her arms, managing not to hit him, as they made their way over to us.

Hilago stopped in front of us. "*Amigos*, should we move on to the next site?" His furry brow furrowed. "Give you time to rest in the cool van?"

I pushed to a stand, then offered my hand to Arielle, who took it. "Yes, I think a rest in the air conditioning would be welcome. Thank you, Hilago." Arielle replied for the both of us.

After we piled into the van and the cool air was blowing, I asked, "How long until the next site?"

His brown eyes met mine in the rearview mirror. "Not long. Twenty minutes, maybe." He shrugged, then refocused on the road. "Just rest, *señoritas*."

Darla and Arielle reclined in their seats, their eyes closed, their chests rising slow and steady as if they'd fallen asleep immediately upon hitting the seat. Maybe Arielle and I had been wrong about the sun and alcohol not getting to Darla.

I didn't want to sleep, but my legs were Jell-O and my head spun more than it had before we went out to see the ruins. My body felt like it had at my one and only spa day. I sank back into the seat and watched the scenery roll past the window. It became a blur of blues, greens, and browns. My eyes drifted closed. I snapped them back open, unaware of how much time passed.

My chest became heavy, my breathing slower. The van was silent besides the slow, rhythmic breathing of my friends. Exhaustion gripped me, then darkness flooded my vision.

Slowly consciousness came back. Sounds were muted as if my brain was under ten feet of snow. I tried to open my eyes, but they felt like they were glued closed. A drumbeat pounded inside my head. I tried again to open my eyes, but they wouldn't budge, so I held still and listened.

The space around me was silent. The air felt heavy and made my breathing hard. I couldn't remember where I was or figure out why my eyes felt so heavy. All that should make me feel anxious, but my insides were sluggish, relaxed, so wrong.

Then I heard what sounded like a door slide open and a light popped on. The small amount of light behind my lids burned. I squeezed my eyes tighter but couldn't find the energy to move my arms to block my eyes. A groan left me. I was sure someone had inserted a sharp object through my temples, and the light only made it worse.

A pair of large, rough hands grabbed my arm and shifted my body. The scent of cigarettes smacked me in the face. My stomach rolled. One arm slipped behind my back and another under my legs, then I was pulled against a muscled chest. The stench of cigarettes increased, with an undercurrent of mint.

Bile rose in the back of my throat. I swallowed as my head rolled back like a newborn baby. The man shifted me in his arms, and my head bobbed against his chest. It was like my mind was awake without my body. Had someone paralyzed me? I tried again to peel my eyes open, but they still refused.

The man moved with me. His chest vibrated against me as he spoke to someone else in a deep and gravelly voice, probably from too many years of smoking. The words were unintelligible, like whatever had happened to me made it difficult to comprehend language. *This is so fucking wrong!*

I felt my body being unceremoniously dropped into the arms of someone else who smelled much better. I instantly felt safer here, in this new man's arms. He smelled like sunshine and coconuts. I tried to ask him where I was, what was happening, but my mouth couldn't form the words. My voice was lost.

As my body relaxed against his muscular form, the darkness took me again.

6

Segundo

After I received El Gato's text to come down and help bring in a last-minute delivery, I walked down a graveled path from the house and saw a blue van parked at the end. El Gato and three other men stood in near darkness, smoking and talking. Only a small bit of light from the house reached us here. I hated being a part of El Gato's human trafficking side of our cartel business. But as second in the Armas Locas cartel, I had to do many things I preferred not to, and this was one of them. The fact was, El Gato made a lot of money for the cartel, no matter how misguided he was. I walked up to the men and caught the tail end of their conversation.

"El Amante did well this time," Serpiente said. Serpiente was an older man who drove a tour van that delivered women for El Gato on occasion. I joined the other men near the passenger door.

"We have three inside," the old man continued in his raspy voice. "All very beautiful, but they drank some alcohol along with the drugs I gave them. They'll be out longer than usual."

El Gato shrugged, then tapped one of his guys on the shoulder and pointed, while snapping his finger, toward the rear of the van. "Go get the one in the back," he growled, then tossed his cigarette on the ground. He glanced my way. "Good of you to join us, Segundo."

I grunted. He'd asked for an additional man, so I came, but I didn't need to join in the banter. "What do you need me to do?" I asked, as the man El Gato had directed to collect the female from the back walked past with a thin woman in his arms. Her long, brown hair was draped over his shoulder. I held back a shudder.

El Gato shot me a wide, knowing grin. "Dito will take the red head. I'll get the third one out of the van, but I'll need you to take her up. I have some unfinished business with Serpiente."

I shrugged as Dito opened the door to the van and scooped out a tanned female with spiked red hair. He winked at me, then headed up toward the basement entrance to the house. I tried to keep the emotion off my face, but it was difficult.

El Gato's hand landed on my shoulder. "These pussies are only good for money, amigo," he said, then moved toward the van. He struggled to squeeze his muscular frame into the van and crawl over the seat to the far side to collect the remaining female. When he had her in his arms, he stepped out and turned to me carrying a pale-white woman with long, blond, almost white, hair. He kept his dark gaze trained on me as he moved my way with the woman trapped in his arms.

Her head flopped back, doll-like, until he repositioned it against his chest. My stomach clenched. This was his thing; I was the computer genius who managed all the weapons, drugs, and money. Even though El Gato brought in plenty of money from trafficking the women he collected, it wasn't right, and no one would ever force me to see it differently.

"You know what to do." El Gato dropped the female in my arms, then stalked away to pick up a conversation with Serpiente, who waited near the driver's door. I swallowed my disgust and pulled the woman's soft body close to my chest.

She moaned, her pink lips parting. She had high cheekbones that narrowed down to a pointed chin with a small, barely there dimple. My chest tightened as I stared at her face. I wanted to trace a line down her cheek, across her lips. Her skin looked smooth, no wrinkles or blemishes, just soft, milky skin with a hint of red at her cheeks. She wore a small silver cross on a delicate chain around her neck.

Everything about her felt soft. From the way her flesh pressed against my arms to the way her body melted against my chest. That's what I hated about the trafficking. The women were soft, beautiful, and innocent in their own way. Maybe some of them were drug addicts or prostitutes, but they all had hopes and dreams and lives somewhere out there. One wrong turn and it was gone.

"Segundo," El Gato snapped.

I blinked and shook my head. "What?" I looked up to see that El Gato stood halfway up the path, fisted hands on his hips. The rest of the men were gone, along with Serpiente's van.

"That's not helpful," he growled, then left me standing in the darkness.

I hugged the blonde tighter. Something inside me didn't want to let her go. I glanced behind me and considered, just for a second, taking her away from here. I blinked, licked my lips, and started up the path after El Gato. The entire cartel would chase us down if I left. They'd claimed her.

Unable to help myself, I leaned down and took a deep breath, inhaling her scent, honey and vanilla. With each slow step, I memorized every contour of her face, every crest and valley of her chest and cleavage. There wasn't enough light to see details, but I could see her shape. She felt so right in my arms.

When I reached the basement entrance, one of El Gato's men stood there with his arms extended. "I can take her from here," he said. He took in the way I held her, then met my gaze. Immediately, his eyes dropped to the ground at my feet. "*Señor, lo siento,*" he said, apologizing.

My mouth went dry at the thought of giving this woman to another man, but I had to, she wasn't mine to keep. Not yet. I stepped forward. "Take care," I whispered, then gently transferred the drugged woman into the other man's arms.

I took the moment to trace a line down her delicate cheek to her kissable lips, over her chin and down to her cross. I picked it up between my thumb and forefinger. Such a delicately religious item, but it wasn't enough to protect her from this horrible fate. Even God had a role in places such as this though.

"Segundo?" the guard asked, shifting the woman in his arms.

As I reached up and unlatched her cross, I met his gaze. I gave him a curt nod, then turned and left him to do his duty with a heavy feeling in my limbs. I tucked the cross into my pocket. They would've removed it anyway; at least this way I'd have something of hers. Something that spoke of her heart.

I made my way through the basement halls to the stairs that led up to the main house. As I walked up the stairs, I glanced up to see El Ratón, the leader of the Armas Locas cartel, standing at the top, a whiskey in one hand and a cigarette in the other. The cigarette smoke drifted up in a snakelike line to the ceiling, catching my eye as I continued to climb toward him. He wasn't a tall man, by most people's standards, but his mere presence exuded power. His eyes held no warmth as they watched me, and he rarely showed mercy. We'd grown up in the same town, and even though he was a few years older, we'd known each other as children, which is what led to me taking up the position of second when El Ratón took over the cartel.

"El Ratón." I inclined my head and joined him on the landing. He backed up so we stood together in the kitchen.

"Segundo," he replied. Members of our cartel were not called by our given names. Part of my job was to assign each member their cartel identity, then destroy all traces of their real selves. "El Gato's business is settled?" He took a sip of the amber liquid.

One of the largest organized cartels, the Armas Locas controlled all the Northwestern states in Mexico, including Sonora, Sinaloa, the western half of Chihuahua, Durango, and Nayarit. El Ratón had taken over the cartel about fifteen years ago when he'd killed his cousin, the boss at the time. After he'd taken control, El Ratón then killed the leader of a rival cartel, while fixing a bad deal his cousin had made, absorbing the other cartel's people and territories.

"*Sí.*" I fought to swallow the acid taste in the back of my throat. El

Ratón's gaze traveled from my face down my body. His eyes were two dark pools of oil.

He lifted his chin, then turned and began walking across the kitchen. The room was large, much more than was needed for the few people who lived in this house year-round. The appliances were stainless steel, the type usually found in a restaurant. El Ratón insisted his house be outfitted to host large parties, although he often ordered from local restaurants rather than make Abuela, our regular housekeeper, make all the food.

I followed his lithe form across the room and out the open doorway onto the pool patio. El Ratón took a seat in one of the padded wooden chairs. He gestured for me to join him. A line of sweat formed on my brow as I sat, straight backed, across from him.

El Ratón set his mostly empty glass down, then lit another cigarette and took a puff. He offered me the pack. I held up my hand and shook my head. My stomach was in knots. He rarely sought me out beyond our usual morning meetings. I wanted to ask so many questions, but I knew better than to push him.

His nostrils flared. "Tell me about Queso's deal."

I rubbed at the back of my neck and looked away from his harsh gaze. Fuck. I'd hoped he wouldn't bring this up. My brother had made a royal mess of the job I'd given him last week and I'd hoped to get it cleaned up before El Ratón heard about it.

"Queso fucked it up." There was no use lying. No use in us both facing punishment. I shook my head. "I want to make it right."

El Ratón swallowed the last of his whiskey and set his glass down, hard. I jolted, then shoved my chair back and stood. I made my way into the kitchen to grab the bottle. It was better to keep him drinking than to let him think too hard on my brother's fuckup. I also needed to think.

"Grab a glass, Segundo." El Ratón's voice carried no room for questions.

I found a glass, then headed back outside. After I'd poured the two of us another finger of whiskey, I retook my seat. I took a sip and savored the sharp burn as it traveled down the back of my throat.

Taken, not Destroyed

"Punishment is necessary," El Ratón said.

I glanced up at my boss over the top of my glass and froze; I couldn't take another drink. My brother couldn't handle a visit to the Black Room. My mother had babied him. Even though Queso had joined the cartel when he turned twenty-five, three years ago, he still hadn't hardened. Queso was the youngest of her surviving children. She'd had a baby after him, from another man, but the baby had died at just a year old. Since then, she'd made Queso the center of her world. It'd killed her when he joined Armas Locas with me. I couldn't let anything bad happen to him.

I set my glass down and rubbed my face. Then it struck me. I could kill two birds with one stone. "Maybe you can forget Queso's mistake, if I find you a distraction." My heart skipped a couple beats as he leaned back in his chair, head cocked.

"Distraction?"

"*Sí.*" I took a deep breath, because this was risky. I could end up in the Black Room right beside my brother for this. "Daniela died two years ago." We both crossed ourselves and El Ratón's brow furrowed. "El Gato has a beauty. A flower. I sense her strength and her faith." I pulled the cross from my pocket and held it up.

His lip lifted in a sneer. "I get pussy."

I shook my head and tucked the cross away. "Not what I meant."

El Ratón held up his hand. My lips pressed firmly together in a tight line. I'd fucked that up. Just when I thought I'd get to keep her, I'd gone and lost her all over again. He rubbed his stubbled chin and studied me with those oil-black eyes of his.

After what felt like a century, he stubbed out his half smoked cigarette. "I enjoy a good tulip," he said, then left me alone on the patio. My heart rate picked up as I remembered the swell of her breast as it pressed against my chest and the soft curve of her lips.

7

Raella

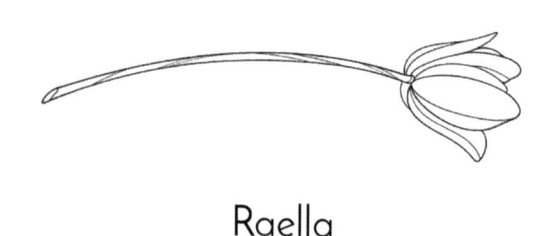

Consciousness came back to me slowly. My whole body felt cold, and I sensed a breeze coming from somewhere above me. Rolling onto my side, I shivered and pulled my knees to my chest, dragging them through something cold and wet. Nausea tore through me, and I retched as a needle of pain shot through my temple. Grabbing my head, I groaned.

I took a deep breath and was struck with the bitter scent of urine and sweat. Acid burned the back of my throat and I swallowed, trying my best not to breathe through my nose. After years of nursing, I'd done it a hundred times when stuck in situations when a patient's wound smelled so bad just being in the room brought your dinner threatening to come back up. I laid there, unable to process where I was or what had happened and took five small breaths through my mouth to settle my stomach.

Once the nausea passed, I tried to pry my eyes open, but my lids felt like hundred-pound weights. A dream took form where a man who smelled like coconuts and sunshine carried me. His arms had been strong, and I'd felt safe next to his body, but I couldn't remember anything else from the dream, nor could I remember what had

Taken, not Destroyed

happened before I fell asleep. I finally tugged my lids open, only to realize it was a place so dark I couldn't see my hand an inch from my nose.

My heart rate spiked. Darkness I could handle. Unknown darkness was terrifying. I reached out and put my hand on the floor. The texture was similar to my parent's kitchen back in Kansas, when I would lie on it as a kid and wait for a cookie after dinner while Mom cleaned up. Before Misti was born, when Mom still cared if I ate a cookie before or after dinner.

Just then a sliver of light came from somewhere beyond my feet. I braced myself and tried to push up. My arms wobbled. "Hello?" My voice cracked, barely sounding like me.

"Shh," someone hissed. "They're coming."

My eyes widened and I pushed harder, forcing myself to sit. My head spun. I wasn't alone here. I'd been so focused on myself that I hadn't heard the people, but now I did. I heard the soft moans, rustling of bodies, and breathing. Lots of different people breathing.

Once I'd managed to sit, I realized the small sliver of light came from under a door across the room. After a few blinks, I could make out shadows of quite a few bodies lying all around me. The draft struck my shoulders, and my nipples hardened. I looked down.

Someone had taken my clothes. I was naked, in a dark room, surrounded by other people. My teeth chattered.

Where the fuck am I? What's going on?

My breathing increased, close to hyperventilation. Before I could lose it entirely, the door to the room slammed open and a bright light flooded the space. My eyes burned and I covered my face. The daggers in my temples were back.

The people around me screamed. Warm bodies pushed against me, and I was shoved to the ground as I felt flesh rub against mine. Nails clawed at my skin and feet slammed against my sides. I rolled into a tight ball with my arms over my head, eyes squeezed shut. Maybe when I opened them this would be over; I'd discover it was a horrible nightmare.

A gun fired and the room fell silent. So silent I could barely hear the others, let alone myself, breathing. I stayed tucked in my ball and took rapid, shallow breaths. My blood whooshed behind my ears. I dared to open my eyes and found the light wasn't so bad inside the safety of my body ball.

A voice growled something in Spanish, but my mind was still moving too slow to process anything. Through a space between my arms, I could see a Hispanic woman with wavy, black hair sitting with her knees pulled to her chest next to me, her wide eyes darted all around. She rocked back and forth, while her lips moved, though I couldn't hear what she was saying.

My knees began to ache, and my legs tingled. I needed to move. I could hear commotion, the soft tinkling of what might've been chains behind me and soft male voices. My arms shook as I tried to remember what'd happened, how I'd gotten there. My whole body felt sluggish, and I knew enough about drugs to recognize the signs. Someone must've drugged me.

Silence fell behind me, then the room fell into darkness. I counted to five as I waited to make sure whoever had fired that gun was truly gone, then released my legs. They burned and tingled as blood rushed through them. I shook them a little and hit a warm body in the process.

"Hey," a female voice snapped.

"Sorry." I flipped onto my back and pushed up to sit. I held my hand over my mouth as my stomach retched against the rapid change in position.

"Shut up, bitches," someone with venom in her voice hissed. "Do you want them to come back?"

My mouth ran dry. I didn't know who would come back, but I needed to know where I was and what was going on. Where was Brian? Why wasn't he here?

"Rae? Arielle?" A heavily Texan-accented voice came from somewhere in the darkness. A voice that brought back a slew of memories. Memories that slammed me somewhat into the present.

I was in Mexico, on a vacation with Brian, if you could call it that.

Instead of lazing at the beach, I'd left the hotel and gone on an excursion to see some ruins. Two women had been with me. We'd had fun together, celebrated my birthday with some vodka and stories. Darla had been one of those women.

"Darla," I gasped, reaching into the darkness toward her voice.

"Rae," she responded, louder than before. "Where're you?" I heard grunting and snide comments, as if Darla were making her way toward me.

My whole body warmed. I wasn't alone here. I knew someone. Even though I wasn't exactly safe, I didn't have to face this nightmare totally alone. "I'm here." I put my arm out again and touched flesh.

A cool hand pushed mine away. Unsure if I'd be stable on my feet, I scooted forward on my knees reaching forward, touching arms, faces and hair. Sometimes the person would push my hand away, but mostly they wouldn't respond and allowed me to move past as if they no longer cared what happened. After I'd moved past three bodies, I stopped. "Darla?"

"Shut the fuck up," the girl with the venomous voice spat from somewhere to my left.

"Rae," Darla responded from directly to my right, then a hand landed on my arm.

I gasped and turned, as if I could see her. My soul soared. "I found you," I whispered.

"Oh my God," she whispered at the same time. "Where the fuck are we?"

Tears welled in my eyes. I hadn't known this woman before we met in the tour van, but after everything we'd talked about, she felt like a close friend. I grabbed her arm and pulled her close. I knew we were both naked, but I needed to be close to someone I knew. To bask in the safety of someone who cared about me, who knew me before I was in this place.

We wrapped our arms around each other. "I don't know," I whimpered, then felt her tears drop against my shoulder. We sat together on the cool floor, holding each other until both of our tears dried up.

I pulled back first. "Do you remember what happened?" Darla moved her hands away, but kept her leg pressed up against mine. Just having her near kept my muscles from tensing and my heartbeat steady.

"Sorta." She exhaled. "This isn't good."

"You don't want them to come back." Venom's voice was sharp even though she whispered.

I took Darla's hand. "My husband's a lawyer. This is illegal."

"Do you think he can find us?" Her voice sounded lighter.

Biting my lip, I looked around as if I could see anything in the dark. For all I knew they were listening to us. Whoever *they* were. I ran my hand up Darla's arm until I cupped the back of her head, then pulled her close so I could whisper in her ear. "He tracks my phone. He has to know where I am."

Darla gasped and turned her head toward me, almost knocking me in the mouth. "Really?"

The light flicked on outside our room again and filtered beneath the door. Tension skyrocketed all around me. I could've sworn not a single one of us moved or breathed.

"Fuckers." Except Venom, who decided to curse us for talking.

The door crashed open and light flooded the room, but I was ready this time. I covered my face and slowly allowed my eyes to adjust before removing my hand. Every muscle in my body shook as the room came into focus. I had no time to register anything before the man dressed in black pointed a nozzle at the middle of the room and let loose a spray of water.

The women who were struck screamed and cursed, then tried to escape from the spray. My heart rate spiked, and my wide-eyed gaze met Darla's. This wasn't like running in the sprinklers during the summer at home. This was downright awful. The spray was cold and harsh. Those being struck with the water ran or crawled away. I scooted back on my bottom, my legs still Jell-O and not completely following commands.

My friend stood, then offered me a hand. I grabbed it and held on while she pulled. The spray came our way and doused us. Darla's hand released mine as she yelled out curses. The water felt like ice pellets against my skin. Goosebumps rose everywhere and my body began to shiver. I wrapped my arms around myself, as the spray redirected toward another group of women who huddled together nearby.

Darla dropped down next to me. Her lips were pale. "That's fucking freezing."

My teeth chattered. "D-d-do you s-see Arielle?"

We both searched the room. There were plenty of female bodies. White. Brown. Black. All shades. Some skinny, in need of extra food. Some with a little extra weight, like me. Hair all different lengths and colors. But nobody looked like Arielle. Darla started biting her nail, then looked at me, her dark brows pulled together.

Before the two of us could see another room, we were all cast into darkness again. The sound of draining water came from somewhere in the room. The door clicked closed, followed shortly by the outside light flicking out.

Total darkness. Again. I wasn't sure if there was a form of torture that included extremes of light and temperature, but if there was, this place fit the bill.

"Why are all these women here?" I whispered, hugging my body. I didn't want to be naïve, but I also didn't want to admit what I'd seen. This couldn't be real. I pinched my arm, hard.

Darla's cold fingers rested on my other arm, then I felt her forehead land against my shoulder. "We can't stay here."

"What the fuck are you going to do?" Venom inserted her opinion again.

I gritted my teeth. That woman was getting on my nerves. "You shut up. Stay out of our conversation."

She scoffed. "You think you can get out of here."

I felt Darla move. "What do you know?" Darla asked, her interest obviously peaked.

"We're not getting out of here. None of us are." Venom's words struck me straight through the gut like a punch.

"W-what?" My voice was barely audible.

"When we leave this room—" I could feel the whole room fall

silent, waiting for Venom to tell us what would happen beyond that door, as if no one else knew. Why was she so knowledgeable? "We'll be auctioned off to the highest bidder."

My stomach dropped, then twisted into ten million loops. I leaned away from Darla and retched against an empty stomach.

8

Raella

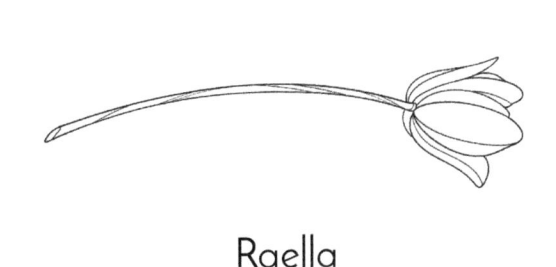

Silence filled the space around me like a living thing. It pressed against my nerves, making them come alive, as if I needed to do something besides just sit here on this floor, waiting. When Venom revealed that we'd all be sold off like chattel, it seemed like everyone around me had taken the news poorly, including Darla. The tension had risen so high that you could cut it with a knife, and I could feel the bodies of the women close to me shaking, their breaths short and staccato.

Time passed in the darkness, but I had no idea how much. Seconds seemed like hours. I shifted every time my butt burned or my legs fell asleep. I tried to imagine Brian making calls and pulling together a search party to come get me. He would find the resources to track me down, even in Mexico. He had to. I couldn't be sold off to some horrible person who could actually buy another human being.

It's inhumane.

I pushed my no longer wet hair off my face and collected it in one hand, pulling it over my shoulder. My hand brushed up against my neck and my breath hitched. I dropped my hair and searched the space on my neck where my cross usually hung. It was bare. No cross. That cross meant the world to me. Where could it have gone?

"Fuck," I swore, then moved to my hands and knees and ran my hands across the cool tile. My chest constricted, the cross was the only connection I had to home, and to God. In my heart I knew it was unreasonable to think I needed a trinket to be connected to God, but it helped. I bumped into someone.

"Ouch," she whined.

"Sorry," I mumbled, as I continued in my blind pursuit.

"Rae?" Darla asked.

I ignored Darla and pressed on, bumping into people and getting cursed at every so often. My eyes burned as my hands continued to come up empty. I was being unreasonable. When I bumped into maybe the fifth or sixth person, a soft, warm hand rested on my arm.

"What you look for?" She spoke broken English with a heavy Spanish accent.

Swallowing the lump that had grown in my throat the longer I looked without success, I sat back on my heels. "My cross," I croaked.

The woman felt along my arms until she had both my hands in her warm ones. How someone could be warm in this place was beyond me. "We pray."

She began to mutter in Spanish beneath her breath. I wondered if she was the young woman I'd seen next to me when the lights had come on the first time. I bowed my head and let her words soak into my soul, even though I couldn't understand them or even really hear her, it was enough to know she was praying.

When she fell silent, I said, "Amen." The woman squeezed my hands. Something about her willingness to touch me, to calm me down even though we were both captives in this place touched my heart. "What's your name?" I asked her.

She pulled her hands away. "No . . . *no utilices nombres aquí.*"

She didn't want to tell me her name. I reached for her hand again. "*Gracias.* For praying." I wished I spoke more Spanish. "How did you get here?"

Her hand fell limp in mine. Maybe I'd scared her off. I couldn't understand why such questions were bad. It wasn't like we could be in a worse position right now. Then I heard a sniffle come from her direction.

"I left market. Then woke here. No, know when." I felt her body shake and she pulled her hand away. "*Mi hijo tiene dos años.*" She sniffled and gasped.

My throat constricted as I reached out in the darkness until I found her shoulder, then pulled her into a hug. I half expected her to pull away, but she didn't. My heart broke for her and her son, who might never see his mother again. I couldn't imagine what it would feel like to be pulled away from your two-year-old child.

"I was here on a vacation with some friends." A light female voice came out of the dark with an accent I couldn't place. "Last thing I remember is going to a club."

The Hispanic mother sniffled, then sat back. "*Gracias, mi amiga,*" she whispered.

"Are your friends in here? With us?" I asked the new storyteller. She'd been brave to speak up, to share her story too.

"Will you guys shut the fuck up?" Venom interjected.

"Butt out, whoever you are. We're talking," Darla snapped. I smiled, happy to know that she still had my back, even in here. Maybe if we felt connected, we could band together and get out of here. Even if we couldn't escape, we could at least feel less alone.

"I'm Rae. What's your name?" The Hispanic mom in front of me slapped my hand, but it was pointless. Darla and I had been using each other's names since we opened our eyes.

"I think the Spanish girl is right," Club Girl said. "And no. My girls aren't here. At least, not that I could see."

I felt the bodies around me shift and someone sat next to me. "Why do they take some and not others?" Darla had found me again. "None of our stories are the same."

I rubbed my chin. "That's true. It doesn't make sense."

"Why you think it should?" the Hispanic mom asked.

The room fell silent, because she was right. What about kidnapping women and selling them needed to make sense? We were just trying to keep our minds busy and rationalize something that would never in a million years be rational.

"I . . . I think . . . " a soft voice started to say in the darkness across the room, but she stopped.

"Don't stop," I encouraged her. We all deserved to have a voice, especially in this place.

"My dad sold me," her voice squeaked. "I traveled for many days in the back of a van before being here."

My heart tore in two—more like shredded. *What could I say to these women?* Nothing. We were all victims here, but I felt like some of them had it so much worse. I leaned against Darla and she snaked her arm around my shoulders. The room fell into silence again, but I didn't feel quite so alone.

"Do you think—" I started just as the door slammed open and the lights blazed on.

There was a collective groan throughout the room. I covered my face until my eyes adjusted to the brightness. Once I could see, my gaze settled on a beast of a man who filled the open doorway with his wide frame. His black hair was cut close on top, and he had a large, bushy beard that came down to a point about his mid chest. He had tattoos on every inch of visible skin.

"Come, *putas*," Tattoos said in a gravelly voice. "We go to the party." He laughed as if he'd just told the best joke.

Frowning, I met Darla's gaze. This man's voice sounded familiar, but that was crazy. Darla's hazel eyes were wide, her arms wrapped around her thighs. I hooked my arm through hers and watched as two men dressed in black from the neck down ducked under Tattoo's arms. They both had rifles slung across their backs, and not hunting shotguns, but the scary kind that shot a lot of bullets at once.

My breath froze. I gripped Darla's arm so tight there would be bruises later. The two men filed into the room, then split off, each one going a different direction. They pointed the tips of their guns at the women and directed them to stand, often wrenching an arm to force them to do it.

I gritted my teeth and pushed to stand. I helped Darla, then offered

Taken, not Destroyed

my hand to the Hispanic mom. I'd been right, she was the same woman who'd been next to me the first time the lights had come on. She took my hand and stood. The three of us supported each other in our small circle. The Hispanic mom started her quiet prayer again, and my legs shook as I squeezed Darla's hand.

A small commotion drew my attention to the door. I didn't think this place could get worse, but my insides threatened to come back up yet again at what I saw. Tattoos secured what looked like a dog collar around each woman's neck who'd been lined up at the door. One of the men with the rifles secured a chain between each collar, connecting the women to each other.

"Come," a gruff voice said, then a hard hand grabbed my arm.

My knees almost gave out as I moved to follow the dark-haired man. He put me in line in front of Darla, then left to go help the others. I touched my neck as I watched Tattoos make his way down the line toward me. I could hear Darla's breaths, mimicking my own, hard and fast.

When Tattoos stopped in front of me. His dark eyes met mine and a shiver raced down my spine. I lifted my chin. His beard twitched as if a smile formed beneath it. He raised the collar and wrapped it around my neck, then leaned close, giving me a full whiff of cigarettes and mint as he secured it in the back.

My lips parted. That smell. I knew I recognized that voice. He stepped back and moved on to Darla. My head began to throb. *Who was this man? Why did I know him?*

Once the guards had the chain secured between all of us, Tattoos stood at the head of the line. His dark eyes surveyed us, then he said, "Follow."

We passed through a few hallways and went up a flight of stairs, the chain between us jingling. The hardest part was trying to maneuver with the chain between our necks. They'd barely given us enough distance and if someone slowed or sped up it would pull, choking the person on one side or the other. I tried to hold the leather away from my skin, but I needed both my hands to prevent myself from toppling over.

It turned out I was so distracted by the collar and the chain that when Tattoos stopped our group and pushed a wall panel aside, bathing the small hall where we stood in light, a bolt of shock ran through me. Venom's voice echoed in my ears, *Auctioned off to the highest bidder.*

My feet froze to the ground. The collar pulled at my neck and Darla slammed into my back. I choked and grabbed at the leather strap.

"Move," one of the guards growled.

Fuck. It's real now.

I followed the dark skinned, black-haired woman in front of me out of the tight hall into the light. The room opened up into one with high ceilings, a chandelier in the center, and endless rows of people. I tripped over my feet as I fixated on the front row.

All men. They all watched us file onto an elevated platform. From somewhere in the distance, lights shone on us. My nipples peaked, sweat ran down my back, and my chest constricted as if someone had captured me in a human-sized vice.

Tattoos guided each one of us into place, shifting our bodies so we stood in just the right spot. He smoothed my hair down and used his thumb to remove something from my cheek. I crossed my arms, but he grabbed them and pushed them down at my sides. Frowning, I looked down at myself, then down the line at the others.

We looked like beaten and battered women. Darla's red hair stuck up in all directions. She had dark circles under her eyes and her face was two shades lighter than her tanned body. The woman to my left looked even worse, her shoulders sagged and her dark-haired head hung forward. I wondered if she was the one whose dad had sold her.

This whole thing was tearing me apart. I buried my face in my hands.

"El Gato," a smooth, male voice said with command behind it.

I lifted my face from my hands and saw Tattoos moving toward another Hispanic male. The newcomer was dressed in a pair of fashionable, dark-washed jeans that hugged him nicely with a black, fitted shirt. The shirt was tight enough to show he had a well-defined chest. Like his counterpart, he was covered in tattoos. It must be a thing with these guys.

While the two men spoke, the sexy man's gaze seemed to seek me out. It burned right through me as it ran up and down my naked body. I'd like to think he looked at the other girls too, but I couldn't be sure. Sexy's lips moved, then he slipped a hand in his front pocket and cocked a hip.

Tattoos, or rather El Gato, frowned, and turned, his gaze pounded against my head like hammers. The two of them stood there, exchanging words, and staring at me as if I had answers to the world's greatest questions. I wanted to run away, even more than before. Everyone in the room was staring at me, at us. Blood rushed behind my ears, and I crossed my arms again. I didn't care what El Gato said.

Sexy turned to face El Gato, his lip curled in a sneer. El Gato squared his shoulders, then spun on his heel, coming at me like a freight train. When he reached me, he gripped my arm in a fist of iron. There'd be bruises later. He unhooked my collar from the chain, then drug me from the stage. I tripped over my feet and struck my knees on the ground before I was able to right myself and stand again.

"*Chingados*, El Gato," Sexy said as we approached him.

El Gato grumbled something I didn't understand, then tossed me at Sexy's feet. "*Esta puta es tuya*," El Gato spat, then spun and stalked off toward the stage again.

My mind was reeling from that little exchange. I glanced up just as Sexy crouched down and held out his hand to me. The scent of sun and coconut washed over me. Something fluttered inside my stomach. He was familiar too.

"Come with me." His voice was like a warm chocolate bath.

I shuddered and clenched my thighs. Who knew a voice could delight the senses? I swallowed hard and stared at his offered hand. This probably wasn't a better option than the auction, but there was something about him. I gazed into his hazel eyes and saw little flecks of gold floating around in them. His lips hooked up into a small smile. I bit my lower lip, then placed the tips of my fingers in his large palm.

He wrapped his warm hand around my cold fingers, then helped me stand. My entire body shook. I glanced back at the line of women still lined up on the stage. Darla stood stock-still, her head turned in my direction. The woman who'd been to my left still stood droopy, like this was the end of her, and maybe it was, maybe she wouldn't last much longer.

The man next to me wrapped an arm around my shoulders and tugged me along, forcing me to tear my gaze away from the others. Away from those I'd left behind. I moved my feet as he led me along the opulent hall, a single tear trailing a silent path down my cheek.

9

Raella

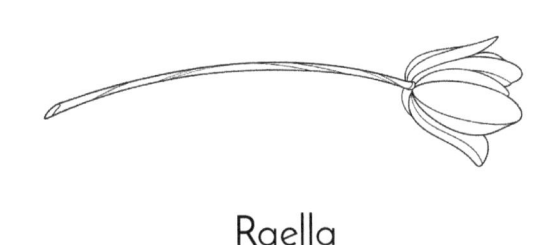

Sexy left me in a large master suite. The bedroom had a king-sized bed with a heavy oak frame, which would be impossible to move, and no other furniture. The bathroom was sparsely stocked too, just the bare essentials, one towel and washcloth, a toothbrush, toothpaste and a hairbrush. In the closet, I found three neat stacks of clothes that would last for two days and a large men's T-shirt that smelled distinctly of coconut. I dropped it on the floor, as flashes of Sexy's face passed across my vision.

I picked a pair of black tights and a plain, white T-shirt from the other piles. No underwear. It felt good to be back in clothes though, and I wrapped my arms around to hug myself. When my fingers touched the nape of my neck, I remembered my lost cross again. *Why had they taken it?* I shook my head, then left the closet. It wasn't the time to get caught up over the cross. I needed to figure out why I was here or even find a way to escape.

Back in the bedroom, I went to the door and pounded on it. "Hey," I yelled at the top of my lungs. "Can anyone hear me?"

Nothing. No response. I spun around and pressed my back to the door, my head falling against it.

When Sexy had first left me here, the sun's light had been bright and had reflected off the bright yellow walls, making the room shiny and almost cheery. Some time had passed since then, and the room seemed less inviting, more like a prison. I walked across the room to the only window and other exit.

A pair of French doors took up most of the wall opposite the door. The glass had mullions in a grid-like pattern inside. The doors opened out onto a huge oval stone balcony that overlooked a pool surrounded by palm trees. Unfortunately, the knobs wouldn't turn, nor would the doors push open. I pushed and shoved with all my body weight, but nothing happened. I slammed my fists against the glass. It shook in its frame but stayed put.

If I could just get one of these pieces to break, I could try to open the door from the outside. I slammed the heel of my hand into a piece close to the handle, hard, with my whole body, like I'd seen fighters do on TV. A small crack formed through the pane. My heart rate kicked up. I rubbed my palm, then ran into the closet to grab the shirt off the floor to protect my hand.

Back in front of the French doors, I squared my shoulders and leaned forward. Bracing myself against the door, I lined my right arm up and jammed it toward the cracked glass. The distinct sound of shattering glass filled the air as my arm slid through the small opening. Before I could celebrate that small victory, a sharp pain lanced up my arm to my shoulder.

"Fuck," I cursed into the silence.

A shard of glass stuck out from the pane. A drop of blood hung from the tip, along with a piece of skin. Blood flowed from my arm and ran down the window like raindrops. My arm shook as I brought it back through the small space, then tightly rewrapped the shirt around the cut to stop the bleeding. I cradled my arm against my chest as my stomach twisted. I'd totally fucked that up.

Just then I heard a series of beeps behind me. I twisted my head in time to see the door open and Sexy amble into the room. I tried to huddle in on myself to hide my injury. Would there be some kind of punishment for this? Fear sliced through my chest.

He looked the same as earlier and carried a tray in his sculpted arms. The delicious smell of food struck my nose. My stomach grumbled. Who knew when I'd eaten last? Then the reason I hadn't eaten in a while slapped me in the face and my empty stomach shoved bile up my throat. I turned away from the food, and the gorgeous man carrying it.

"*¿Hambrienta?*" His voice was as enticing as I remembered, making me want to look. He'd asked if I was hungry, but I didn't know enough Spanish for him to continue using it.

I shook my head and turned to him. "*No hablo español.*"

He raised one brow. "You will need to learn," he said matter-of-factly, as if I had access to Rosetta Stone or a Spanish tutor. His eyes traveled over me, stopped on the French doors, then darted back to me, a deep crease between his gold-flecked, hazel eyes. "What have you been doing in here?" His voice sounded harsher than a moment ago.

Unsure if I should answer, I backed up, hoping to hide the broken window, then froze when my foot squished in the carpet. I lifted my foot and saw the line of blood leading from the French doors right to me. My eyes widened, my chest tightened, and my vision blurred out for a second.

Sexy's nostrils flared. "You made a mess." He seemed angry, but his voice didn't sound like it. He moved toward me with swift movements and grasped my injured arm. I tried to pull it away, but he held tight. He pulled back the shirt and saw the cut, which had stopped bleeding now and didn't look as bad as I had initially thought. He cursed in Spanish.

I reached up for my cross, then bit my lower lip when my fingers met empty skin. Sexy's eyes followed the path of my fingers, then landed on my eyes. His gaze was so intense I wanted to hide. I didn't know what to say or do in this moment, but I had to do something.

"Why am I here?" My voice sounded weak. I didn't want to be weak, but my whole body shook. I'd been kidnapped by strangers and stripped of my dignity. My husband hadn't come to rescue me like he should've. My entire world had been flipped upside down.

Sexy smiled, then reached up and ran his thumb along the arc of my cheek. He didn't respond, just stood there taking in my features and making me feel more self-conscious than I'd felt in a very long time.

I tried to step back, but his hand tightened on my arm. I glanced down and willed him to let go. He shouldn't touch me, though his touch was kinder than I thought it'd be.

Sexy leaned in closer and took a deep breath, then wrinkled his nose. "You need a shower."

I opened and closed my mouth, trying to wriggle out of his grasp. "Do you have a name?"

"Segundo." He smirked, then moved toward the bathroom, pulling me with him.

"Second? Don't you have a real name?" If I kept him talking maybe I'd learn something. He didn't seem to want to hurt me, but he was awful bossy. He pulled me through the doorway into the bathroom, not caring he was squeezing my injured arm.

He chuckled and craned his neck to look back at me. "Sí. Segundo is my name here and yours is Tulipán," he said with finality in his voice.

I frowned as he resisted my efforts to free my injured arm. I tried to dig in my heels, but he forced me to keep moving. "Tulipán? But my name is—"

"No." He stopped and turned to face me, pulling me close to him. "Your name is Tulipán." He leaned in, his breath hot against my face. My whole body flushed with heat and a tingling sensation raced through me at his nearness. He stood there for a minute, then abruptly dropped my arm to turn on the shower.

I hugged myself while I watched him prepare the shower he so badly wanted me to take. My arm stung, but it wasn't bleeding any longer. These people had kidnapped me and now they'd changed my name. What else were they going to do with me? How long had I been here? A day? Two?

"What's today?" It was a simple question. There was no harm in me knowing.

Segundo's eyes flashed as he glanced at me. "Tuesday. Why?"

I buried my face in my hands and listened to the water strike the

Taken, not Destroyed

shower tiles. A warm, calloused hand began to rub a path up and down both my upper arms. I lifted my face. Segundo stood just in front of me. He was almost the same height as me, maybe a couple inches taller. He had a five-o'clock shadow and plump, pink lips that tipped up as I stared at them. I shouldn't be appreciating this man, he'd been a part of my kidnapping.

I swallowed against a thickness that had formed in my throat and stepped to the side. "I should shower now." I stared at him and cocked out a hip, waiting for him to leave.

His gaze raked up and down my body, then he turned and moved to stand in the bathroom door with his back to me. "You need to be clean," he said, his voice muffled.

I began stripping, feeling more exposed than I had before. "Why?"

"El Ratón will expect it."

"Wh-Who's El Ratón?" I stammered. "And why . . . "

"Shower, Tulipán," he commanded, no longer patient.

I climbed into the shower and my body seemed to melt as the hot water struck my skin. My heart ached as the past two days rushed back. The other women. What had happened to them? Darla. The Hispanic mom. The girl whose dad had sold her. Club Girl. All of them, even Venom. I'd left them. I let the water flow over my face as my eyes burned with tears I didn't want to shed. Tears wouldn't help them or me.

Blowing out a breath, I reached out and grabbed the bodywash and almost dropped the bottle. It was the same wash I used every day. How had they known? My breaths shuttered and my jaw shook as chills raced through my body. I stared at the bottle in my hand, unable to move.

A knock sounded on the glass and I jumped, dropping the bodywash. I turned to see Segundo standing outside the glass shower. I covered my chest even though I knew it was pointless, he'd seen every inch of me already.

He opened the door and chuckled as a wry smile formed on his lips. *"Todos te vimos desnuda."*

That bit of Spanish I didn't follow. "What?" I demanded and shivered from the cool air. "Can you close that door?"

Segundo licked his lips as his eyes roamed over my naked form beneath the running water. My breaths increased despite the fact that I wanted to be repulsed. He reached out and ran a finger from the nape of my neck to my cleavage. "Hurry. I have business to attend to."

I licked my suddenly dry lips. His eyes followed the movement. I nodded and he left, closing the door and allowing the steam to build again. I quickly scrubbed myself, shoving away thoughts about the other women and the bodywash until later. I grabbed the towel that hung just outside the shower and wrapped it around me.

"What should I wear now?" I asked Segundo, who'd returned to his spot in the doorway.

His shoulders tensed, then he turned around. His hazel eyes sparkled as they traveled over my towel-clad body as if they could see right through it. His tongue darted out between his lips. I'd never been alone with a man besides Brian like this before. The one time I'd had sex in high school had been a complete first-time disaster for both of us. Did all women have these thoughts about their captors? Or just dumb, inexperienced women like me?

Segundo walked over to me and stopped about six inches away. He looked at me like he wanted to devour me, rather than I was the biggest disappointment—like Brian usually did. He leaned in so his breath brushed against the crook of my neck. A prickling sensation traveled down my neck and my nipples peaked. Then he walked off and disappeared into the closet, leaving me there, breathless.

I shifted and felt like I needed another shower, maybe a cold one this time. Just one look from that gorgeous man had wetness gathering between my legs and that had never happened to me before. *What was happening to me?*

When Segundo returned, he handed me a stack of clothes, then leaned against the counter with his arms crossed, gaze pinned on me. He looked relaxed, as if he'd found the most comfortable spot in the room.

I raised a brow. "Do you mind?"

Taken, not Destroyed

"Nope." He looked like a gorgeous statue. One covered in dangerous looking tattoos that did all kinds of things to my libido.

We stared at each other in silence for a beat. Gritting my teeth, I turned around and met his gaze in the mirror. He planned to watch one way or another. I made sure the towel was tucked in tight at the top, then pulled on the shorts he'd brought me.

Segundo's eyes followed every move I made in the mirror, making my skin burn. No one had ever been so interested in watching me dress. Especially not Brian. I was almost successful at changing without showing too much skin, but the towel fell moments before I had my shirt pulled over my head. I yanked my shirt down, but I was positive Segundo got a full view of my tits by the glow in his eyes. Damn mirrors. My cheeks burned so hot you could almost fry an egg on them.

Segundo stepped in front of me, his sun and coconut scent washing over me. "You must not be so . . . " He frowned and waved his hand, and I smiled for the first time. He looked so damn cute. "*Avergonzada*, I do not know the English word."

He ran his thumb across my cheek, where I could feel the heat of my embarrassment. I closed my eyes at his gentle touch. He caressed me as if he was trying to wash the embarrassment away.

"Embarrassed?" How could this man be so gentle?

Segundo had leaned closer so his breath mingled with mine, like he planned to kiss me. The desire to know what his lips felt like washed through me. His lips looked so soft. His gaze was locked on mine. My heart raced, even though this was wrong, it almost felt right. Before one of us could lean closer, he dropped his hand and stepped away. I shook my head and wanted to slap myself.

"I have work." He raked his fingers through his thick, black hair. "You will be expected tomorrow for dinner."

I blinked at the rapid shift in mood. He continued to talk, even though I had questions I couldn't find an opening to ask.

"I will bring you an outfit for dinner. Abuela will see to you in the morning." He left the bathroom before I could collect myself.

I shook myself from my stupor and ran after him. I still had a million questions. I didn't know why I was here. Or what had happened to the others. I pushed myself to move faster, but by the time I'd made it to the bedroom, he was knocking on the door with the empty tray in hand.

The door opened. He glanced back at me and his lips tipped up.

"*Buenas noches, mi tulipán,*" he said, then was gone. Just like a wraith in the night.

If I was meeting this El Ratón guy tomorrow, why had he made me shower tonight? And who was El Ratón? What made him so special? When I reached the door, I tried the handle, but it was locked again. I screamed and pounded on it until my throat was sore and my arms gave out.

They had no right to lock me up. They'd stolen me from my family. Took my freedom, which was guaranteed to me as an American citizen. I had to get out of this place. My kids and my sister needed me. Even Paige needed me.

When my cries went unanswered yet again, I turned and slid down the door to the floor. I had to find a way to escape.

10

Segundo

After I'd left Tulipán last night, I'd updated El Ratón that his gift wasn't quite ready. She needed time to accept her role and I needed time to help her understand the need to obey. Like I thought, he refused to speak English or change his plans. I needed to find a way to help her learn Spanish and to behave, it would save us all heartache in the long run.

I walked into the large, modern kitchen and inhaled the wonderful smell of fresh tortillas. "Abuela, it smells wonderful." I stretched my arms behind me.

Abuela was a grandmother to one of the cartel members and she'd been the main housekeeper here since El Ratón's cousin ran things. She was the best cook and acted like a mother to us all, even El Ratón. He avoided her scolding whenever he could.

At my voice, she turned from her work and smiled, the wrinkles on her cheeks becoming more prominent. "Segundo, I made it for you."

She didn't do anything in this house just for me, but I took her in my arms for a hug anyway. Her gray-haired head stopped about the center of my chest. She wrapped her short arms around me and said, "Oh. So strong." She chuckled.

I rolled my eyes, then stepped back. "*Gracias*, Abuela. I have a favor." She would help. She had a soft spot for people in need. She'd cared for Daniela, at her bedside every day, until the moment the cancer took her. El Ratón couldn't watch her die, so Abuela took his place. He loved Daniela in his own way, but the cancer made her weak and he couldn't stand it.

Abuela's rheumy gaze met mine. She gave me a curt nod, then turned back to her work.

"You know of the new female?" Her thin lips tipped up as she kneaded some dough. "She is Tulipán. Please see to her meals, linens, and that she cares for herself." I watched Abuela's face, but it remained stoic.

I couldn't bring myself to supervise another shower no matter how much I enjoyed last night. It'd been too tempting not to ravage her. The way she'd looked at me, I swore she wanted me to kiss her as much as I wanted it. I'd wanted nothing less from the minute I'd held her in my arms. There was no way I could touch the gift I meant for El Ratón without his permission. My throat tightened as I forced my thoughts back to the present.

"She also needs to learn Spanish." I cocked my head when she paused and looked at me.

Abuela shook her head and tsked. "I can do as you ask, *mi hijo*." Abuela's pale blue eyes ringed with white met mine and pierced my skull, straight through to my soul.

Her eyes were unusual for a Hispanic woman. She'd been a beauty in her younger days, but now those eyes made grown men shiver. She knew how to scold without words.

I glanced away and swallowed, my tongue suddenly dry. "Is there coffee?" I searched for a cup, desperately looking anywhere but at her. She knew I was up to something. I didn't even know if I should feel guilty, but strangely enough, I did.

"Of course." She chuckled. I heard the water running as I found a cup, then filled it with coffee. "Speak to her in Spanish, then repeat in English," Abuela explained as I took a sip.

Staring at the dark liquid in my cup with my brows pulled together, I asked, "Will she really learn to speak that way?" I lifted my gaze to her.

She shrugged her small shoulder, then returned to the counter and her dough, which could be more tortillas or something else. Clearly, she was satisfied that she'd given me an answer and was done with our conversation.

"*Gracias*," I thanked her, then turned with my coffee to leave. I wasn't entirely sure if I was doing this to save Tulipán from El Ratón's violence or me from having to see her endure it.

At the doorway, I bumped into Tocino, one of our information runners, and almost spilled the cup on both of us. The teenager's face was flushed. I lifted the cup to save us from the hot coffee. "Whoa, Tocino. What's up?"

He was a wily, skinny kid about eighteen years old. He shouldn't have gotten caught up in our business, but he had a knack for getting information which meant I had use for him. I did my best to only use him for information gathering, keeping him away from the drugs, for now. It was probably the only way his family kept food on their table.

Tocino's eyes met mine. "I have information." He huffed as if he'd run the whole way from the front gate.

I put my hand on the back of his neck and led him out of the kitchen and into my old office down the hall. "Yes, of course," I said once we'd arrived. "What is it?" A little curious since he rarely brought me information I hadn't asked for.

"That girl you took from El Gato." He lifted his chin, pointing it at the second floor.

"Yeah, what about her?" I leaned on the desk and bounced my knee. He needed to get to the point, I had business to take care of today.

"She has a husband. He's making a fuss at the hotel about her being missing." He spoke so fast I almost didn't catch it all, but I did.

My heart stalled, then restarted at a marathon pace as I gaped at the kid. "A fucking husband?"

She hadn't had a ring on her finger. El Amante was supposed to choose women who wouldn't be missed, who didn't have any fucking connections in Mexico to throw a fit. That was the whole point of having a guy at the resorts. What a colossal fuckup. I needed to fix this before El Ratón found out my gift was a liability to the cartel. He'd kill her, or worse, he'd make me kill her. I stood and turned my back on Tocino. I dug in my back pocket, grabbed my phone, then dialed El Amante's number.

He answered with a bright, cheery voice on the second ring. "*Hola?*"

"You fucking idiot," I seethed, not just for his fuckup but because I'd have to deal with the consequences. I couldn't imagine killing Tulipán, I'd just gotten her.

"Segundo?" His voice shook. "What—"

"The woman has a husband, who's in Mexico." I took a deep breath. "My woman, El Amante." I clarified.

"*Sí.*" All the sunshine from earlier had drained from his voice. "Both from this hotel do. The blond is traveling with hers." I gritted my teeth and growled deep in my throat at his confession. I heard the door slam behind me and turned to find that Tocino had abandoned me.

Rubbing my hand down my face, I tried to wipe away my fury. I needed to hold it together to fix this situation before El Ratón found out and fixed it his way. "Is it a problem?"

He exhaled. "No. I don't think so, or I wouldn't have sent either with Serpiente."

I walked around the large, dark oak desk and dropped into the plush leather chair. I leaned back and stared at the ceiling, imagining that I could see the woman we spoke of through the thick floor. "Tell me."

In the silence, I could hear conversations from people at the resort. Soon the sound disappeared as El Amante, known as David at the hotel, sought privacy. "He came to visit me since she left here. Twice now. It's not a problem though. I have it handled."

I sat forward and rested my elbows on the desk. Something about his tone didn't sit right. "How?"

"No worries, Boss." I could almost hear the smile in his voice, the confidence even. "It's taken care of."

"Not good enough." This couldn't blow back on me or the cartel. The others were sold off to unknown agents, but Tulipán was here, if the Americans found her, we'd be in a world of shit. "This needs to be contained."

El Amante tsked. "I can cover my end."

I rolled out my shoulders. "Will it hold up against the Americans if they investigate?"

"*Sí*, Segundo. I'll work it out with Serpiente." He sounded even more confident now.

Pushing back the chair, I stood and filled my lungs with air, then let it out slowly. "I want all the details sent to me. Everything. Nothing can be left to chance."

"I don't understand. Why is this so important?"

Rubbing my jaw, I considered what he needed to know to get the job done and what I was willing to do to keep Tulipán safe. "I'm trying to protect you from the Black Room and the cartel from the Americans."

He gasped. "*Gracias. Gracias.*"

I cut the line with my head spinning from that entire conversation. I had no control over any of it beyond leaving here to go supervise the situation, which I had no desire to do. I had to trust that they'd take care of it to protect their asses and the cartel.

I spent the rest of the day in front of my computer trying to focus on siphoning the money El Gato had made through the many accounts we had set up to launder money. But my mind kept wandering to the female in the room next door. When I'd made the decision to take her as a gift for El Ratón, I'd had Daniela's suite cleaned out and added the door lock. Then I'd taken the room next door, so I could be close. It was a balm and a curse.

When the sun touched the horizon, I powered down my computer and went to clean up for Tulipán's first dinner with El Ratón. I'd ordered a floor-length, red dress for her this evening. I grabbed it from my closet and headed to her room with my heart jammed up in my throat. I took a moment outside the door to pray that this night would go well, for both our sakes, because she would either stay here or be buried somewhere in the back forest. I typed in the six-digit code and pushed open the door.

A pale arm swung at my face. I reached up and grabbed her forearm before it connected with my nose. I couldn't stop the laugh that erupted. She was perfect. I twisted her arm, wrenched it behind her body, spun us both, and pressed her front against the wall next to the door. My heart rate picked up and my dick swelled in my pants as I breathed in her scent of vanilla and honey.

I pressed my front against her back, and lightly brushed my lips against her ear. "¿*Qué esperabas lograr, mi tulipán?*" I took a breath, then said it in English, "What did you hope to achieve, my tulip?"

Her body stiffened in response to my words, and maybe she sensed the fact that I was pressing a raging hard-on into her ass. El Ratón had a point about women who fought, it was a turn-on, this woman in particular. I stepped back, releasing her arm, and closed the door. I tried to calm the beast that raged inside my pants.

Keeping to what Abuela suggested I said everything to Tulipán in Spanish first, then English. "I brought your dress for this evening." I leaned down and picked it up from the floor where I'd dropped it.

Her chest heaved up and down and her face was flushed. She stared at me with desire-filled, blazing blue eyes. I raked my fingers through my thick hair. I wasn't entirely prepared to deal with my feelings, let alone hers. I held the dress out and took a small step back. I needed to play this right with her and El Ratón. Besides she wasn't ready, no matter what her body said. I needed to focus on convincing her to obey and play along tonight, not worry about what I wanted. Not yet anyway.

Tulipán's eyes moved from my face to the dress, then back to my face. She looked better this evening. The puffiness had gone from around her sparkling blue eyes. Eyes that told stories, stories of how she'd lived a sheltered life. This experience was going to test her and everything she knew. I resisted the urge to touch her flushed cheeks and feel if they were as heated as they looked.

Without a word, she took the dress out of my hands and moved past me into the bathroom. I exhaled as the tension followed her. Fuck, this woman was going to be a challenge. Maybe I should've found another way to save Queso. But the thought of her being with someone else brought bile to the back of my throat.

A few minutes later, a screech sounded from the bathroom. I rushed to the doorway to find her dressed and staring at herself in the full-length mirror. My heart stopped and my breath caught in my chest. The wine-red dress had wide straps that connected to the skirt and crossed over her breasts, then traveled over each shoulder to meet at the nape of her neck. The back was completely open. The skirt hugged her hips and flowed down in a gentle wave to her ankle bones. It had a slit up the right side that stopped mid-thigh. There was just the right amount of skin showing to make a man's cock hard. I had proof.

Fucking hell. She's a wet dream come true.

"What's wrong?" Eyes wide, I searched the room for spiders or something dangerous.

"I'm barely covered," she gasped, while trying to cover the areas where her ample cleavage was exposed.

I scoffed and shook my head. El Ratón would be happy and that was all that mattered. I stepped up behind her and caught her gaze in the mirror. I lightly ran my fingertips down her upper arms, leaving goosebumps in their wake. "We should go."

Her eyes hooded and the muscles in her shoulders relaxed as her arms fell down to her sides. My gaze fell to her peaked nipples, and I bit my tongue. Her soft skin felt so good, so right beneath my fingers. I needed to stop before I took this too far.

"Who are you people? Why am I here?" Her voice was strong and insistent.

I tucked my hands into my pockets and stepped away from the heat of her body. Someday she'd be ready, and she'd give herself to me. She turned as soon as I stepped away, her bright blue eyes pinned to mine.

The fire inside me burned like an inferno. I needed her to trust me, but I didn't know what to tell her. "El Ratón's the leader of a cartel."

She dropped her head and pushed her fingers against her forehead. She mumbled and shook her head. I pulled her hands away and tipped her chin up.

"Relax," I said, not just for her benefit. "Tonight, will only be the three of us." There really was no reason for her to trust me, but she didn't have a choice. Her throat bobbed on a heavy swallow, then she nodded slightly.

"*Bien*." I tore my gaze from hers and turned to leave. My desire for her a living current beneath my skin.

"Are there shoes?" Her soft voice stopped me. I glanced over my shoulder. She had her eyes pinned on my bare feet.

"No shoes in the house." My response was more curt than I'd intended, but she was the last person who needed shoes. Shoes gave her a sense of security. Security offered her the ability to try to escape. There was no escape for her unless El Ratón chose to sell or kill her. Neither of those were options in my mind.

I grasped her small hand and wrapped her arm through mine, then glanced sideways at her as I made my way toward the door. "Are you married, Tulipán?" I studied her face, wondering if she'd lie.

She tucked her lower lip between her teeth and glanced away. I paused with my hand on the door and raised a brow, certain she was going to try to lie to me, but happy that she didn't have a poker face worth a shit.

"Yes." She hung her head. Maybe this husband wouldn't come looking for her after all? Maybe the marriage wasn't good. I definitely didn't want her thinking about another man when I came inside her.

Without another word, I opened the door and directed her through the ornately decorated hall and down the marble front stairs. She walked next to me with her eyes downcast and one hand absently touching the space at the nape of her neck. My stomach twisted. Her cross hung on a hook in my bedroom next to my computer.

When we reached the doors to the dining room on the first floor, I leaned into her space and touched her ear with my lips. "Do not lie to him. Do as he says. Always. He's always in control."

She exhaled as a shiver moved down her body. I straightened my shoulders. I'd calmed and prepared her as much as I could. There was no telling how this evening would progress. The Boss was just as unpredictable as he was predictable.

11

Tulipán

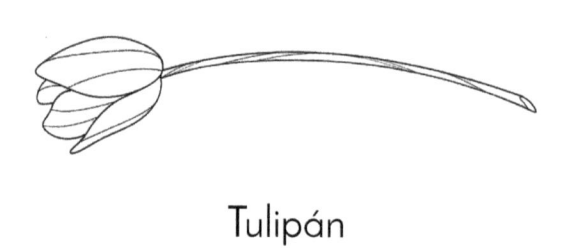

Segundo guided me down some marble curving stairs, my arm hooked through his. The only thing I could focus on as we moved was the set of large, wooden double doors at the bottom. They looked like entry doors. Doors that opened to freedom. At the bottom, my feet faltered when Segundo turned left, then paused in front of a different set of double doors. Blood rushed through my head.

After he'd given his warning and pushed into the massive dining room, my eyes widened as I took in my new surroundings. There was no doubt that this cartel leader was wealthy and liked to show it. A dark wood, rectangular table took up the entirety of the room and was surrounded by at least twenty cushioned chairs with arms. To my right, there were three large arches that spanned the room and opened to the dark night. A soft breeze struck my cheek.

Segundo tugged my arm. My mind felt foggy, and I didn't want to go where he wanted me to go. Freedom screamed my name. If I could just get out of here, maybe I could find the others before they disappeared forever. I couldn't pull my gaze away from the darkness beyond the archways.

Taken, not Destroyed

"*Pinche pecaminosa.*" A deep voice growled, yanking me from my musings.

I turned and saw a short, thin-framed man standing on the far side of the room. I felt the power he exuded down to my bones. His salt-and-pepper hair was cut close on the sides with a longer wave on top, and he wore a red, long sleeved, button-down. The sleeves were folded back, which exposed the various tattoos on his forearms. They even covered his fingers. He had a tattoo on his neck of a skull perched on top of a gun with some writing, which I couldn't read from here. I glanced over at Segundo and saw the same tattoo on the right side of his neck.

I turned back and met the gaze of the new man. When our eyes met, I could've sworn I saw the depths of Hell in the black pools. I squeezed Segundo's arm tighter. Even though I had no reason to trust the man next to me, there was no way I trusted the one in red across the room.

One side of Segundo's lip tipped up briefly. He gently removed my arm from his and took up a guard-like pose in the corner near one of the arches. My feet froze to the floor as I watched him leave me, his face a mask of indifference, so like what Brian would do when he turned on lawyer mode. Segundo waved his hand to encourage me to continue. I hugged my middle and took measured steps toward what could've been my doom as much as anything else.

"*Ven a comer conmigo.*" El Ratón gestured toward the chair to the right of the head of the table, where he stood.

Segundo had said this was a dinner. I didn't need to speak Spanish to understand he'd invited me to eat, but my stomach was in so many knots that I couldn't imagine putting a speck of food inside it. I stopped by the chair, dropped my gaze, and reached for my cross. I gritted my teeth over its absence yet again. I needed to ask Segundo where it went.

El Ratón stepped around the table and pulled the chair out. He leaned in close and his words struck me in the gut. "*Tomaré más de lo que doy, Tulipán.*"

I sat quickly and met Segundo's gaze. Even though I didn't know the words, I knew a threat when I heard it. My hair stuck to the back of my neck. I folded my hands in my lap and stared straight ahead, only glancing at El Ratón out the side of my eyes every so often. He'd taken his seat and was pouring red wine into two long-stemmed wine glasses.

The minute he set the bottle down, the older woman, who'd introduced herself earlier today as Abuela, came in and served us plates heaping with food. She didn't speak a word before she bustled out a hidden door near the head of the table. The smell of food wafted up from the plate. I wanted to be hungry, but the scent and sight of food only flipped my stomach.

Unconcerned with me, El Ratón leaned forward, pushed my wine glass toward me, then picked up his fork and began to eat. My stomach rolled and twisted with each bite he took. My hands twisted in my lap. It was hard to just sit back and eat when I was so close to an open door, but Segundo had warned me to obey. El Ratón stabbed at his food, bit it off his fork, and chewed in a manner that was almost violent, working his jaw like a starved lion. If I didn't eat something, he'd be done before I took my next breath.

Tentatively, I picked up my fork, then chanced a glance at Segundo. He stared daggers at me. I blew out a breath and pushed a few bits of chicken and vegetables around on the plate before picking one up and dropping it in my mouth. I knew from the smell that the food should taste good, but it all tasted like sand. I took a sip of the bitter wine. My mouth felt like the Sahara Desert.

When I glanced up from my plate, El Ratón's cold, hard gaze followed my movements. His plate was completely empty, and he lounged back in his chair holding his glass of wine. He took a sip, then lifted the glass toward me. My jaw quivered. I didn't know what to do. What did these men want from me?

He sneered. *"No sabes porque estas aqui."*

"No." I didn't know why I was there. I couldn't understand why anyone would kidnap another human being and hold them against their will. Nothing about this situation made any sense to me. If he was anything like Brian, and I suspected he was, less words were better.

Without warning, he pushed his chair back and stood. Then he grabbed mine by the arms and spun it so I was facing him. He threaded his fingers in my hair. *"Porque lo que quiero lo consigo."*

My heart raced out of my chest as he gazed down at me. His hand fisted in the hair at the back of my head, pulling sharply at the ends until my eyes watered. I refused to make a sound or cry. But I couldn't prevent myself from trying to pull away. His grip hurt, and the food I'd just forced down threatened to come back up. I pressed my lips together and swallowed to keep it all down.

He stared down at me with those dark, evil eyes. When the pressure on my head got to be too much, I reached up and dug my nails into El Ratón's inked forearm. I wanted to beg him to let go, but I knew words wouldn't convince him to stop. Instead of releasing my hair, he shot me the evilest of grins, then unfastened his pants, dropping them to the floor and releasing his erect penis.

I tried to turn my head, but he only gripped my hair tighter. The ends burned as tears flowed freely down my cheeks. I pressed back against the chair and grabbed the armrests. An ice cage gripped my chest. There had to be an escape.

El Ratón yanked my head forward and aimed his hard cock for my lips. I tried to turn away, but he held tight, controlling my head with his strong arm and directing his hard-on with the other. I sealed my lips together and used my grip on the chair's arms to push back.

"Tomarás lo que te doy o serás castigado," he commanded as he thrust his cock hard against my lips. I could feel the bead of precum moistening my outer lip. I grunted as I tried to struggle away, sweat coating every inch of my body.

Segundo cleared his throat, but El Ratón's black eyes remained pinned to mine. I couldn't tell if Segundo was reminding me to obey or if the interruption was meant for his boss; either way, neither of us responded. El Ratón wasn't in control of my body. I didn't even do this for Brian anymore. No one could make me do this. I curled my lips inside and bit on them.

The deranged man seemed to get harder and more excited the longer I refused. He stroked his cock, then groaned. A little more moisture landed on my lips. Acid burned the back of my throat, and I tried to turn my head, but his grip was so tight it felt like my head would explode. I shook my head as far as I could against his hold, on the verge of sobbing, wanting to beg him to stop, but not wanting to open my mouth to speak.

Time passed, maybe one minute, maybe twenty, I couldn't tell, but it was too long. When he released my hair and moved away, I wiped my face, then held my burning head, rocking back and forth. Maybe he'd let me go back to my room.

As I lifted my head, he reached out and wrapped his hand around my neck. With his other arm, El Ratón swiped it across the table, dumping our leftover plates, glasses, and silverware onto the floor. I gasped and latched on to his hand. He tightened his grip and pulled me to stand. Our eyes met for the briefest of seconds before he spun me around, bent me at the waist, and planted me face down on the table. He leaned over me so I could feel his hardness pressed against my ass.

"Know you are punished for your actions, Tulip," he whispered in my ear, the name they gave me a curse on his lips, his breath like acid on my skin.

His voice was nothing like Segundo's, it was rough and laced with evil.

My entire body shook. I could barely pull in a breath as I waited for whatever he had planned. It couldn't be good. He'd just tried to force me to suck his cock. Was he going to rape me? Getting close to hyperventilating, I rested my cheek on the table, so I could see Segundo. He'd moved out of the dark corner and now stood with his hands tightly gripping the back of one of the chairs. Our eyes met, just as El Ratón's weight lifted off me.

My heart slowed a fraction, and I tried to push up. El Ratón's hot hand wrapped around the back of my neck, shoving me back down and squishing my chest against the table. My chest burned.

"*Permanecer*," he commanded. Stay.

Segundo's eyes flashed seconds before I heard a slashing sound, then felt the hot slice of pain across my back from my right shoulder to the bottom of my left ribs. My arms shot out to the side and I

Taken, not Destroyed

screamed, unable to stop the response. After the initial shock of pain, a slow burning sensation followed the same path.

My mind emptied. Everything centered on the burning strip across my back.

Then the whoosh came again, followed quickly by the slicing pain across another area on my back and the slow burn. The process repeated. Again and again. I screamed with each strike. On the third one, I arched my back and tried to push away from the table. The pain was almost unbearable, so I stopped trying to move and lay limp on the table.

The whip came one more time across another area on my back, followed by another scream. My throat felt raw, my mouth dry. My back had hot coals roasting on it. I wanted to escape, to protect myself, but none of my parts would respond.

I met Segundo's gaze again and felt the icy hand of betrayal building in my gut. Nothing he'd said had warned me this could happen. He'd said not to lie and to remember El Ratón was in control. He hadn't mentioned punishment or a sexual act requirement. Not that either would've mattered. He'd just stood there while El Ratón whipped me bloody. I needed to ignore my body and listen to my head. No matter how attractive that man was, he wasn't good for me.

After a minute of silence, El Ratón grunted behind me, and I heard what sounded like him jacking off. I squeezed my eyes closed to stop the tears that burned behind them. He didn't deserve any more of my tears.

I felt his body press against the backs of my legs. Then he groaned loudly as a hot, sticky liquid squirted across my freshly whipped back. I retched and pressed a hand to my mouth as it filled with vomit. My stomach rolled and flipped, but I squeezed my eyes and swallowed the acid back down.

El Ratón zipped his pants, then appeared in my vision next to Segundo. They exchanged a few quiet words before El Ratón left through the doorway out into the night like a phantom who wrought pain and suffering. I wouldn't underestimate that man again, but I didn't know if I could just let him use my body to avoid another whipping.

Every muscle in my body shook as the smallest movement sent shockwaves of pain all the way up and down my spine. I was drenched in sweat, and I might've wet myself at some point, I couldn't be sure. Instead of trying to stand, I slid over the edge of the table onto the ground in a puddle.

Segundo had seemed safe, but there wasn't any safety in this place. Somehow, I was going to have to save myself. Not just for me. If this was happening to me. What was happening to the other girls? I couldn't leave them to be forgotten. I had to get out of here, for myself, for Misti, for Landon and Shannon, for the girls.

People needed me.

12

Segundo

Almost a week later, I stood on the balcony that both my and Tulipán's rooms opened onto and watched Bernard, a local worker, replace the glass she'd broken on her first day. Up until now, I'd covered the space with a piece of wood to keep her from attempting another escape. Though that was unlikely after El Ratón had whipped her on her second day here.

The two of us were cast in shadow as the sun was just peeking over the horizon on the other side of the house. I crossed my arms and watched Tulipán through the window as her back moved in a peaceful sleep. Abuela reported twice a day on her progress, and I'd often come here to watch her. She only moved from her prone position on the bed when Abuela forced her to the bathroom or to eat. My throat tightened as I considered her wasting away in that bed.

She took a deep breath, then her bright blue eyes opened and pinned on me. A shiver traced down my spine. I hadn't spoken to or been in her presence since the incident, and I had no idea how she felt about me. Her eyes narrowed and she turned her head. I swallowed hard as a stone settled in my gut.

Just then, my phone buzzed in my pocket. I turned away, dug it out, and brought it to my ear without looking at the caller ID. "Yes?"

"Segundo?" A male voice I recognized, but couldn't place, responded.

Frowning, I glanced at the phone's face and saw it was El Amante calling. So much had happened since I'd last spoken with him that I'd completely forgotten he was supposed to clean up the mess with Tulipán's husband. "You have something to report?"

I raked my fingers through my hair and turned back to gaze at her, even though she'd turned away. She'd been so strong, refusing to take his cock in her mouth. Even though I knew deep in my gut that it wouldn't turn out well, I'd wanted to praise her for her strength and worship her for saving herself for me. But it had all ended so horribly for us both. The look in her eyes tore my heart right out of my chest. I knew it would only be that much harder to get her to trust me now.

"I do." El Amante's voice cut through my musings. "Her husband flew out this morning."

I rubbed my stubbled jaw as a weight seemed to lift from my shoulders, one I hadn't noticed before now. "Did he cause much trouble?"

"No. It all worked as expected." He paused, breathing heavy through the phone. "You received the information I sent you?"

The email had come the following day after our last conversation. El Amante had been thorough in covering our tracks. No one, not even the American government, would find her here. She was a ghost now. My ghostly flower.

"I did."

She moved, faced me again, grimaced, then returned to the same position on her front, her head turned my way again. The sheet fell, exposing the side of her bare, round breast. My gaze darted to Bernard, who had just put the finishing touches on the glass. "*Adios.*" I closed the call, then stepped up behind the worker. "Finished?" My voice sounded rougher than I intended, but he could easily look up and see her. She was too vulnerable. No other man should see her now.

Bernard's hands shook as he finished with the last bits of caulk, then packed away his bag. He stood quickly, but didn't raise his eyes to meet mine. "*Sí.*"

"Segundo," El Ratón growled from behind me. Bernard's eyes

Taken, not Destroyed

widened as he took in the leader of the Armas Locas cartel. He wrapped his arms around his work bag and pulled it close to his chest.

Schooling my face, I turned and nodded at the cartel leader. "El Ratón." I thanked God he hadn't caught me drooling over Tulipán as I'd done so many times over the last few days.

His dark eyes surveyed the work and the worker, then returned to me. His thick brows pinched. "Inside." He spun and headed into my room.

I took one last glance at my sleeping beauty, then followed my boss. Bernard darted past us both and out my bedroom door, slamming it in his wake. I tried not to smile but couldn't help it. El Ratón took the seat at my computer desk. I bit the inside of my cheek, then pulled over a file box from across the room and sat in front of him.

He smirked. "She'll be better next time."

Swallowing the lump that'd formed, I nodded. He wasn't commenting on her health. "*Sí.*"

El Ratón brushed the front of his shirt as if it were covered with dirt, then leaned back in the leather chair, propping his ankle on the opposite knee. "I have business out of the country."

My gut twisted. I hated when he left the country. It meant I became responsible for the entire cartel. Everyone came to me with their problems. "Where?" I twiddled my thumbs.

His gaze dropped to my hands in my lap, and I flattened my palms on my thighs. "Columbia first. I'll meet with El Mil. We need to deal with a supply issue in India."

I pushed my tongue into my cheek. India supplied pseudoephedrine. I hadn't heard about any issues. Money had been coming out of the account like usual. "Do I need to stop payments?"

He cocked his head and rubbed his jaw. "Not today. I'll call if that changes."

The muscles in my shoulders relaxed. I shifted on the box and gazed at El Ratón, wondering if there was more. He twisted the chair, then leaned forward and took Tulipán's cross between his fingers.

My focus zeroed in on his fingers and my heart rate kicked up. He couldn't take it. I leaned forward and dug my elbows into my thighs.

He rolled the small, silver cross around between his thumb and forefinger while I struggled to maintain my position and not rip it out of his hand.

Finally, El Ratón released the trinket, and I barely recovered my relaxed mask before he swiveled back around in the chair. "El Mil and I will come back here with his wife. I want to have a party."

I took slow, measured breaths to quiet my pounding heart. "When?"

He wrinkled his nose. "A month." El Ratón stood. "Arrange everything."

"I will," I said, then pushed up from the low box, stretching my back when my legs were straight. "What kind of party?" El Ratón had varied tastes, and I never knew which to cater to.

He exited my room and headed down the hall toward the front doors. I followed with tension building in my gut. Messing up the party was just another way to earn a punishment. It might not be a trip to the Black Room, but he'd make his disappointment known. "For El Mil," he finally responded.

That was the best news he could've given me. El Mil was a simple man, with simple needs. To make him happy a party only needed to have music, food, alcohol, drugs, and people. "Is there any pressing business I need to know about before you leave?"

El Ratón stepped through the front doors onto the front stoop, then turned and pinned me with his dark gaze. The bright yellow sun was just peaking over the treetops behind him. "The notes and files are in my office, Segundo, as always."

The head of the Armas Locas cartel spun on his heel and strode down the steps into the light of the rising sun. He climbed into the passenger seat of a black SUV with blacked-out windows. As it took off down the gravel drive toward the gate, I ran my hand down my day-old scruff.

I watched the taillights disappear around the bend beyond the gate, then leaned against the doorjamb and closed my eyes, taking in the soft twittering of the birds that lived in the trees throughout the property. I could use his absence to my advantage. It would give me

Taken, not Destroyed

time to get to know Tulipán better, to earn her trust, to convince her to play along so she wouldn't get punished again. I could tell she felt the pull to me, like I did to her. I just had to balance my time. I couldn't let cartel business fall short, or I'd be the one facing punishment.

A motorcycle engine revved, then hummed as it slowed down in front of me. I opened my eyes as Queso swung his leg off the dirt bike he'd been riding since he'd grown tall enough to reach the ground while seated on it. I walked down to the gravel drive, opening my arms to my youngest brother.

Queso tucked himself against my body and pulled me in close. "Hugo," he whispered in my ear.

I cringed at my brother's insistence on using our given names, even on cartel property. I stepped back and grabbed his thin face. "Queso." I stressed the nickname.

Even though I sent money home, and my family hadn't been poor since I'd joined Armas Locas, my twenty-eight-year-old brother was still skin and bones, like he'd been all his life. He dropped his gaze and nodded.

I kissed his forehead and released his face. "Why're you here?" I was happy to see him, but there had to be a reason for his visit.

The smile he offered barely reached his eyes and wasn't like my overly happy brother. "I need to talk to you. I waited until El Ratón left." He glanced behind him as if he could still see our boss driving away.

I raised my brows, wondering how Queso knew about El Ratón's travel plans before me. Shaking my head, because it truly didn't matter, I slapped my brother on the back. "We can talk in my office. I'll have Abuela bring us breakfast."

After I'd arranged for Abuela to bring us some food, I met Queso in the office that seemed to be my meeting space nowadays. Queso was sat on a chair in front of the desk, so I chose the one next to him. I turned it to face him and propped my ankle on my knee.

"Tell me, what's this about," I prompted.

He popped his knuckles and stared at the wall above my head. My mouth went dry, I'd thought this was a good visit. "Look, Hu—Segundo." He glanced away, then back at me. "Mamá's sick."

A chill raced through me and sweat broke out on the back of my neck. "What do you mean, *sick*?"

He dropped his head and rubbed at his face. "She's been this way for a while." His response was muffled. "Not eating. Sleeping all the time. She's losing weight."

My chest constricted. I sat forward, gripping my brother's thin leg. "Explain." My voice was harsh and I winced.

His head popped up, his brown, watery eyes wide. "I'm sorry. It's been hard to do both." A single tear rolled down his cheek.

A crisp knock sounded at the door and Abuela entered the room. Queso wiped his face in his shirt and sniffled. I sat back and stared at the old woman. She stopped short with the tray of food in her hand, her wise eyes darting between the two of us.

"Come to the kitchen when you want food," she replied, then disappeared just as quickly as she'd appeared.

I closed my eyes and took a moment to collect myself, then took Queso's cool, damp hand in mine. "Did you take her to the doctor?"

He screwed up his face and nodded. "The doctor in our town doesn't know. He says we have to go to the hospital, either Puerto Vallarta or Guadalajara."

"Fuck!" I pushed the chair back and began to pace the room. He couldn't take her all the way to Guadalajara. That was too far to go on his own. I could arrange for cartel help, but not without El Ratón's okay. This was a disaster. I turned to him. "Take her to Puerto Vallarta."

He looked up at me with red-rimmed eyes. "I'm so sorry. I tried, but she's getting worse." The tears flowed freely now.

My heart ached, not only for what my brother had been trying to handle, but for my mother and this entire fucked up situation. What was wrong with my mother? How was I supposed to balance the cartel, my mother's illness, and Tulipán?

I walked around the desk and dug out a pen and piece of paper. I set it in front of my brother. "Write down all your responsibilities to the cartel for the next month. Runs. Deals. Everything."

His brown eyes moved from the paper to me, then back down to the paper. "Wha—"

"Just do it," I snapped. He couldn't care for my mother and keep up with his cartel work. That was obvious after his last fuckup. I barely saved his ass from the Black Room, and now I had Tulipán to worry about. She caught a glimpse of the Black Room's justice on that dining room table. That couldn't happen again. I wasn't sure she'd survive it.

When Queso finished writing, he set the pen down and dropped his head onto the desk. I put my palm against the back of his head and closed my eyes. Somehow it would all work out. Everything. I knew it in my soul. Queso would take care of our mother, and I would get the situation straightened out with Tulipán.

"Tell Mamá I love her," I said as I reached over and picked up the paper, then left Queso to collect himself. I had a shit ton of stuff to do. He should be happy I'd emptied his plate a little.

13

Tulipán

One morning I woke before Abuela came in with my breakfast and sat on the edge of the bed. The muscles in my back were tight, but it no longer sent bolts of lightning from my scalp to my butt every time I moved. Time had passed in a blur of Abuela's visits when she'd brought me small meals and provided wound care. During my time of healing, it had become clear that I'd lived a privileged life of very little pain and suffering. If I'd whined, Abuela commented about rich American people who knew nothing. Eventually, I'd learned to suffer the wound care in silence.

The phrase, "What doesn't kill you makes you stronger," had dug into my soul and taken root. I repeated it to myself over and over while I healed, because there had been a point when I thought about quitting, just giving up completely. But then I remembered the others who'd been in the darkness with me, my kids, and my sister. If I didn't grow a pair and get out of here, they'd all suffer.

The keypad beeped, then the door opened. "Good morning, Tulipán." Abuela sang, chipper as ever. I no longer needed her to speak Spanish and English, but I still couldn't form an intelligent sentence in Spanish. She carried in my breakfast tray and her bag of cleaning supplies, which she sat near the door.

Warmth spread through my chest, I smiled and gripped the bedpost for support as I stood. "Good morning, Abuela. What's for breakfast?"

Wordlessly, she set the tray filled with eggs, black beans, and tortillas on the bed. It was the same meal she brought every morning. She never brought me silverware, though I looked every time. My chest tightened and I forced a small smile. Abuela left the tray and disappeared into the bathroom with her supplies and fresh laundry. They'd finally provided me with underwear. Even though my appetite wasn't what it used to be, I plopped down and picked at the eggs.

"I need to move around. Strengthen my muscles," I said loud enough for Abuela to hear between bites. Her small, gray-haired head poked out from the bathroom with her brow pinched. "Do you think I can leave the room?"

Her gaze dropped and she shifted on her feet. "I'm not sure, *mi hija*. El Ratón, he's not here."

I cocked my head. "Oh? When is he coming back?"

Waving her hand, she shook her head. She turned to head back into the bathroom. I leaned forward, almost tipping the tray over. "How long have I been here?"

Abuela's eyes wondered the room, then landed on me. She shrugged. "Many weeks. I no longer keep track."

Sighing, I pushed the tray back and joined her in the bathroom. I sat on the counter and watched her scrub the shower tiles as if twenty people used it rather than just one. I hadn't seen Segundo or El Ratón since dinner that night. I still had no idea why I was here. Abuela had explained that, as the head of this cartel, El Ratón needed to be commanding and punish disobedience. But that sounded like an excuse to me. He was just an asshole, plain and simple.

My throat tightened, but I managed to speak anyway. "Do you know why I'm here?" My quiet question sliced through the comfortable silence.

Abuela glanced up at me, then shook her head and dropped her gaze back to her work. "I do not know exactly." My gut clenched. She knew more than she let on.

"What—" I started, then froze when the door to the room slammed shut. I hadn't heard the door panel beep, which I'd really come to rely on to let me know someone was entering the room.

Segundo stepped into the bathroom doorway, then gave Abuela a sharp look. She gathered her cleaning supplies and scurried from the room without another word. Segundo turned that look on me. I straightened my shoulders, refusing to be cowed by this man. The man who hadn't protected me from being whipped or the cruelty of El Ratón despite his obvious attraction to me. No, I wouldn't let him bully me too.

Segundo's jaw flexed. He moved to stand directly in front of me. "You need to eat better."

Scowling, I leaned against the mirror. "Don't treat me like he does."

His eyes hooded as he stepped closer, moving between my legs and pressing his body against the countertop. He reached up and ran his thumb across my cheekbone. "You need to eat more." His voice was softer this time, more caring.

My breaths came in short gasps. I searched for the right words, but he was too close. His pupils were dilated, the hazel lighter but almost completely blacked out. Segundo leaned closer, his hands resting on the counter on either side of me, his tattooed biceps flexing. A lava like heat began to spread from my belly button down.

"You've healed." I focused on the movement of his plump lips as he spoke. His voice a balm on my frazzled senses.

Tipping my chin up, I squeezed my eyes shut. I didn't want him to make me feel better. I wanted to be angry with him. "You let him *beat* me."

Segundo rested his head on my shoulder. His coconut and sunshine scent overwhelmed my senses. "*Sí.* I couldn't stop him." He sighed heavily. "But I truly wanted to. It took all that I had not to."

Segundo raised his head and took my chin in his hand, directing me to meet his gaze. The pain I saw there was like a punch to the gut. He spoke the truth, but that didn't excuse what I'd gone through.

"If I had intervened, he would've killed me. Then you would've been left here alone." His voice dropped to a whisper at the end as if the thought of me being here alone was the worst conclusion possible.

My heart dropped like an elevator from the top floor. Alone. Even though I didn't feel entirely safe with Segundo, but he'd shown me some kindness. He was a sliver of light in the darkness that surrounded me. He wouldn't get me out of here, but he could be a safe haven on this island of despair. I needed to save myself from this hellhole, but I didn't have to find the strength to survive here alone. I leaned forward and gently brushed my lips across his forehead.

"Okay." Although I didn't entirely understand, I wanted to keep him as a friend, as someone who'd look out for me when he could. The tension between us seemed to drain away, along with the tightness in my muscles.

Segundo adjusted so his lips hovered over mine, our breaths mixing. His thumb traced the line of my right cheekbone. I swear I could feel his heartbeat pounding in time with mine. His eyes darted from my eyes to my lips, then back.

My tongue stuck to the roof of my mouth. I pulled it away and licked my lips, tracing the edge of his lips. Little sparks lit up against my tongue. His eyes widened. I was unable to breathe. Was he going to kiss me? He shouldn't kiss me. But I wanted him to. Oh God, I wanted him to. It was so wrong, but fuck, my body wanted him to kiss me.

Abruptly, Segundo backed away, his eyes the size of golf balls. He raked his fingers through his thick, jet-black hair. His chest heaved as he turned away from me.

Words failed me in that moment as I opened and closed my mouth. Nothing good would come from this heat between us. I shouldn't even feel it for this man who held me in this place against my will. But I couldn't help the way my body responded to him.

He glanced back and his eyes burned a path along my face, then down my body. I pressed my legs together. My privates were on fire. Segundo's gaze followed the movement of my legs. He shifted his feet, then bit his lower lip as his gaze pinned on my rapidly moving chest. I found some satisfaction that I wasn't the only one here with a war going on inside.

After what seemed like ages, Segundo stepped forward, pressed himself between my legs, cupped my cheek in his large hand, then closed the distance between us, pressing his lips against mine. His tongue licked along the seam of mine softly, asking to be let in. It only took a moment before I relaxed into the kiss. Our tongues met in a dance. He slid his hand around and cupped the back of my head, while the other hand grabbed my ass and pulled me against his body.

My insides lit up. Shockwaves raced through me from my mouth all the way down to my toes. He pressed his hard length against my groin. Wetness pooled in my panties, and I clenched my thighs together, effectively wrapping my legs around him. Oh God, I'd never gotten wet from just a kiss in my life.

He stopped the kiss as quickly as he'd started, then leaned his head back. I could still feel his hardness against my center. He met my gaze with his hazel eyes. His throat bobbed on a swallow. "I have something I should tell you," he said with a hoarse voice. "If I don't say it now, I may not tell you."

My insides twisted, hoping I hadn't just fucked up by letting him kiss me. I nodded, unable to form words.

"I wanted you the moment I saw you." He traced my cheekbone with his thumb again. Closing my eyes, I turned my face into his touch. At least I understood why I was the only one not sold. "El Ratón craves control and obedience. He demands punishment for disobedience and —" He pressed his lips together and looked up at the ceiling. "Play along."

I straightened and pulled away. "What? What do you mean?"

"He won't rape you, but he will use us both to get what he wants." He cupped my face in his hands.

My whole body went rigid. I wasn't sure what Segundo classified as rape, but El Ratón had come super fucking close to it when he tried to force me to suck his dick. But I guess in this man's world rape only included my pussy. What I really didn't understand was how El Ratón would use us both to get what he wanted. What did he want? Why did it include me at all? There were so many fucking problems with what he'd just said I didn't even know where to start. I tried to move out of his grasp, but he held me still.

"I don't know what to say." I averted my eyes and relaxed, since he obviously didn't plan to let me go.

He kissed my nose, then ran his lips along the angle of my jaw until he reached my chin. We remained there in silence while Segundo ran his finger along my face as if he were waiting for me to decide on what to say, even though I'd just said I didn't know.

"Why would he use us? What does he want?" I asked.

Segundo brushed a strand of hair back behind my ear. "He suspects why I chose you." His gaze dropped. "He has to control everything and my desire threatens that control. There is always punishment for disobedience," he said, his voice barely audible.

Chills ran up my arms. "For what disobedience?"

Segundo's fingers traced a line down my neck to my left nipple. Both of them instantly peaked. He pinched it through my shirt. My breath shuddered and my back arched as pinpricks danced down my spine.

"Wha-what're you doing?" I asked, breathless.

His lips tipped up, but his eyes were focused on the path of his fingers as they moved toward my right breast.

Unable to concentrate, I gripped his strong shoulders and pushed his body away from mine with all the force I could muster. I rested my elbows on my thighs and dropped my face into my hands. I didn't know what this man wanted from me. His boss practically raped me, then whipped me as a punishment. And now he wanted me to do what? Admit I wanted to fuck him or let his boss do whatever he wanted to me?

Any woman with eyes would want to fuck Segundo, but to play along with El Ratón's games was another beast I wasn't sure I could go along with.

"I enjoy this very much, but I shouldn't." I slipped off the counter, maneuvering away from his body, and ran my hands down the front of my shirt.

Segundo chuckled as he came up behind me. He was a dark god, with his toned body full of tattoos and easy, yet bossy attitude. He was that off-limits bad boy your mom told you to stay away from, yet you just couldn't.

"You're right, we shouldn't enjoy each other." He rested his hands on my arms and kissed the curve of my neck where it met my shoulder. A shiver ran the length of my body. "El Ratón is having a party for some important people in a couple days," he said, all business again. "You'll be expected to come."

I spun around and gaped. "Me? At a party? What for?"

Segundo stepped away and pushed his shoulders back. "I'll have Abuela bring you books and magazines, now that you're better. I'll return with your outfit for the party and to escort you." Then he walked out without a backward glance.

My jaw dropped open. The man was an enigma, one minute he was all up in my grill ready to fuck me on the countertop. The next he was all business and acting as if I was a nobody. I turned on the shower with the water set to cold.

14

Tulipán

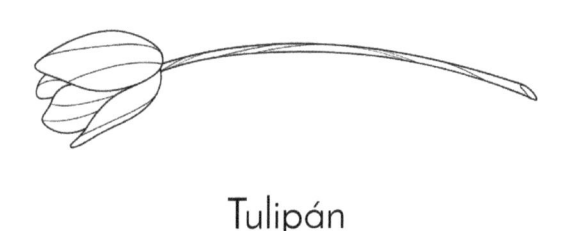

The next day, I gazed out the French doors and traced my finger along the clear, solid glass of the pane I'd broken when I first arrived in this horrid place. At some point, they'd replaced it. I sighed, then returned my gaze to the treetops beyond the wall that surrounded the property. Those trees held hope and the potential for freedom. I just needed to get out of this room. Then I could find a way to get beyond that wall.

I'd been here long enough. Yesterday had been a mistake. I'd let my hormones take over and forgot Segundo was my captor, not just a sexy man who knew how to make me feel all warm inside. I shouldn't consider him anyway. What would Brian say? I dropped my head against the cool window and groaned.

Brian.

My gut clenched. He should've found me by now. What was preventing him from coming? The other women whose stories I knew didn't have someone with unlimited money to raise the US government to search for them. There was something wrong with this picture. I'd let him bring me on this vacation. Let him ruin my fortieth birthday party. He'd pushed me around our entire marriage, the least he could do was rescue me.

I fisted my hands, straightened up, and stamped my foot. No longer. I wouldn't let him tell me what to do. If it came to an argument, then fuck it. I'd fight from now on. I'd fight for myself and for Shannon. I needed to get out of here and put Brian in his place, not only for myself but for Shannon. He would make her life miserable without me.

I glanced back at the door. Yesterday, Segundo had come in after Abuela and the keypad hadn't beeped. She'd left the door unlocked behind her. I didn't know if that was typical or if there was a guard on the other side, but I needed to take advantage. Segundo never took his eyes off me, but Abuela frequently left me alone while she cleaned the bathroom. And after he interrupted her yesterday, she would definitely return to clean the shower today. I began to pace a half circle around the bed while playing with the ends of my hair.

This situation was so unreal. Whoever imagined themselves being held hostage in an actual mansion by the Mexican cartel? How could anyone ever plan for a situation like this? My back had mostly healed, but it still ached when I moved and there were still scabs in places where the whip had bitten extra deep. I'd survived the whip once, and I knew I could survive it again, but that didn't mean I wanted to.

The keypad beeped. My feet froze to the floor. I dropped my hands, pinning my eyes on the door, while holding my breath. It had to be Abuela. She always came first thing in the morning. This plan would only work if it was her. Sweat rolled down my back.

Abuela's short, plump body popped through the open door carrying my usual tray of food and her cleaning bag. The door closed behind her, and I listened with bated breath for any beeps to signify that they'd locked the door, but nothing came. I shifted and did my best to keep my face neutral as she shuffled her way over to me.

"Good morning, Tulipán," she said brightly. "Segundo asked that I bring you some reading material to help you stay busy." Abuela set the tray on the floor near my feet. It held a plate of my normal morning fare with a short stack of books next to it.

I swallowed the lump in my throat. "Thank you," I croaked.

She gave me a toothy smile. "You feel well today?"

Unable to move, I forced a smile and nodded. My heart ached. This woman had been so kind. She took care of me. Unlike my own mom, who'd barely given me a cough drop.

Abuela stepped close, took my face in her warm, calloused hands and squeezed it gently. "You must smile more, *mi hija*. You have such a beautiful face."

My eyes burned. I wrapped my arms around her as my heart swelled with love. "Thank you for everything you've done for me." I sniffled, breathing in the scent of lemon cleaner and tortillas.

She chuckled and unwrapped my arms, then wiped my cheek with her thumb. "I must work. You eat." She turned and began to strip my bed.

I gazed down at the plate of food and my stomach revolted. Even though I was completely justified in escaping, it still felt like I was betraying her trust by sneaking out behind her back. Everything about this place was messed up. All the feelings I had were so wrong. I shouldn't feel any loyalty toward this woman, but I did.

When satisfied with the bedsheets, Abuela turned and shuffled into the bathroom, not sparing me a second glance. My heart clenched. She trusted me to stay here. She knew the door to the room was unlocked, yet she didn't even check to see what I was doing before she walked out of the bedroom. She started to hum while she cleaned, which was my clue that she was deep into her work.

I shoved whatever loyalty I felt toward her aside and rushed across the room on the balls of my bare feet. At the door, I gripped the knob and turned, letting out a silent cheer when I found it unlocked. A quick glance behind me showed Abuela still inside the bathroom, so I pulled the door open a crack and peeked out. When I was sure no one stood there, I pulled it open and stepped into the wide hall.

Just like when Segundo had taken me to dinner, it was crickets in the hall. A red carpet ran down the center, covering the white marble floor. I glanced around. Every door in my path was closed. There weren't any decorations I could use as a weapon, only a couple pictures that were so large I probably couldn't carry them. I started down the hall with my heart pounding against my breastbone.

Halfway down the hall, I glanced back. The hall remained miraculously empty. The silence pressed in around me. So far, so good. At the end of the hall, I pressed my back against the wall. A bead of sweat trailed down my forehead. I wiped it away as I took three deep breaths and listened. Before I stuck my head around the corner, I needed to be sure no one stood right there. I tried to take shallow, quiet breaths. When I was sure there were no sounds, I peeked around the corner to find the area empty as well.

The tension drained down my body like a waterfall. I leaned over and rested my hands on my knees, trying to catch my breath. I'd reached the top of the stairs that overlooked the main entrance. I just needed to get down those stairs and I'd be at the front doors. I closed my eyes and saw them in my mind, two large, mahogany doors with bronze handles. Wooden gates that exited Hell.

Then I heard male voices echoing in the entryway. I dropped to the ground, face down. My stomach felt like a lead weight holding me against the ground. Biting my lip, I scooted over to the railing. Once there, I crouched on shaky legs. Two men stood talking near the doors. Both carried rifles like the guards who'd corralled me to the auction when I'd first gotten here. Seconds before I dropped back down, I could've sworn one of them glanced up at me, but I was already on my stomach again. *Fuck. I hope they didn't see me!* I covered my mouth to quiet my breathing.

After a couple minutes I heard their booted feet leave the entryway. I counted to fifty and when nothing else happened, I stood, checking around me. I glanced down the hall toward my room and couldn't believe Abuela hadn't noticed me yet. I thought for sure this delay would've been my end. God was definitely with me in this moment.

I crossed myself. *Thank you, God.*

With my gaze pinned on the set of stairs closest to me, I moved cautiously toward the top. My heart hammered in my chest. I was so close, I could see the front doors, right there. I reached out my foot to step down. Seconds before my foot struck the cool, marble step, a pair of strong arms wrapped around my center. My body was pulled against a hard and unyielding chest, then I was surrounded by the familiar scent of coconut and sunshine.

Taken, not Destroyed

I yelped in shock as my dreams of escape vanished. I was so close. "No!" I reached out my arms and kicked.

"Where do you think you're going?" Segundo asked with a hint of humor in his voice. Even though I struggled, he still managed to press his cheek against mine as he spoke.

"Let me go," I demanded. I'd almost made it, almost made it out that door. It wasn't funny. A hundred-pound weight pressed against my chest.

"You cannot escape me." Segundo ran his tongue along the curve of my ear, then bit down on the lobe, hard enough to draw blood.

My body froze as liquid fire replaced the blood in my veins. *Holy fuck, that was hot.*

Segundo lifted me and cradled me in his arms like a baby, carrying me back toward my prison. The front door and entryway disappeared along with the hope of escape. The hope of not letting men tell me what to do, of getting my shit straight over this man. I wanted to fight against his hold, to wiggle out of his arms and take my chances in a race toward the front door.

But I couldn't deny that I felt safe in his arms. The way he held me gave me a sense of peace and he sure as fuck knew how to turn me on. I didn't know what he'd done to my ear, but holy hell. I reached up and touched it as I studied the sharp angle of his jaw, the small, almost unnoticeable cleft in his narrow chin.

Back in my prison room, Segundo set me down. I backed away until my legs struck the bed. He followed until he stood close enough he could touch me, but not so close I felt crowded.

He watched me intently. His face unreadable. I couldn't tell if he was mad at me for trying to leave or indifferent. I didn't know what I wanted from him in that moment, but any normal man who admitted an attraction might try to be comforting, but this wasn't a normal situation. Was it?

Segundo raked his fingers through his raven hair, then shifted and sighed. "I'll do my best to make sure El Ratón isn't informed of this."

My jaw dropped open. "Wha—"

He turned and left me. This time I heard him activate the electronic lock on my door. I stared, wide-eyed at the door to my prison. It seemed he was going to remind me how little control I had at every opportunity. I really needed to get out of this place.

15

Tulipán

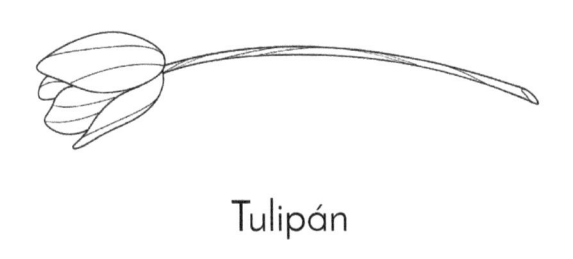

The next day, Abuela didn't bring me breakfast or lunch. She didn't come in to change my sheets or clean my bathroom, which had been her routine for every day I could remember. My meals were pushed inside by an armed guard, who didn't speak a single word, despite my multiple attempts to find out what was going on. They gave me no chance to escape, and I suspected that guard stayed outside the door even though it was locked.

Feeling like lead pumped through my veins, I leaned against the French door and stared out the window. The yellow-white sun mocked me from its spot just above the treetops in the bright blue sky. It was outside, moving through the sky, doing what it was supposed to do. While I was trapped in here, unable to help the people I needed to help, unable to be the woman I was meant to be. I hated that it took me being kidnapped to see what a doormat I'd been. But I wouldn't let anyone push me around anymore, if I could help it. I pressed my hand against the cool glass, as if I could feel the warmth through it.

My gaze dropped to the wall surrounding the property. That escape attempt was probably futile anyway. They probably had guards with guns at the only gate to the property. If I were a cartel leader, I sure would. I needed to come up with a smarter plan than just running out the front door. My chest constricted.

But how?

Segundo had said El Ratón expected me to go to a party. They didn't give me access to anything I could use as a weapon in here, but maybe I could find something at a party. A fork or a knife. Anything sharp or stabby. I didn't really want to hurt Segundo or Abuela. But El Ratón? Yeah, I could find it in my heart to stab him if it wouldn't blow back and get me killed.

The keypad beeped; I glanced behind me just in time to see Segundo walking in dressed in his typical all-black outfit. Though this evening he wore a button-up that was open enough at the top so I could see the planes of his tattoo covered pec muscles. Saliva gathered in my mouth.

Segundo's lip twitched up. "Good evening, Tulipán." His voice brought a whole number of inappropriate sexual thoughts to mind.

I ducked my head and pressed my thighs together. Who the hell was this man? How could he shut my intelligent brain off and kick my hormones into high gear just by speaking? "H-hi."

He cleared his throat. I glanced up out the tops of my eyes. He leaned against the bedpost, holding out a small, plastic sack.

Tentatively, I took the bag and glanced inside to see a very scant amount of gold fabric bundled there. I pursed my lips and returned my gaze to the gorgeous man who I couldn't quite figure out what to do with. "What's this?"

He took a step closer. "Your outfit."

I hooked two fingers around a strap and pulled it out, letting the bag drift to the floor. What I held in my hand looked more like a few thick straps some swimsuit model with a great body might wear. Not something I'd ever put on. "No." I dropped it.

I hated this place. Too many conflicting feelings. I shouldn't care if I pissed Segundo off or worry about how he turned me on with a mere look. I needed to focus on escaping. On getting back to Shannon and Misti, and helping the authorities find those other women. That was it. Fuck Segundo and his issues.

Taken, not Destroyed

"No." I backed up and planted my fists on my hips. "I'm not wearing that. No fucking way."

Segundo raised one brow and smirked. "You can go naked." His eyes flashed as if that idea would be fine with him.

Gritting my teeth, I squeezed my fists tighter and reveled in the feeling of my nails as they dug into my palms. Naked or almost naked. I bent over and grabbed the fabric, then stormed off into the bathroom. I swear I heard him chuckling behind me, but I didn't want to deal with that.

After I'd maneuvered into the strappy suit, Segundo led me back to the dining room where I'd first met El Ratón. I tried to distract myself from replaying everything that'd happened last time by scanning for a weapon, anything I could get ahold of. Even though it was ridiculous to think I could hide anything in this outfit.

Segundo walked through the double doors and took my hand to guide me inside when I'd stopped dead at the entrance. It wasn't a conscious decision, my feet had just frozen like they'd hit an invisible wall. Segundo tugged until I moved through the doors. A headache was already forming between my eyes.

Just inside, El Ratón stood waiting with his hands clasped behind him and a look of indifference on his scruffy face. His outfit was similar to the previous one except the shirt was a deep royal-blue, which shimmered in the light. He'd left the top few buttons open exposing the hair that marred his chest and made the tattoo on his neck stand out.

"*Buenos noches*, El Ratón," Segundo said after closing us in.

El Ratón glared, while rubbing the salt-and-pepper stubble on his chin. The tension in the room climbed. My gaze darted between the two men, who seemed to be having a silent conversation, and I could sense Segundo's muscles tightening next to me. He dropped my hand and stuck his hand in his pocket.

I reached for my cross and almost spat curses when I found it missing again. El Ratón's black gaze landed on my hand and his lips pulled up in a sneer. I clasped my fingers in front of me, squeezing tight to prevent fidgeting. Sweat gathered on my neck. A cool breeze struck it from the windows, making me regret pulling my hair up in a ponytail.

Without a word, El Ratón pulled something out of his pocket. He set a box on the table, then stepped in front of Segundo, meeting his gaze for a minute. As he moved to leave the room, he paused at the door and said, "Bring Tulipán to the Black Room at ten."

The door slammed behind him and silence reigned once more. None of this made any sense. There was still no clear reason for my presence in this house and those two men obviously had some serious issues. I chewed on my lower lip and side glanced at Segundo. He stood with his gaze fixed on the box, his brow furrowed.

"What's in the box?" I whispered, unsure if I really wanted to know.

He shook his head, then met my gaze. "It's for you." He gestured for me to open the box.

Cocking my head, I reached over and lifted the lid. My stomach fluttered and my cheeks heated. A silver bullet device sat on a velvet pad. Attached to the end of the bullet were multiple black ribbons about five or six inches long. Next to the device sat a small tube of lube. Frowning, I glanced up at him, then back down. I lightly ran a finger over the sleek, silver surface. "What is it?" I'd never seen anything like it. What was I supposed to do with it?

Segundo groaned and pinched the bridge of his nose. "Fuck."

I stepped back from him. "What?"

He moved closer and whispered, "It goes in your ass."

My jaw dropped and I covered my ass. "What? No," I practically shrieked. "You can't. No!" What the hell were these two playing at?

"He'll punish you if you don't." Segundo spoke as if what they were asking was completely normal, but it wasn't normal. If he put that in me, it would look like I had a tail. That was so much more than fucked up. It was a whole different level of fucked up.

"Please, Segundo." I shook my head and covered my bottom.

He gave me a pleading look. "Please don't fight this. Just let me put it in." He picked up the tail and lube and moved toward me.

My heart rate kicked up. I wanted to run away, to fight against this.

Taken, not Destroyed

But I could tell from the determined look on Segundo's face that I wasn't getting out of this no matter how much I protested. "Why? Why does he do this?"

Segundo pressed his front against mine and shrugged. "I don't know, *mi tulipán*. I can't question if I want to live, and neither can you."

He wrapped his strong arm around my waist and pulled my body tight to his. I could feel the press of his hard length against my stomach. This whole thing might turn him on, but I was ready to run for the hills. With gentle fingers Segundo moved the scrap of fabric that covered my butt to the side, then spread my cheeks. I squeezed my eyes closed and buried my face in his chest, breathing in his scent.

The cold tip of the object pressed against my butthole. Clamping down, I gasped as the device stretched a part of my body that wasn't meant to accept items into it. It wasn't a painful sensation, but as he seated the device fully into my ass, I felt uncomfortable. It was a constant fullness that I just wanted to push out. I dug my nails into Segundo's back to stop my body from rejecting the object.

He leaned down and kissed my neck from the curve where it met my shoulder all the way up to my earlobe. Chills ran down my spine. The pressure from the butt device lessened as my focus shifted to the desire he'd sparked inside my core. *Fuck*. He nipped my ear, then pulled away.

"Better?" he asked.

Tingles and shivers ran along my body. I wouldn't ever be anything good or okay here, but whatever he'd done made it possible for me to tolerate that device. For now. I nodded ever so slightly.

"Good, now you must endure," he warned. "Don't take it out."

Segundo gripped my hand and led me from the room. Walking proved to be a challenge, since it was difficult not to hunch forward. Segundo corrected me many times on our walk to the party. The tail swished against my legs, a light tickling sensation that made me want something more. I just didn't know what.

16

Tulipán

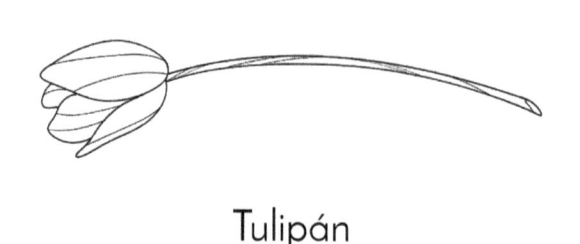

Segundo led me to a room at the other end of the house. The deep thump of bass beat beyond a pair of tall, gilded doors. The sound traveled through my body and seemed to connect with the small muscles in my bottom, causing me to clench each time it struck. I glanced over at Segundo's profile as he paused just outside the ornate doors.

"Behave tonight," he said, staring straight ahead. "Please don't do anything to anger him." He turned his beautiful, gold-flecked hazel eyes my way and butterflies danced in my stomach. "Can you do that for me? Please?"

I swallowed deeply. This man was confusing. He seemed to want to protect me from his boss, yet he allowed him to whip and humiliate me. I pulled my lower lip between my teeth, searching for some skin to bite off. His eyes followed the movement, pinned to my lips. He took a deep breath.

His gorgeous face screwed up, making my hand twitch to comfort whatever hurt he felt. "Tulipán? You *can* obey?"

Sweat gathered on his temples as we stood staring at each other, waiting to enter the party. The muscles in my bottom burned already, yet I wanted this man to put his lips on me to take my mind off it.

Taken, not Destroyed

Could I play along? I had to, at least until I could figure out how to protect myself or get this thing out of me. I nodded, unable to speak against the knot in my throat.

Segundo's lips tipped up slightly, then he turned and pushed one door open. He took my hand and ushered me into a huge room that appeared to run the entire width of the house, front to back. The walls were painted a creamy white color with only a few pictures randomly hung on the wall. The red carpet stopped at the door. My foot struck the cool marble sending chills up my legs.

One side of the room held a group of people dancing to the Latin beat that resounded through my body. It was much louder in here. The other side of the room had a series of lounge chairs, couches, and tables set up with people clustered in groups, talking, drinking, and eating. My eyes found the food table set up between the groups of people along the back wall, half of which was a series of open arches just like in the dining room.

Segundo grasped my arm, his eyes darting around the room as if he didn't know where to take me. His grip on my arm felt like an iron band. A few people stopped dancing and watched as he guided me toward a group of women near the food table.

"Stay here," he said. I stared at the three scantily dressed females. "I have some business. I'll find you later. Try to stay out of trouble."

With that, Segundo dropped my arm and strode across the room to a group of men seated on a lounge chair. I bit the inside of my lip as I assessed the group he'd left me in. The women had revealing dresses on, but at least they were more covered than myself. None of them had a fucking tail either. I clenched my cheeks at the reminder of it and electricity jolted up to my belly button. I really needed to get rid of this thing.

A rail-thin female wearing a black sequined dress said something in Spanish, then gave me a smile full of teeth much in need of a dentist. I tried to think only of the sadness I felt for her and smiled back, then turned to search the food table. They couldn't feed these people without silverware.

One of the women said something, then said my name, or at least the name Segundo called me. I frowned and turned back. "What?"

The three of them laughed and began to chatter in Spanish. It wasn't that I didn't understand, it was that I chose not to pay attention. They spoke fast and were hard to hear over the music. "Fuck this," I said, but when I turned to search the food table, I slammed into a body.

Blinking rapidly, I backed up and found myself face-to-face with a Hispanic male with a disgusting mustache. He was about my height and smoking a cigarette. His beady eyes traveled over my body like I was a chocolate cake with a cherry on top.

He smirked. *"Te ves lo suficientemente buena para comer,"* he said in a slithery voice.

Clenching my butt cheeks, I chose to ignore him as well. I glanced over his shoulder and tried to sidestep him, but the snake stepped to block me, smiling like he'd won the lottery or something. I hugged myself to hide what I could of my body, then tried again, but he blocked me again. I didn't know what to do. I glanced over at the three women who'd magically disappeared.

"What do you want?" I asked.

Mustache reached out. I flinched back just as a hand landed on his shoulder. I glanced up to see Segundo behind him. He leaned in close to the man and spoke. I couldn't hear what Segundo said, but the man's beady eyes widened until they looked like snake eyes on dice. Mustache scampered away. Segundo's gaze met mine briefly before he left me there without a word. A warm feeling pooled in my lower belly. He'd saved me even though he could've let that man harass me.

This place still sucks.

I rubbed my face and pinned my gaze on the white, linen-covered food table, that was piled high with different varieties of foods. At the far end, I could see plates stacked, but there were people lined up. They were in my way, but I swore they had silverware. Gritting my teeth, I took two steps, then felt an iron hand clamp down on my upper arm. Damn it.

I twisted, then shrieked when my eyes met El Ratón's hard black gaze. My breath froze in my chest. His gaze traveled down my body

Taken, not Destroyed

as if he could see beneath the small scraps of cloth covering my skin. This outfit was a joke. Every man, including Segundo, looked at me like they could see beneath it anyway. I might as well have been naked. One corner of El Ratón's lips quirked up as he reached out. He traced a finger from the nape of my neck down between my breasts.

My whole body tensed, including the muscles in my butt. I let out a sound. I had no clue what it meant—maybe it was from being surprised—but whatever it was, it made El Ratón genuinely smile. He obviously took the sound to mean something good. He hadn't shaved in a few days, and the dark hair, dotted with white, made him look older, more sophisticated than he had when we'd eaten dinner. I closed my eyes and took a deep breath, trying to get a hold of myself in front of this horrid man.

"Where are you going?" He sounded almost curious.

My eyes popped open to find him closer, much closer. From this distance, his eyes looked like two swirling pools of darkness. My teeth chattered and muscles in my whole body clenched, sending shockwaves up to my belly from my bottom. What did he want? No one openly looked at us, but people glanced our way, as if they knew better than to stare.

I blew out a breath and shook my head rapidly. "N-n-nowhere," I managed to spit out.

El Ratón forced me to move back, until my back pressed against a cool wall. I could feel his breath on my face. "You're mine. Don't forget." His voice was like acid running down my back.

Pressing farther against the wall, I wanted to argue. I didn't want to belong to anyone, but it was obvious I had no control here. I was trapped until I could find an escape. If I didn't play along, I'd find myself battered again by this man. Biting my lip, I nodded. I couldn't form the words to agree, because I didn't believe them.

His eyes softened slightly as he reached up and ran a finger over my lips. My stomach turned with nausea and revulsion. My eyes widened, and I pressed my lips into a hard line. This was nothing like when Segundo touched me. His touch felt good, even though it shouldn't. El Ratón's fingers made me want to peel the skin from my body just to forget he'd ever touched me.

El Ratón watched the progress of his finger as he moved it down my body. He stopped at my breast, then pinched my nipple. My traitorous nipple hardened under his touch. I whimpered as every muscle clenched again, including my butt. This stupid thing needed to come out.

All the little muscles in my body began to shake as his hand moved lower, closer to my sex. I didn't want him there, especially not in front of this room full of people. I glanced around quickly, but I didn't want to take my eyes off him for too long in case he tried something like what he'd done after dinner. I felt like everything inside me dried up and tried to curl away from him. I clenched my thighs together.

Please, no. Please, don't do this to me.

His hand traveled down past my belly button. The device in my bottom seemed to intensify everything. My body wanted to be touched, to be satisfied, even though I didn't want any of it. I hated this. Was this why he'd made me wear it? Why was he doing this to me? He ran his wretched finger along the seam at the top of the triangle of fabric just above my sex. Wriggling my hips back, I let out a huge breath of air and met his hard gaze.

His eyes were narrowed, and his lips pulled up in a sneer. I didn't want this, just like I hadn't wanted to suck his dick. I couldn't force myself to want him. He was repulsive to me. He was evil and I didn't want an evil man to touch my body. I clenched my teeth, my body completely rigid.

El Ratón's jaw flexed as he pressed his calloused palm on my shoulder, his face set in a hard line. This was it; I was in trouble for refusing him yet again. He pushed against my shoulder until my knees buckled. My heart rate spiked. He couldn't possibly want me to suck his dick. Not here. Not in front of all these people!

Squeezing my eyes closed, I dropped my head and turned it away. *Please God, save me from this.* I felt him move to stand next to me, then his rough hand clasped on the back of my neck, hard. The music cut off abruptly, followed quickly by all the voices, coating the room in silence. It was deafening.

"This female is mine," he growled, voice echoing through the room. A shiver rushed down my spine. I couldn't bring myself to look up at a single one of them. "No one is to touch her, look at her, or talk to her. *¿Compredne?*"

The room erupted in words of agreement. I pinched my eyes tighter. El Ratón crouched down next to me and spoke in my ear, his breath hot on my face.

"*¿Compredne, Tulipán?*" he asked me as if it wasn't clear by the way he treated me. When I didn't say or do anything, he gripped my chin painfully and moved my head to look at him. He raised his brows.

"*Si*, El Ratón. I understand." He could've done so much worse. Maybe my prayers had been answered. Now that he'd announced to the room that I belonged to him, maybe he'd leave me alone and go back to his business.

The room blurred away while our eyes warred with each other. While I waited for him to release me.

17

Tulipán

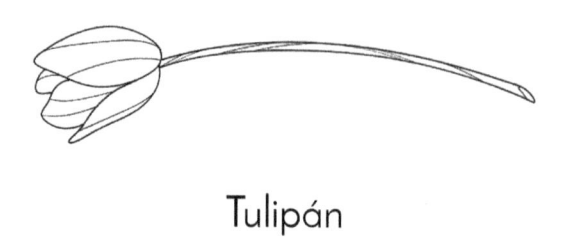

Just when I thought my eyes might burn out of my skull, a beautiful woman dressed in a sparkly blue gown approached us. Almost like an avenging angel. She gave El Ratón a wide smile, full of straight, white teeth. She swayed her hips seductively as if trying to catch his eye. El Ratón stood, grabbing my arm and pulling me along with him.

As I stood, the tension in my legs drained away from kneeling on the marble floor, and my knees almost gave out. El Ratón didn't seem to notice as his entire focus was on our new guest. I reached out and supported myself against the cool wall.

"Camila." He addressed her with familiarity, but not like he was happy to see her.

Her smile changed into a smirk as if she knew something he didn't. She spoke in rapid Spanish that I tuned out until the very end. "El Mil has need of you." Her voice was cultured, and she exuded confidence even in the wake of El Ratón's evil stare.

El Ratón gave her a curt nod, shot me a quick glare, then left us. He strolled through the crowd, which parted for him like the Red Sea, as if he were a god among them. I watched until the bodies filled back in, and he was no longer visible. My entire body relaxed, and I felt like I'd run a marathon. Not that I ever had, but I imagined this was what people felt like after such an event. Exhaling, I fell against the cool marble wall, closing my eyes and taking a minute to collect myself.

"You must be Tulipán," the woman El Ratón had addressed as Camila said.

She was my height in three-inch heels with long, shiny, chocolate-colored hair that hung in waves past her mid back. Camila gazed at me with deep-brown eyes surrounded by thick, manicured black lashes. They were eyes that held secrets and compassion. She gave me a slow, almost sad smile.

I gave her a half smile back. "Yes. I don't speak Spanish well," I responded. "But I understand you."

Camila brought her manicured hands together in a soft clap. "*Maravillosa*," she exclaimed.

I shifted uncomfortably as the butt device reared its ugly, uncomfortable head again. Now that I was out of El Ratón's clutches, I was able to focus on my body again. I needed to get this thing out. Desperately, I looked around for somewhere I could hide and slip it out.

"No, Tulipán." She rested her cool fingers against my forearm. "Stay and speak with me."

Pulling my attention back to her, I bit at my lower lip. She'd saved me from El Ratón, but I really needed to get this thing out. "Camila? Right?"

She nodded and giggled, like full-on high school girl giggle. "Yes, darling, I'm Camila Rosco."

She waved her hand, as if I should know her. And maybe if drug selling, people stealing, money laundering people were the type I hung with on a normal day, I would know her. But they weren't, so I didn't.

I cleared my throat. "Nice to meet you, Camila," I said honestly. She was the first person in this place who'd actually given me their real name. Maybe I should find out more about her. I shifted my hips and a groan escaped my lips as the thing in my bottom began to chafe. The lube Segundo had put on it was long gone. I rubbed my glute, afraid to even touch the ribbons.

"I can help you," she whispered, angling her head down.

My eyes popped open and I met her gaze. "What?" Was she really offering to help defy El Ratón?

She held out the crook of her arm. I glanced at it, unsure what to do. Just when I thought I could trust someone, they'd proved me wrong. Everyone was loyal to El Ratón. I was a no one. Why should I trust her? My stomach flipped over as sweat gathered at the base of my neck.

A breeze blew in from the outside and brought goosebumps across my flesh. I examined the slim, bronze arm she offered. I could figure out a way to take this thing out on my own or I could maybe make a friend. Taking a risk, I slipped my arm into Camila's and mentally held my breath that this wouldn't backfire on me. The risk was huge if I pissed off El Ratón again.

Camila walked briskly across the room. I did my best to move with her, even though fire spread up the curve of my back from the little device. As we walked, she leaned close to my ear and whispered. "There are plants over here, you can press against the wall and remove it. Hide it in the plant. I'll stand in front of you."

Her plan sounded solid, but I couldn't believe she was going to help. At this point I'd do anything to get this thing out of my butt. A lump formed in my throat as I gave a short nod.

She continued, "I also have the means to help you escape."

My steps faltered and I almost tripped over my own two feet. Camila clamped down on my arm and shot me a dirty look.

"Can you really . . . " I paused, barely able to breathe. "Help me?"

Camila's lips tipped up in a secretive sort of smile, then she focused on steering me around a group of men dressed in everyday jeans and T-shirts. This probably wasn't the best idea, but I felt like I was being ripped open. She'd also just dropped a bigger bomb on me.

Escape! My heart could hardly handle the possibility. How could she so casually mention that, then act like she hadn't mentioned it at all? With her lips pressed into a thin line, Camila guided me along the wall, then stopped on the opposite side of the room next to a tall plant with wide green leaves. The scent of marijuana drifted our way from a

Taken, not Destroyed

group of men who sat together, talking in low voices on some nearby couches.

Segundo and El Ratón were among the group.

I chewed my lower lip as I watched the two of them. Segundo's eyes scanned the opposite side of the room, while El Ratón was deep in conversation with a bearded man who had a different style of tattoos marking his neck and forearms. "Are you sure this is safe?" I whispered, my voice shaking.

Camila grabbed both my upper arms and moved me back against the wall, behind the thick leaves, then stood in front of me. "Remove it now." She glanced around. "Leave it in the pot. We shouldn't stand here long."

All the tiny muscles in my body shook, but I wasn't cold. I couldn't move for a moment. Even though I could tell I was completely hidden by the large green leaves, the memory of that whip and El Ratón's soulless eyes flashed across my mind.

"Either you do it, or I will," she hissed. "We shouldn't be here." She glanced quickly over her shoulder, and I saw her confidence slip for a brief moment.

That spurred me into action. I reached back and grabbed onto the ribbons, then yanked. It was difficult because I clenched on reflex and hot, fireballs arched out from my ass. I bit down on the knuckle of my opposite hand. Camila watched intently as I dropped it in the pot, then she hooked her arm back in mine.

"Thank you." I couldn't express my gratitude to her enough. I didn't even know what El Ratón's goal was in having me wear that thing, but I felt liberated in getting rid of it.

Her chocolate eyes met mine and she smiled conspiratorially, then turned and began to walk quickly back to the other side of the room. It was easier to keep up with her pace now. The burn had dissipated into a slight ache. Before we'd made it past the food tables, Segundo stepped into our path.

Camila straightened her shoulders and flipped her hair back.

"What are you two up to?" Segundo asked.

Camila fluttered her eyes at him, like she was trying to flirt.

Segundo didn't appear at all interested as he turned his hazel gaze directly to me. My chest tightened and I shrunk back a bit at the look on his face. I knew it was risky and would be completely obvious once I took that thing out, but I had to, it was so uncomfortable. He needed to understand that.

I opened my mouth. Segundo put up his hand, then glared at Camila. She squeezed my arm against her body and leaned close to me. "We'll speak again soon," she whispered. She sauntered off with a sway in her hips that drew every eye as she passed.

Segundo turned his glare on me, then grabbed my upper arm, his fingers digging in hard enough to bruise. "Tulipán," he growled. "Time to go."

I tripped over my feet in an attempt to keep up with him. Glancing up at his face, his jaw was set and I could see the muscles flexing in his neck beneath his tattoo. I rubbed my hands together and did my best to keep up with him as he rushed me through the crowd. The same people who had watched El Ratón claim me not twenty minutes before, now watched his second drag me from the party. I could only imagine what they thought.

My jaw shook at what was going to happen to me. The last time I got in trouble the night ended with me face down in my bed, bleeding from whip marks. Had I just signed myself up for that again? At least I could count myself one friend and one possible escape route richer, because nothing else good had come of this evening.

18

Segundo

I ground my teeth as I led Tulipán through the large hall toward our shared doom, because surely El Ratón would blame me as much as he would her for this failure. She had no idea how much trouble we were both in at this moment. Damn Camila Rosco for helping her make this situation even worse. My fingers tightened on Tulipán's arm.

She'd been doomed to the Black Room before this night even began, but his plan might've been mild. With El Ratón one could never be sure. In some deep pocket of Camila's mind, she likely thought she'd helped Tulipán tonight, but her actions had only caused her more harm. She'd blocked whatever dominance game El Ratón had wanted to play.

Tulipán whimpered as she struggled to keep up with my swift stride. I glanced to the side and slowed. Her normally bright blue eyes were a darker, cobalt color and were glazed with unshed tears. I paused, releasing her arm and pinched the bridge of my nose.

"You realize what you've done?" I ground out, still angry, but doing my best to calm down.

She hugged herself. The triangles that were supposed to cover her nipples pulled to the sides, exposing those delicious looking peaks. I closed my eyes and took a deep breath. This woman had no fucking idea how much I wanted to ravage her. Even though we were both facing punishment, I could barely keep my head on straight in her presence. Slowly, I reached out and pulled the small pieces of fabric back over, hiding her nipples from my eyes.

Tulipán flinched at my touch, then glanced down to watch me, her chest still as if she held her breath. Feeling calmer now, even though our situation hadn't changed, I stepped back, offering her my hand. "Come, it's almost ten."

She touched the hollow of her neck, then winced. She seemed to search out her cross necklace whenever her emotions ran high, and its absence was obviously disconcerting. I bit my tongue. I'd never give it back. It would remain hanging next to my computer. She may find comfort in its presence, but so did I. Besides, El Ratón wouldn't allow her to have it even though it was a symbol of the faith.

Her gaze darted from my hand to my face, then back to my hand before she slipped her delicate hand in mine. Her fingers were soft and cold. I wrapped them easily within my palm, then turned to lead her up the stairs. Her hand looked so innocent next to mine. Clean, pale white skin next to my tanned, tattooed skin marked with the sins of cartel life.

Tulipán walked next to me in silence, which seemed to scream at me to whisk her away from here and protect her from El Ratón's wrath. Only certain people enjoyed what he had to offer when he wasn't angry. His level of play went a few levels beyond mine.

We crossed into El Ratón's section of the house. The only indication was the carpet changed from red to black lined with gold. Tulipán's eyes scanned the walls and decorations as if she were filing it away for another time. I barely saw any of it, my mind was swirling with the possibilities. It had my stomach in knots.

As we passed El Ratón's bedroom suite, I squeezed her hand. We came to a stop at a tall, black door with black inlaid markings. If you didn't know the markings were there, you likely wouldn't see them. They were pictures of people having sex, like a Kama Sutra and BDSM manual rolled into one. This was El Ratón's favorite room in the whole house, as far as I could tell. I'd only been inside once before and preferred to never enter it again. It wasn't just a room for pleasure, he punished here as well.

Tonight, I had no choice. I paused before the door and gazed down at Tulipán. She stared at the black door. Her wide eyes darted around the door. Her hand became slick with sweat. I swallowed against a tight throat. I needed to show her a face of strength. I straightened my shoulders and reached for the door.

"What is this?" she asked, her voice sounding too loud in the dead silent hall.

My hand froze on the door handle, my heart the same in my chest. "The Black Room," I replied, then opened the door and stepped inside. I couldn't delay the inevitable any longer.

Bright white lights flickered on the moment the door opened. True to its name, every surface that wasn't mirror was painted black. Three of the walls were covered, floor to ceiling, with mirrors. The far wall, opposite the door, held a built-in shelving unit and peg board for hanging equipment. There was an oversized bed along the wall to the left with black silk sheets.

Tulipán gasped, and her hand pulled out of mine to cover her lips. "What is this place?"

Unfortunately, the walls weren't what made this room shocking. "It's where El Ratón finds pleasure. And deals out punishment." I closed the door and continued to guide her into the room, but her footsteps had slowed as she resisted me.

The room held a variety of objects, most I couldn't name, describe, or provide the function of if asked. The last time I'd been in here, El Ratón secured me to a device that held my arms out as if I was on a cross, then he'd whipped me for disobedience. Cartel members weren't allowed to get tattoos on their backs since he whipped members to keep them in line and he respected our tattoo artist too much to damage his work. If a member pissed him off enough, he shot them, plain and simple.

"Why am I here?" She tried to back out of the room, her hand still over her mouth.

I ached to let her go. To not leave her here with El Ratón and whatever he had planned for her. I wanted to wrap her in my arms and protect her. To run away with her. But I couldn't, it wasn't meant to be that way for us. If I ran with Tulipán, I'd condemn Queso and my mother. El Ratón would find us eventually.

Tulipán shivered and hugged herself once again. Her eyes were wide as she looked around the room. Much like the butt plug, she acted as if all of this were new. Like no one had ever introduced her to the racy side of sex. I sighed and brushed my thumb across her cheekbone.

"You have to obey this time." I tugged on her arm and began walking toward a couple chairs in the middle of the room. "Please." My chest clenched as I met her ocean-blue gaze.

She bit her lower lip, then nodded. "I'll try."

Not five minutes passed before El Ratón appeared through the door. He approached us, still in his navy shirt, but he'd unbuttoned it all the way, exposing his entire chest. His gaze darted between the two of us, then he pinned Tulipán with his assessing gaze. "You disobeyed. Again," he growled.

Tulipán twitched in the chair. She looked at me as if pleading for me to save her. She didn't know how much I wanted to do just that, but I couldn't. I'd warned her. Yet she'd still taken the butt plug out. *I wonder what Camila told her to get her to do that.* I pressed my shoulders back as she turned her gaze back to him.

"I-I . . . " she stammered.

"No!" He slammed his fist on the small table. His dark gaze shifted to me. "Secure her in the Cross, then go."

"What?" Wide-eyed, she gasped, then tried to stand. He pushed her down by the shoulder.

My worst nightmare was realized in that moment as I fisted my hands. "Yes," I said through clenched teeth. I couldn't say more. I was lucky I could speak at all. He was sending me out. Not that I could stop whatever he planned if I'd been allowed to stay, but maybe he wouldn't whip her again or maybe she'd obey. Or maybe my imagination wouldn't drive me absolutely fucking insane.

Stiffly, I stood and offered her my hand again. She glared up at me, her chest rising and falling rapidly. I couldn't blame her, not in the least, but she didn't understand that neither of us had a choice if we wanted to be breathing tomorrow. El Ratón wouldn't hesitate to kill either of us if we pushed him too far. When she didn't move, I reached down and wrapped my arm around her shoulders, then bent over.

"Please, Tulipán, I beg you to cooperate," I whispered in her ear, wishing I could kiss her neck or any part of her body for that matter.

She tensed for a minute, then, as if resigning to her fate, she relaxed and stood. I grasped her delicate hand, then guided her to the rectangular device El Ratón had referred to. It wasn't a cross, but a device that held a person's body in the shape of a T. It had a metal frame with leather straps that secured a person's wrists and ankles in place. The arm straps were adjustable to accommodate people of different sizes. I had no idea where he'd gotten it, but I'd hated every second of being tied into it and putting her in this spot brought acid to the back of my throat.

My fingers shook as I secured the leather straps around her dainty wrists and ankles. I stood behind her and met her gaze in the mirror. The position thrust her breasts forward in a delectable sort of way. I licked my lips as my cock hardened. Despite everything, I wanted this woman for myself, and I'd take her just like this if I could.

"*Gracias*, Segundo," El Ratón's voice came from way too close. I jerked and glanced over my shoulder. He stood barely three meters away. "Leave us."

Her jaw shook as she craned her neck, twisting her body to try to make eye contact with me. Every fiber of my being swore that she was pleading with me to steal her away and not leave her here. My feet froze to the ground as I stared at her tied to the Cross.

My hands ached to release her. Or to at least be able to offer her some comfort, assure her she wouldn't be harmed, but there was nothing I could do. I was helpless and that was the worst feeling in the whole world. I gave her the most apologetic look I could muster. I turned and walked from the room with my head hanging and my heart breaking into a thousand pieces for the woman I'd chosen. For the woman who I knew was mine. Not his.

19

Segundo

After El Ratón kicked me out of the Black Room, I ran back down to the party and grabbed a couple beers to help pass the time and settle my nerves. There was no way I would leave her to suffer him alone. Even if we were separated by a door, I had to believe she could feel my presence.

Hours passed as I waited for El Ratón to exit. Now that the beers were gone, I clasped my hands behind me and paced the hall outside the Black Room. The black door had soundproofing, so I couldn't hear a thing. Electricity raced through my body every time I thought about what he was doing to *mi tulipán*. Visions of her destroyed back danced behind my eyes every time I blinked.

Across the hall from El Ratón's suite of rooms was a large balcony that looked out onto the backyard. The full moon cast its ominous glow through the open balcony doors. Despite the cool breeze, sweat beaded on my forehead. I wiped my face, sure the wait would never end.

I froze when the door clicked, then opened. El Ratón appeared with Carol in toe. Carol was the cartel's designated tattoo artist. He stood a head taller than our boss and waddled to support his potbelly. Carol carried his battered, black tattoo bag and puffed on a joint, his beady green eyes pinned to mine over El Ratón's head.

My gaze darted between the two men. I hadn't seen Carol enter the room. I shifted my feet and wiped my palms on my jeans. El Ratón raised one brow, but didn't answer the question he knew I wanted an answer to.

"Return her to her room," he ordered. "Don't miss our breakfast meeting." With that he and Carol disappeared, their voices low in a conversation not meant for my ears.

"*Sí*," I said in answer, almost for myself since El Ratón was long gone.

With heart hammering, I walked slowly back into the Black Room. I wasn't sure what he'd left for me to find. I caught sight of her immediately, in the same place I'd left her. My heart stalled at the pale pink color of her hair as it stuck to the new bloodied lashes across her back. New whip welts marked her buttocks and blood ran down her legs, collecting in small puddles on the floor. Her arms were slack in the holders.

My throat thickened, I almost choked as I rushed to her side. "Tulipán?" I touched a small space on her shoulder that appeared unmarred, praying she was still conscious.

She moaned, her eyes fluttering open, then closed. *God, what did he do to her?*

I wiped the sweat and hair off her face, then wrapped my arm around her waist to support her. I reached up and released her arms from the holders. Her body fell slack like a sack of potatoes. When I leaned over to release her legs, I saw the ink on her right breast. Carol's presence made sense now.

El Ratón had tattooed the Armas Locas cartel symbol on her. Every cartel member had the tattoo somewhere on their body, usually it was somewhere visible, unless that member was responsible for a covert duty. It signified loyalty and made members dependent on the organization. The tattoo was *el Día de Muertos* skull sitting on top a hand gun with the cartel's name along the side. He'd not only whipped her but, for some reason, branded her too. I shook my head and gently traced the line of the skull's face. I needed to get her cleaned up.

After releasing her legs, I swept her up in my arms and snuggled her close to me. Even in this state she still smelled of honey and vanilla. She pressed closer to my chest, her face pinched as if in pain. I imagined my arm on her back hurt, but I had to get her to her room.

Once in her room, I laid her on her stomach and leaned close to her face. "I'm so sorry." I brushed my lips against her dry, cracked lips. My stomach twisted at how ruined she looked, at what he'd done to her. Again. What I couldn't save her from. Again.

I pulled out my cell, typed out a message to Abuela to bring up supplies to clean and dress the wounds, then stepped into the bathroom to run some warm water. My nerves were shot over this whole situation. I'd expected El Ratón to punish her, but not to this extent. She was barely conscious, and I wasn't sure why. Was it from the blood loss or the pain? There hadn't been that much blood on the floor, but what did I know about blood loss?

When Abuela arrived, she almost dropped the load of supplies in her hands when she caught sight of Tulipán lying prone on the bed. "*Mi hijo*," she gasped. "What did he do?" Her face drained of blood as she shuffled over next to me.

I shook my head, then took the bowl and clean towels from her, unable to form a single word to explain or defend his actions. Because there wasn't any this time. He'd gone too far. It felt like he'd beat her within an inch of her life. It should've been me. I would've hung there and let him beat me.

My eyes burned as Abuela and I worked together in silence to clean the wounds on Tulipán's back. Her face scrunched with each touch, but she never opened her mouth to cry out. Her eyes remained closed as if in a distressed state of sleep. I couldn't tell if she knew what was going on or if she was having a nightmare. Neither seemed good. I wished she could find a peaceful sleep while we cleaned her up.

When I tilted Tulipán to put a dressing on her new tattoo. Abuela frowned. "What is this?"

I shrugged. "El Ratón." It was all I could say. Maybe he saw it as his way of reminding her that she belonged to him, but the tattoo wasn't visible, so he only meant it to be a reminder for her, not for the

Taken, not Destroyed

world. *And a reminder for any man who would see her naked.* I rubbed at my eyes and shoved the thought from my head.

It didn't matter. Only she could choose who her heart belonged to, and I planned to convince her to give it to me. El Ratón could claim her body, but her soul belonged to me. I'd known that from the moment I'd held her in my arms.

Once Tulipán's wounds were cleaned and dressed, Abuela took the dirty supplies and left. Tulipán slept, her breathing slow and calm. If I was ever going to shed a tear, now would've been that time. I'd chosen her. I should've done more to prevent this from happening again. I should've prepared her better for El Ratón. Should've explained better how obeying him was in her best interests no matter how much she didn't like it. I'd failed her.

The room began to lighten with the coming day. *Fuck.* I needed to shower and change before my meeting with El Ratón. My gaze flowed over her still naked form. I pulled the sheet gently up to cover her and knelt down so I was close to her head.

"Tulipán?" I whispered, wanting to wake her, but knowing she needed her sleep.

She moaned, and her eyelids cracked open. "Segundo?"

I gave her a small smile. It was the best I could do at the moment. I rested my forehead against hers. "I'm so sorry, Raella." I said her name as anyone would who spoke Spanish given the spelling, *Rae-ya.*

She pulled back, her mouth open. "Wha-what did you call me?" She seemed fully awake now. Her blue eyes were wide.

"Did I say it wrong?"

"Yes, but no." Her voice was breathless. She shifted and winced, as if just now remembering that she had fresh whip marks all over her back and buttocks. She groaned again.

"Turn on your side." I reached out to help her and she flinched at my touch. I pulled my hand back.

"I'm sorry, Segundo. It's just . . . he . . . " A solitary tear rolled down her pale cheek. She pulled her bottom lip between her teeth and bit down.

My stomach turned. I couldn't even ask her why she'd disobeyed him, because it didn't matter. He did what he was going to do no matter what she did. And we both knew it. I didn't want to know what else he'd done, I just wanted to offer her some comfort. To show her that not all the hands in this place were here to cause her pain.

I wiped the tear away and said, "It's Hugo. You don't have to tell me." I swallowed against the thickness in my throat. "I'm not sure I want to know."

Her eyes sparkled as the rising sun's light began to brighten the room more. "Hugo." She smiled. "I like that, and I like the way you say my name."

We stayed like that for a few minutes, locked in the gaze of the other, my thumb stroking gentle waves over her cheekbone. I took a deep breath. I still didn't want to leave, but I needed to go meet El Ratón. His patience was likely thin after last night. I didn't want to be late for our meeting.

"You can only use my name in this room, when it's just us." I cupped her cheek. She nodded. "I have to go." With care, I leaned up and pressed my lips to her forehead.

"Will you be back?" Her voice cracked at the end.

A smile pulled at my lips. "When I can. Abuela will care for you. You are strong." I believed it, and she needed to as well.

I stood and moved swiftly to the door before I changed my mind and stayed in that bed with her all day. This woman was doing something to me. I never thought I'd see the day when I'd want to spend time physically caring for another person. Even though I cared about my family, I still wasn't the one who took care of them physically. I took one last glance at her lying in the bed before I stepped into the hall.

I rubbed my face and squeezed my eyes. I needed to get my shit together. I couldn't be this emotional piece of shit when I met with El Ratón. I needed to find the me who was second in the Armas Locas cartel. Who kept El Ratón's arms and drug empire running smoothly. I took a deep breath, squared my shoulders and wiped my face of all emotion.

There was no room for emotion in cartel business.

20

Tulipán

I managed to keep track of time during my recovery this time. After two weeks, I forced myself to get out of bed, pushing through the pain, to take care of myself. Up to this point, I'd been relying on Abuela and Segundo a lot. They'd both cared for me that first night. I remembered bits and pieces before my mind shut down after the tenth lashing.

Stepping into the steamy shower, I let the hot water roll down my front as the past week played through my mind. What I remembered the most was Segundo's face as he gazed at me in the morning sun. In that moment, I'd felt like he was an angel sent down to care for me. It was hard to reconcile those feelings with the man who'd trapped me here and continuously left me in the hands of the beast who whipped me within an inch of my life.

I squirted soap on the loofah and ran its scratchy surface over my arms, careful not to let the direct spray land on my back or buttocks. Even though the wounds were starting to heal, they weren't quite closed. I asked Abuela to rub antibiotic ointment on them every day. Whether it was the better wound care or my determination to heal, I felt better in two weeks than I had in three last time.

Once I was clean, I stepped out of the glass enclosure and

grabbed the closest towel. As I dabbed off the water, I considered how I could get out of this situation. Nothing I'd tried so far had worked, and I wasn't sure I could handle another beating like this last one. It had been rough. I turned and looked at my backside in the mirror.

My eyes burned and throat tightened as I stared at the mishmash of white scarred lines, mixed in with pink lines, scabbed lines, and some lines that were still open wounds trying to pull together at the edges. This mess of wounds started just behind the curve of my shoulder and traveled the length of my back all the way down to the ledge of my buttocks.

I turned my head away and buried my face in my hands. I refused to cry over this. I couldn't become a sniveling mess. I had to get stronger so I could get the fuck out of here. That woman, Camila, had offered to help me escape. I had no clue what that entailed, but it couldn't possibly be easy. I'd never been a gym bunny, but my time here had weakened me. If I wanted even a slim chance at getting out, I needed to build my muscles and my stamina.

I pulled on some breathable clothes and decided to start easy. Jumping jacks. For the next three days, I did jumping jacks three times a day, increasing the number each day. Then I added sit-ups and lunges. A week later, I had a whole exercise routine going, so I was sweating and short of breath at the end.

One afternoon, three weeks after the party, the keypad beeped and the door opened enough for Camila to peek her head in. *"Hola, chica."* She gave me a bright, toothy smile. "Can I come visit?"

Huffing from my workout, I paused, mid jumping jack. Eyes wide, I shrugged. "Of course," I said, then wiped my face with the bottom of my shirt.

Camila hopped into the room and closed the door. She wore a bright yellow sun dress with spaghetti straps. Her long, brown hair was up in a loose ponytail, with a pair of sunglasses pushed up onto the top of her head. Her face was flushed as if she'd just come in from outdoors and, unlike the other night, she wore the bare minimum for makeup.

Taken, not Destroyed

"Thank you." She tapped the end of her red, manicured nail against her teeth.

I raised my brows and watched as her brown eyes scanned my sparse room. I wondered what she thought about the space I'd been given here.

"Honestly, I'm surprised to see you," I said to break the silence.

"Oh." She turned her long-lashed eyes on me. "Yes. My husband has business in Mexico. El Ratón often allows me to stay here," she explained dismissively, almost like I should've known or maybe she didn't like explaining herself. I couldn't tell.

"Okay?" I tried to say the word as a question, hoping she'd expand on the reason for her visit.

The woman seemed to genuinely want to help me. I couldn't help but wonder if I hadn't removed that butt thing. Would El Ratón still have whipped me? I turned away from her and rubbed my eye. I couldn't let thoughts of "What if?" cloud my brain. She'd offered me some light in this eternal darkness. I couldn't treat her like shit just because I felt like shit. I took a deep breath and plastered a smile on my face.

She touched my shoulder with soft fingers. "I'm so sorry."

I kept the fake-as-shit smile on my face. I touched my right breast where my new, and only tattoo, sat. El Ratón had given me a permanent memory of this place and his possessive nature. "I know." I didn't want to tell her it was okay, because it would never be okay.

"Do you want to talk about it?" Her eyes seemed kind and at face value her question was good intentioned, but I didn't know her and wasn't going to share my deepest thoughts with a stranger.

"Thank you for the offer"—I moved to the bed and sat—"but it's not easy to talk about."

She pursed her lips, followed, and sat next to me. "I meant it . . . that I want to help you."

I frowned. I wanted to believe her, wanted so badly to have someone purely on my side. Not straddling the divide between the cartel and me, like Segundo. But it was difficult to trust her. Yes, she was a woman, but she was also a cartel boss's wife. "Why?" I asked.

Camila clicked her nails. She wore multiple rings with large stones such as diamonds, sapphires, and one with a pearl. She stared down at her hands. The only sound was the click, click, click of her nails. I wanted to slap her hands. I balled my fists and gritted my teeth.

She took a deep breath and stopped the nail clicking. "I have a sister. She's ten years younger," she began, her gaze focused on her hands, which now rested calmly in her lap. I remained quiet during the lengthy silence, this seemed like an important story. "I was married to El Mil when she was very little, my parents arranged it."

I nodded as she cleared her throat. This story was visibly difficult for her to tell. "Estrella was kidnapped when she was sixteen, much like you've been by the Armas Locas."

"Armas Locas?" I raised my brows. The name caught my attention.

Camila straightened. "Oh, yes. El Ratón's cartel." She waved her hand at me.

Filing the name away, I touched her hand, and she grasped ahold of it as if it were a lifeline. "Where is she now?" I asked. Her shiny, chocolate eyes met mine.

"For many years, El Mil has used his resources to look for her." Her voice rose, then cracked. "Nothing. She's gone. Lost." Camila dabbed at the corner of her eye with her finger. "I fear for what she's going through. What all women go through like her, like you." She grabbed both my hands in her cool ones with a death grip. "I do not like this business. It's vile."

My gut clenched. She truly wanted to help me. She may not know everything I'd been through, but she saw what was happening to me and linked it in her mind to what had happened to her sister. But she didn't see how her actions the other night resulted in more pain for me. All she saw was her sister and, if she helped, I'd be a symbol for her sister's escape. I pressed my lips together. If I wanted out of here, I could deal with that, even if it wasn't entirely right.

I took my hands back and straightened my shoulders. "It is awful. But I'm not the only one they've kidnapped." I remembered all the other women they sold the day Segundo kept me. I could never forget them, not in a million years. My stomach churned at the thought of what could be happening to them. Their lives could be so much worse than mine. "They're lost too."

Camila stood abruptly and brushed a hand down her front. "I know, but I can help you. Not the others." Her voice turned stern, and I saw the woman who stood beside a cartel boss in her posture.

Sensing that I shouldn't push her, I nodded. It seemed this was how she chose to cope with her sister. "Okay. How do I get out of here?" I could help the others myself, once I'd escaped.

"El Ratón and my husband are gone on business right now," she explained. "When they come back, there will be another party."

I groaned and rubbed my face, not another party. My hand fell to my right breast, to El Ratón's idea of a reminder that I belong to him. Whatever happened after I escaped, I wouldn't allow myself to be ruled by another man. Camilla watched my hand.

"You shouldn't see the party's end." Her gaze darted back to mine.

My heart pounded a rapid beat in my chest. "Really?"

Her bright red lips tipped up and she nodded. "I'm working on it. El Mil has contacts." Her voice dropped as if someone might be listening. "Once you're out of the house and off property. The rest is easier."

She continued to explain how I would leave here and find myself reliant on her husband's contacts. On her. But I would never allow myself to be trapped in the hands of another man, or woman, again. I let her voice drift into background noise, nodding and smiling, as I imagined what I would do once I arrived back in Kansas.

I couldn't go back home to Brian. He wasn't as controlling as El Ratón, but he was a close second. I never saw it before, but I did now. I let it go on all those years because I didn't want to argue. I lied, and told myself it was for the kids, but it was because I didn't want to deal with the blowback of fighting against Brian's commanding nature. It was easier just to give him what he wanted, rather than to stand up for myself.

Blinking rapidly, I realized Camila had fallen silent and stared at me as if she'd said something and expected a response. Rather than admit I hadn't been listening, I asked, "How do I get out of this house?"

"Oh. Right." Her gaze darted around. "There will be a go-bag on your balcony. You must wait until I give the okay to go."

My balcony was locked, I couldn't get out there. "Camila..."

She waved her hand, then stood. My mouth stayed open, the words dead on my tongue. She gave me a half-hearted hug, kissed my cheek, then vanished like a genie in a cloud of smoke.

My mind was reeling. It had all happened so fast, and she'd barely given me any explanation. Or at least any information that was important. It left my stomach feeling rotten, and I didn't like my entire escape plan hinging on the efforts of someone I wasn't entirely sure I could trust. But what choice did I have?

Abso-fucking-lutely none!

21

Segundo

Late one afternoon, I sat at a table in one of El Ratón's restaurants in Nuevo Vallarta. It'd been almost a month since I'd found Tulipán whipped and bloodied in the Black Room, and I hadn't had time to visit her. I'd been so busy with cartel work and covering for Queso that the only time I'd seen her was when I spied through her balcony window late at night. Abuela reported that she'd healed much quicker this time and seemed in better spirits despite my inability to visit. My stomach twisted. Maybe I wouldn't be able to win her trust.

My laptop sat open and my fingers hovered over the keys. My eyes burned as I stared at the bright light in the darkening room, lost in thought about the woman who I'd rather be with than here. It'd been too long since I'd touched the silky skin of her face, seen the way her breasts swelled when she breathed, and watched as she squirmed when I implied how much I wanted her. My cock swelled and throbbed. I bit the inside of my cheek.

Fuck! I needed to get ahold of myself.

I wiped a hand down my face, then looked around the almost empty room. Late last night I'd gotten intel that the Zapas, a rival cartel, were on their way to Nuevo Vallarta to intercept one of the drug deliveries scheduled to arrive just after dark. El Ratón met me here with extra men, though neither of our plans had included supervising this deal. I shifted in my seat, lit a cigarette, then focused on the dock surveillance I'd hacked into earlier in the evening.

Five of our guys stood on the dock waiting for the delivery as the sun kissed the horizon in the distance. Three of the five cameras caught different angles of the deal, the other two gave me a view of the dock's entrance and gatehouse. I'd also managed to hack into a camera from a nearby bank down the street. If the Zapas wanted to join our party, I'd have a heads-up.

I set the cigarette down, the smoke drifting up like a snake, then took a drink of beer. I didn't smoke or drink often, but both seemed to keep my thoughts in the present and off the blond-haired goddess back home. I pressed my arms up in the air, stretching my back. I'd been sitting in front of this computer for hours, hacking camera networks, and we were nowhere near the end of the night. I glanced at the clock; the drugs weren't due for another hour. El Ratón liked to arrive early to prevent fuckups. I half wanted this to erupt in a fight; it'd make my purpose here worth it, but the other half of me wanted the deal to go down without a hitch, so I could get the fuck out of here.

"Everything quiet?" El Ratón leaned on my chairback and a cloud of smoke enveloped my head.

I nodded. "So far. I can't see the boat yet. Our guys are ready though. There's no one else around." Acid turned in my stomach.

The intel I'd gotten was solid though. The likelihood that the Zapas weren't going to try and heist our deal was low. They were here, somewhere. I just hadn't found them yet, and that bugged the shit out of me.

"Zero?" he growled. He knew the sicario was ready with his team but expected me to check anyway.

I pulled out my walkie and checked in with Zero. "All's quiet," I reported. The tension between us was palpable. He wanted something and I wasn't sure I wanted to know.

El Ratón leaned close and stabbed out his cigarette in the tray next

Taken, not Destroyed

to me, then stood back up. I could feel his presence behind me, like a weight on my shoulders. Sweat gathered on my back, sticking my shirt to it.

I ran my fingers through my hair, cleared my throat, and scooted forward a bit in the chair. I needed some space and some air. I fanned myself with the front of my shirt. "Is it hot in here?"

El Ratón grunted, but didn't respond. I felt the back of the chair shift with his movements. I almost relaxed, thinking he got what he'd come for, an update on the drug delivery, but then he spoke. "Where's your brother?"

I closed my eyes and wiped my palms down my jeans. He generally left personnel to me, so I didn't think he'd noticed Queso had been missing these past few weeks. My mom hadn't been doing well. The doctors in Puerto Vallarta hadn't been able to tell us anymore about her illness than the one in our home village. The last time Queso had called, Mom had lost another five kilos. They wanted her to stay in the hospital, but she refused, forcing Queso to stay in the hotel and take care of her.

Rubbing my face, I hung my head. "He's with our mamá."

"Why?" His voice softened a bit, but not so much that I relaxed.

I propped my elbow on the desk and rested my head on my hand. "She's sick. The doctors don't know what's wrong."

"You want to care for her." Again, his voice changed. It sent a chill down my spine. It made me think he wasn't talking about my mom.

I swallowed against a lump in my throat and nodded, placing both my hands in my lap and returning my gaze to the black and white surveillance videos. Our men formed a line along the dock's edge, while a mid-sized yacht pulled up to the dock. I wasn't sure where he was going with this or what he wanted from me.

I interlaced my fingers. "It's the right thing to do." It was dumb to think he didn't see how I wanted Tulipán. How I wanted to protect her even from him. El Ratón saw everything that happened in that house.

He gripped my shoulders at the base of my neck and dug his fingers in. "I see. The right thing."

My throat constricted. I wasn't sure I could breathe properly, but I managed a single nod. I had no clue what to say. We'd disagreed before, but this was different. It wasn't that I disagreed with his methods, per se. If she were some other female, I wouldn't have batted an eye. It was her. I gave a shit about her.

El Ratón's grip lightened. "You want her."

Exhaling lightly, I hesitated and his fingers bit down into my shoulder again. Somehow, I knew he no longer spoke about my mom, but referred to Tulipán instead. "Yes, very much," I agreed quickly, my heart racing in my chest.

Trying to keep an eye on the situation at the docks while talking about Tulipán was complicated, so I shifted my focus back to the screen. Two of our men stood guard while the others unloaded the boat, along with a couple from the delivery team. They put the drugs into the back of a van that was parked close by. One of our guys sat in the front, the engine running like I'd told him. The delivery would be complete soon, and if El Ratón hadn't been grilling me about Tulipán, I'd be able to relax a bit.

"*Bien.*" His hands left my shoulders. "Go home tomorrow. I'll be back Friday." The lighter flicked as he lit another cigarette. "We'll party Saturday."

I nodded briefly with each command. My boss didn't offer his possessions out to others so easily. There had to be a reason he was sending me home to be with Tulipán, knowing I wanted her. Sweat beaded on my brow and my stomach twisted as I waited for him to give me more of an explanation. I pressed my lips together.

"Okay," I whispered.

"She's disobedient," he growled. I felt the anger in his words down in my bones.

"I can help," I blurted, desperate to fix the situation.

El Ratón walked past me to stand in front of the window. His body cast in shadow. The orange light from his cigarette cast an ominous glow on his face. He exhaled a cloud of smoke. "I have a potential buyer coming on Saturday."

My heart stalled and I coughed. Why had he tattooed her if he

Taken, not Destroyed

planned to sell her? So many questions ran through my mind, but that one stuck out the most. The tattoo meant she was property of the Armas Locas cartel. It made no sense. But he'd never explain himself to me. I just needed to fix this somehow.

"Please . . . I . . . " I started.

El Ratón turned his depthless, dark eyes on me. My entire insides burned as if the devil himself were here lighting me on fire. I straightened my shoulders. There wasn't anything I could say right now to deter him. I needed to start with her. I needed to win Tulipán over, then I'd work on El Ratón. Right now, I needed to focus on cartel business.

I blinked and returned my gaze to the computer screen, shoving aside all thoughts of Tulipán. It appeared like all the drugs had been loaded in the van. Two Armas Locas men talked to one of the boat workers, likely exchanging money. The other three walked in a group back toward the van. It looked like the deal had gone off successfully.

Seconds before I opened my mouth to report that to El Ratón, one of the men walking toward the van dropped to the ground and pulled a weapon. The other two followed suit. I glanced to the video that showed the driver of the van. He slumped forward with his head on the steering wheel. It looked like there was a hole in the front windshield.

"Fuck!" I slammed my hands on the desk, then stood, shoving my chair over.

The acid that had built in my stomach earlier returned in a rush and climbed up my throat, coating my mouth with a foul taste. Six Zapas came running up the dock toward the deal location, firing weapons.

I ripped the walkie off the hook of my jeans. "Zero. Go!" I yelled.

"Gone." His response came as if he had been watching the feed with me. The man was a genius fighter. He'd have half those Zapas dead before El Ratón and I could make it out the front door of this restaurant.

Zero's group showed up on the screen and chaos descended. Once the initial shock of the attack wore off, my heart rate accelerated with the need to get out there and join my brothers in battle. I shook myself back to reality.

El Ratón was halfway to the door. He glanced back at me with a maniacal grin on his face. "Let's kill those fuckers." He waved his favorite golden gun, then disappeared out the door.

I grabbed my gun off the desk and followed him, wondering if the day would ever come when I was on the wrong side of his weapon. Especially if I ever decided to defend Tulipán against him.

22

Tulipán

It'd been a few days since Camila visited me. I'd stuck to my workout routine, but in between those times all I'd been able to do was stare out the window and imagine myself running free through the forest. My bare feet as they pounded against the dry dirt in pursuit of escape from this marble cage. My heart ached to feel the warm sun on my face and the breeze brush my skin.

The sun burned a bright, orangey red as it said its last goodbye to me. I wrapped my arms around my stomach as the tension in my back pulled my thoughts into the past.

I was strung up in the torture device that held my arms out and legs apart, as if on a cross like Jesus, but there was nothing spiritual about this device.

El Ratón talked to the rotund white man behind me, their voices too low for me to hear. My whole body shook after I'd slammed my forehead into his. I needed to survive this, whatever he had planned, but I couldn't reconcile what this wretched man had made me feel. Even though I was appalled by him, he'd turned me on. It was disgusting.

The men finished their conversation and El Ratón stalked back toward me, while the other man dug through a black bag on the table. My gaze darted to El Ratón. When he reached me, he stepped up next to me and growled in my ear, *"There's a fine line between pleasure and pain, Tulipán."*

I blinked and looked at myself. My face had drained of any color. I looked like a ghost. I glanced back at his dark form. He stepped back, his face contorted in an evil sort of smile. I pulled at my arms. I needed to get away. "Don't, please." *I wasn't beyond begging at this point.*

El Ratón spanked my bare butt cheek, the sound like a thunderclap in the empty space. A lightning bolt shot straight to my pussy. Warmth gathered in my core. Holy fuck! He repeated the gesture three more times. Each time the sensation increased. My eyes rolled back, and my body writhed in pleasure. I wanted, no needed, something to press my pubis up against.

"You disobeyed." His voice sliced through my pleasure.

My eyes popped opened. He stood with his legs apart, hands behind his back and his empty eyes pinned on mine in the mirror. I swallowed against the lump in my throat. What had just happened? I tried to press my thighs together, but I couldn't.

He sneered, then turned toward the other man in the room. "You may begin."

The beeps from the keypad behind me yanked me back to the present. My core was warm and my panties were wet from the memory. I shifted and rubbed my thighs together. Had I always been like this or had El Ratón done something to me?

The door opened and Segundo appeared with a chair. He didn't offer me a second glance as he stalked into the room toward me.

Frowning, I took a step back. "What are you doing?"

Ignoring my question, he carried the chair to the corner a few feet away, set it down, then stood on it. He pulled something out of his pocket, then reached over his head where the wall met the ceiling.

I leaned to the side to get a better look. "What are you doing?"

He glanced over his shoulder, his eyes flashing golden. He pursed his lips, then slowly ran his tongue along the bottom one. I stiffened. I couldn't tear my eyes away from his tongue. It was like he knew how to get my attention. My lips parted and my breaths came heavier.

Segundo's lips tipped up. He stepped off the chair and removed it the same way he brought it in. I ran my finger along the edge of my lip as I stared at the place where he'd just stood. *What the hell was that?* I squeezed my eyes closed and took a deep breath. This place was doing strange things to me. I needed to get ahold of myself.

I heard Segundo speaking to another man just outside my door, then the door closed, followed by the beeps of the door lock. I exhaled heavily and opened my eyes. Segundo stood a few paces away, his hazel eyes pinned on my face.

I jolted. "What's going on?"

He moved closer and rested his warm fingers against my cheek. "Raella." His voice rolled along my spine like warm honey.

I covered his hand with mine. We shouldn't be comfortable calling each other by our real names. Everything this man did confused me. One minute he acted like I was his whole world, then the next he left me to the evils that prowled in it. This place was nightmare enough, without my emotions being drug through the ringer like that.

I gripped his hand and removed it, then dropped my gaze. "Don't. Please."

"You're so beautiful." He tipped my chin up.

My eyes burned. "Segundo . . . "

"Hugo," he corrected.

I winced. None of this felt right. I wanted him. God, I really wanted him, but I shouldn't want him. Just like I shouldn't have been turned on by what El Ratón did to me. My face heated at that last memory. I shook my head and backed away.

He reached for me. "Raella. Please," he pleaded. His thick brows knit together.

Never in my life would I have guessed that a man who ran in a cartel would beg me like this. I froze and gnawed at my lower lip. His eyes looked so sad. "Seg—Hugo. We can't do this." I shook my head.

He took my hands in his large, calloused ones and led me to the bed. He sat and guided me to sit facing him. "I need you." He brought the knuckles of my right hand to his lips. "I'm so sorry I let him hurt you."

My gut wrenched and I pressed my lips together. What could I say to him? It wasn't okay. What happened to me here would never be okay. But I could see how much he needed me to accept his apology. I squeezed his hands. "I know. You've said as much before."

He cupped my face. "I wish I could take you away."

My heart skipped a beat, then took off at a mile a minute. "Take me . . . away?" Was he offering to help me escape? "What do you mean?"

He dropped his hand, then stood and turned his back on me. I hadn't noticed before, but he looked less put together than normal. His jeans were lined with dark stains and his black T-shirt had wrinkles as if he'd pulled a dirty shirt out of a pile. He raked a hand through his hair, then began to pace in front of my bed.

"It could work," he said, more to himself than me. "I'd have to find a place to hide you. Somewhere he'd never look."

I pulled my legs under me and bounced up on my knees. This was beginning to sound like a plan. Maybe Hugo could get me out of here and we could be together. "Where?" I prompted.

He shook his head, spun to face me, his jaw flexing. "I don't know. He has eyes everywhere." He continued to pace. My head began to spin as I watched him. Then he slammed his fist into the palm of his opposite hand. "It'd never work." He spun, his golden eyes on fire.

I clenched my hands. He stalked toward me, and I turned to face him. "What won't work?" I asked.

Hugo stood only inches from me, enveloping me in his coconut and sunshine scent. He cocked his head, then ran his thumb along my cheekbone. The muscles in my legs shook as a warm heat gathered in my core. *Why did my body make this so easy for him?* I wanted to be strong, not so easily manipulated by these men. I closed my eyes.

"Please don't," I whispered, but there was no strength in my voice. I licked my lips and tasted his salty fingers. I opened my eyes to find him even closer, his eyes hooded and pinned on mine.

His lips tipped up slightly, almost challenging me to deny him what he wanted right now. To deny that I wanted it too. My lips parted as my breathing grew heavy and my panties grew wet. I wanted to tell him to back away. Tell him that we couldn't do this. But no words left my mouth as I remembered the way his lips felt against mine.

Hugo's fingers trailed lightly down my neck, leaving a line of tingles in their wake. I shivered as he circled each of my nipples. Even through the shirt, my nipples peaked, wanting more of his touch. I arched my back.

He leaned close and ran his tongue along the shell of my ear. "Should I stop?"

Goosebumps formed a line up my spine, and I arched into him. My breasts rubbed up against his solid chest, the friction sending thrills over my nipples. I moaned as Hugo lightly trailed his fingers down my back. He tickled the skin at the bottom edge of my shirt, then ran his fingers up my back again.

The respect he showed me in this moment set my heart on fire. I wanted him more than anything. He knew that El Ratón had done things to shame me. He was in control of this whole thing, yet he still gave me the power to stop it.

I reached behind me and took hold of his wrists. He straightened and looked at me questioningly. "I just have some questions."

He nodded.

"What changed? Why can we do this now and not before?" I wanted this, I couldn't deny it, but Hugo had stopped us before. He'd said El Ratón wouldn't approve. I needed to know what made now okay. I couldn't risk another whipping. It took too long to heal, and I'd miss the escape Camila had for me.

Hugo brushed some hair that had fallen out of my ponytail off my forehead. "I need to figure something out."

I frowned. "That's vague."

He reached up and tugged at the band holding my hair up. "I love your hair." He ran his fingers through its length.

Shaking my head, I pulled his hands away. "Don't ignore my question."

He threaded his fingers in my hair and gripped the back of my head, then pulled me close to him so our faces were inches apart. "I'm not ignoring you." He brushed his lips against mine.

Sparks lit across my lips and danced down my front, igniting my desire for this man. *Holy shit! What were we talking about?*

"Please. Trust me," he said.

He pulled me closer and captured my lips with his. Electricity erupted throughout my body and lava pooled in my panties. Hugo parted my lips with his tongue. I ran my hands up his sculpted arms, then over the broad planes of his back as our tongues met in an exquisite dance. The kiss was slow, hot, and everything a kiss should be.

By the time my heart felt like it was about to bust out of my chest, Hugo pulled back and ran his hand down my cheek. He took my bottom lip between his thumb and finger. "Trust me?"

I'd never been kissed like that before in my life. How could I not trust him right now? I felt like my entire world had been turned upside down. I nodded, and he gave me a smile that lit up his entire face.

23

Tulipán

"**G**ood." Hugo ran his hands down my back and gripped my ass, then hooked one leg up over his hip. "Tell me what you want." His voice dropped, and I could feel his length pressed against my center.

I swallowed hard against my suddenly dry mouth. My breathing increased. I opened and closed my mouth, unable to form a single word. He slapped my butt cheek, then grabbed it hard and pulled my center against him. His eyes flashed with desire as he ground his hard-on against me.

"Tell me, Raella. What do you want?" He traced the edge of my ear with his tongue, then bit the lobe. "Who do you truly belong to?"

Fuck! I couldn't hold back any longer. He was driving me insane. Touching and rubbing through the clothes was a special kind of torture. I could tell this man knew how to make a woman feel good. He was just waiting for me to give him the go-ahead. I wasn't sure why I was holding back. At this point, once I escaped, I didn't plan to go back to my marriage in the US, so there was no reason for me to deny what I so clearly wanted.

"You, Hugo," I gasped and dug my nails into his back. "I belong to you. I want you."

That was all the man needed to hear. He grabbed my other leg, picked me up, and tossed me onto the bed. In the next breath, he took hold of the top of my stretch pants and panties and pulled them both off in one swift motion. I gripped the sheets in my hands, resisting the urge to cover myself as his eyes feasted on my bare flesh.

Hugo crawled onto the bed at my feet, then lightly touched my right calf just below the knee. I shivered at the contact and propped myself up on my elbows so I could watch him. I bit my lower lip as his touch traveled up my thigh, closer to the center of my desire. Brian only touched me there to get his cock inside. There'd been no one else. My chest constricted as Hugo's fingers and face moved closer to my core.

He licked the inside of my leg, right where it met the outside fold of my sex, and I squirmed and exhaled loudly. Hugo's head lifted and his eyes met mine. He cocked his head. My whole body shook. His mouth was hidden below my pelvis, but I swore he smiled before I felt the warm wetness of his tongue run the length of my seam.

I arched my back. "Holy. Fuck." I tried to scoot away.

His strong arm wrapped around my hips and pressed down. "No." He parted my folds with his fingers. "Wet." He ran his hot tongue up my center. "Delicious."

My pussy was on fire. I'd never felt so many sensations in my core before. He pressed his tongue against the bundle of nerves at the top and shoved two fingers inside me. Spasms of pleasure shot out from my sex, and I got wetter, if that was possible. He growled deep in his throat.

"Holy fuck." I tried to grind my hips against him as the pressure built in my pussy. It seemed my new mantra was going to be *Holy fuck*. I couldn't think of anything else to say.

Hugo slid his fingers deep inside, then curled them up, while he circled my clit with his tongue. I moaned and fought against his hold, trying to grind my hips, while the coil of pleasure in my core tightened. I couldn't figure out what to do with my hands. I kept grabbing his head, then the sheets, then his head. My entire body was on fire.

"Oh God, Hugo . . . Fuck . . . I can't . . . " I wasn't sure what I was trying to say. I arched my back as my entire body exploded in orgasm.

The motion of his fingers slowed. I lifted my head. He pulled back and sucked on his fingers. I sank into the bed, my body heavy and satisfied. Hugo crawled up and rested on his side next to me. He propped his head on his hand, a lopsided smile on his face.

I pursed my lips. "Proud of yourself?" He looked adorable like that.

He reached out and pulled my shirt up exposing my chest. As he began to trace the lines of the tattoo on my chest, his eyes grew distant. I got the feeling something about the tattoo bothered him. He'd made me admit that I belonged to him, not El Ratón. There was something with these two men. They needed to feel like they owned me, but it wasn't enough that they believed it; I had to believe it too.

"Why did he give me this tattoo?" My voice sliced through the silence like a knife.

Hugo's eyes moved to mine as if he'd forgotten I was there. "That's just who he is."

My fingers traced a circle at the nape of my neck. "Doesn't it mean that he won't like . . . this? Us?"

His gaze returned to my tattoo, then his finger began to pinch at my nipple, which peaked at the new attention. Chills ran along my neck and my breathing grew heavy. This man was going to be the death of me. He was also trying to distract me. He didn't want to talk about El Ratón for some reason. I needed to stay focused.

I pushed his hand away. "Hugo. You're trying to distract me."

"Hmm." He leaned over and licked a circle around my nipple, then teased it with his teeth. He pinched the other between two fingers. The dual sensations had pinpricks racing through my chest straight down to my pussy.

I cupped his face in my hands and pushed him back. "Wait." It was one of the hardest things I'd ever done, but I couldn't lose myself. There was too much at stake. I had to keep my mind clear somehow.

He lifted his head, breathing heavily, a questioning look on his face. He continued to trace a path along my chest aimlessly, which kept my nipples peaked and my pussy wet and ready.

I rubbed my face. The dynamic right now was so skewed. I was practically naked and he was fully dressed. I wasn't used to getting all the attention in the bedroom, my mind was reeling. I needed to focus. "Tell me what this tattoo means, Hugo. There's something important. I can tell."

He scrunched his face, then traced a line between my breasts to my belly button. "He's difficult to predict. I don't always understand him." I grabbed his hand as it began to travel lower. He took control of my hand, then slipped it between my legs so I felt the folds of my sopping pussy beneath his fingers. Hugo leaned down close to my ear. "Have you ever touched yourself?"

I pressed my lips together. This was another distraction, but it was good. He worked our fingers through the warm wetness, then circled them at the bundle of nerves that sent a lightning sensation straight up through my center the second we touched it. I groaned, then shook my head, unable to say anything intelligent.

I rocked my hips as he worked our fingers and shoved them inside. My lips parted as I tried to stretch my arm so my finger could reach, but his were just angled better. He slipped another one of his inside and I felt full. I pulled my hand out as Hugo moved his faster. My core contracted.

"Come for me, *mi tulipán*," he growled, his breath hot against my ear as he curled his fingers and rubbed his palm against the bundle of nerves.

My body exploded. I grabbed his arm and writhed against his hand as I came. It was like nothing I'd ever felt before. "Holy fuck!"

After I'd come, he put the finger I'd just come all over in my mouth. It tasted a little salty, but what got me was the look of unbridled desire on his face. I sucked in my cheeks as he pulled his finger out slowly, then pinched my nipple. I gave him a satisfied smile.

"There's an interested buyer coming to the party Saturday," he whispered as I was basking in the glory of that last orgasm.

My body went rigid and, what had once been flaming hot, shot through with ice. "Excuse me? What did you just say?" I stared, wide-eyed at the man who'd just sent me over the moon so many times I couldn't count.

He closed his eyes and shook his head. "I wish I could explain him, but I can't. All I know is that he's given me time to fix things." He met my gaze, his eyes pleading. "I need you to trust that I can, and trust me when I tell you to do things."

I sat up and drew my knees to my chest. My nakedness more of a problem now that he'd told me about this possibility. How could he have kept this from me? If I hadn't pushed, would he have even told me? Maybe I should've stayed ignorant; I couldn't do anything about it. But if El Ratón sold me before Camila could help me escape, I was completely fucked. I didn't want to stay here, but this place was better than somewhere else.

I turned and met Hugo's hazel eyes in the now dark room. "There must be something you can do to stop him." My gut twisted. I rested my cheek on my knees to look at him as I hugged them tighter.

His eyes scanned my back. It was the first time he'd seen it since the Black Room. Hugo sat and traced some of the lines. "That's why I'm here. I can't let you go." He kissed my shoulder. "You're mine."

Closing my eyes, I leaned in as he trailed kisses up my neck to my ear. I could so live like this for the rest of my life. Having a man kiss me like this, treating me like a goddess. Even though he was a bit possessive, he still seemed to respect my wants and desires.

"What about running away together?" I threaded my fingers in his hair as he continued to kiss my neck and knead my breasts.

"Hmm," he hummed between kisses. "I haven't thought of a way to get you out yet." He ran his hand down my front until it rested at the wetness between my thighs. I had no idea I could get wet this much or feel this good without a dick inside me. "We would have to walk for about thirty kilometers through the forest behind us before the closest village."

I took his hand and put one finger in my mouth, then spoke around it. "Is that a long way?" My words were muffled, but I still made sense.

Hugo moaned. "Uh."

I couldn't tell if that was a yes or a no. I needed to get more information from him. This was important. Camila said I would escape out my balcony. Since I had no plans to get in a car with her or one of her men, I needed to know more about what was around this fortress. I circled his finger with my tongue, then asked, "What's the forest like?"

"Huh?" Hugo slipped a finger from his other hand between my folds. I leaned back into his hard body. He lifted his chin and stared out my patio door, then leaned in and ran his tongue along my neck.

My eyes rolled back as I tried to keep my thoughts straight. "Is there a road or path?"

He groaned.

"Hugo. What's the land like?" He slicked his fingers through my wetness, then rubbed and circled my clit. While pulling his finger in and out of my mouth, I reached behind me and grabbed onto his hard cock through his jeans, stroking it.

His fingers paused, then disappeared. I felt the bed shift behind me. Hugo picked me up, then placed me face down. He leaned against me, his chest now bare against my back. "You're being naughty."

My heart rate kicked up as I twisted my head to see him. He knelt on the bed next to me. He wasn't a large man, but his muscles were defined. Every available space along his neck, arms, hands and chest held a tattoo of some sort. His Armas Locas tattoo stood out on the right side of his neck. He scooted a little closer, then lifted his hand and spanked me.

The sharp sting sung through my veins, then pooled in my pussy. I had no idea why he decided to spank me, but I sure as fuck wasn't going to complain. I lifted my hips a bit, but instead of another spank, Hugo slipped his hand between my legs and jammed two fingers inside my wet heat. My core contracted and I almost came right then and there.

"Be a good girl for me." He brought his fingers out and spanked me again.

I laced my fingers in my hair, arched my head back, and yelled, "Holy fuck!" I wasn't sure I could take any more. He was driving me insane. I wanted to beg him to fuck me. Was I beyond begging?

24

Segundo

I pleasured Raella until her eyes were heavy. I felt like I was floating on a cloud. She'd given herself to me, mostly. Bare chested, I leaned back into the pillows and put my hands behind my head. She turned on her side and rested her head on my chest. In the darkness, I couldn't see her, but I could feel every inch of her as she pressed against me.

"Hugo?" Her voice sounded as if she were on the edge of sleep.

"Hmm?" I ran my fingers up and down her scarred back. The damage he'd done to her turned my stomach, but she remained strong. She didn't even wince or pull away when I touched the scars or scabs. It filled my heart with a pride I had no right to feel, but still did.

"Why did you pick me?" She tilted her head, her eyes filled with curiosity. "There were other girls. Younger, prettier ones. Why me?"

It was a fair question, but my jaw clenched nonetheless. None of those women could've held a candle to her. How could I explain that my soul felt drawn to hers? That I knew deep in my bones that I needed to keep her here? Those were the things that romantics said, not cartel leaders.

"I helped the day you were brought in." I played with her white-blond hair. "I just knew you were mine." I shrugged a shoulder. It was the best explanation I could give her.

Her finger began to trace the lines of a cross tattoo on my left pec. I shivered and my cock twitched to life. The woman had the softest fingers, even though they felt like ice against my heated skin. The curves of her warm body pressed against my side. I ran my hand over the roundness of her ass, then squeezed. I wanted to spank her again. She'd gotten so wet.

"I lost mine, you know," she mused.

I blinked and glanced down at her fingers, trying to pull my mind back to the here and now. "What?"

"My cross. It was a graduation gift from my sister." Her voice cracked. "I . . . "

I pinched the bridge of my nose. I'd taken that cross on an impulse when I thought I'd never see her again. A way to remember her. Now, it was my connection to her when I couldn't be next to her. I ran my fingers through her silky hair.

"I took it," I admitted through the lump in my throat. I wanted her to know what I'd done, but more I wanted her to know about the connection I felt. "I felt this connection, but at the time I didn't know I could keep you here." Her body stiffened. "It was my way to remember you."

She tilted her head up, resting her chin on my chest. Her eyes sparkled with unshed tears. I could see how much that cross meant to her, and it stung that I couldn't give it back.

"Can I—"

I shook my head, cutting her off. "He won't let you have it." It was easier to put all the blame on El Ratón, though I didn't want to give it back either.

Cupping her delicate face in my hands, I pulled her up to give her a gentle kiss. An apology of sorts. At first her lips resisted me, then she became pliant and melted into the kiss with a moan. I was rock hard again, any thoughts of allowing her to rest had vanished with that sound from her mouth.

Desperate to feel her body against mine, I positioned her so her legs straddled my body, grinding my cock against her center. I was tired of wearing clothes, but I wanted her to beg me to fuck her. No, I needed it. Her body wanted it, but I needed her to know how much she wanted me. I slipped my hand between our bodies and pressed two fingers into her dripping wet cunt.

She moaned and my cock swelled even more, pressing against the confines of my jeans. I leaned up and took her nipple in my mouth, then rolled the pebble around with my tongue. Her body was so responsive. I barely had to touch her and she was ready.

"Holy fuck, Hugo." She laced her fingers in her hair and pulled.

I hummed as the position thrust her breasts into my mouth. She gasped again. "What do you want, Raella?" I rested back and fucked her with my fingers, hard. I felt the walls of her pussy contract. Her eyes rolled back as her hips rocked against my hand. "Tell me," I urged. I needed to hear it. She wanted me. I knew she did.

She licked her lips, then pressed them into a thin line. She ground her hips against my hand.

I pulled my fingers out. "Tell me what you want." I grabbed her hips and flipped her onto her back, hovering over her so close my breath landed on her face. "I'm right here."

Her cerulean eyes sparkled as she scanned my face. "I . . . " She bit her lip.

"Tell me, Raella." Fuck, she was stubborn. She dug her fingers into my ass and tried to pull me against her needy core, but I held back, refusing to meet her needs until she admitted what she wanted. I leaned close and whispered in her ear, "I know you want my cock in your needy pussy. Tell me. Tell me to fuck you like a good girl."

She inhaled sharply. "I need you, Hugo." Her words were breathless. "P-p-please, fuck me."

Unable to wait a second longer, I sat back on my heels, unbuttoned my pants, and pulled them off. My cock pulsed with the need to be inside her tight, hot pussy. Her wide eyes landed on my raging hard cock as I moved between her legs. I took her hand and wrapped her delicate fingers around the base. Fire ignited inside me.

"I've wanted this from the moment I laid eyes on you." I pressed her knees apart, then ran the head of my cock along the folds of her center. Wetness dripped out. "You're so wet for me," I rasped.

She reached around and dug her nails into my ass. "Please."

I smirked. Now she was needy. But I wanted to enter her slowly. To feel each and every inch of my cock as it spread her cunt until I was seated deep inside. I pressed forward. Sweat beaded on my forehead. Raella's legs squeezed against my hips as I slipped in past midway.

"Fuck. Hugo." She rolled her hips beneath me and pulled my hips.

My name on her delicate lips almost made me come. I had to keep this under control. Once I was seated all the way inside her warm center, my cock throbbed. I took a deep breath, then backed out. This was everything I'd ever wanted. The way she wanted and needed me. The way she gave herself to me. The desire burning in her eyes as she gazed up at me. This was why I needed to find a way for El Ratón to keep her. She was mine. Not his.

I slammed back inside her. I couldn't help it. "Tell me you're mine." I leaned on both my arms and pulled out, my cock screaming for more.

"I'm yours. Fuck, yes. I'm yours." Her nails dug into my ass to the point of drawing blood. "Please, Hugo. Don't stop." Bracing myself, I took both her hands in mine and held them above her head in one hand, then kissed her deeply.

"*Sí*, Tulipán, you're mine," I growled, then held still so the head of my cock was just inside her wet pussy. She wriggled and writhed against me as I sat there. She clenched against me. My cock ached with the need to explode. I tightened my hold on her wrists.

"Be a good girl for me," I said. She whimpered. "Come and scream my name."

"Fuck." She lifted her hips and I slammed into her, hard and fast.

With each thrust, her pussy contracted around me, and she grunted, her orgasm close. A coil began to tighten as I stroked my cock through her hot pussy juices. I wanted to brand this woman with my own tattoo, but I'd have to settle with spilling my cum inside her and branding her that way.

"Come on my cock," I commanded. Sweat rolled down my back as

I kept a tight hold on that coil inside. I grabbed one of her legs and held it up by her head. She gasped, her bright blue eyes wide. Her pussy contracted hard, then started to spasm.

"Oh God! Holy fuck! Hugo!" She pulled at her arms, still clasped above her head in my hand, as she fell apart for me.

My balls contracted as I roared my release, spilling my hot seed inside her. I tried to keep moving, to keep pleasuring her through her orgasm and my own, but it was too much. I'd held back too long. When we were both spent, I released her arms and rested my forehead against hers. I kissed her lips gently.

"There are no words, Raella," I whispered against her lips.

She bit her lower lip and smiled, but didn't respond. She'd given herself to me and I was going to do everything in my power to keep her. Even if I had to defy El Ratón, I wouldn't let him sell her. I couldn't survive without knowing where she was. I pulled my completely satisfied cock out of her, grabbed the sheet, and curled up next to her.

"I don't know what to say, Hugo." She turned and pressed her back up against my front.

I wrapped my arm around her and pulled her body close. It wouldn't take long before I'd want her again if we stayed like this. I couldn't get enough. I'd never loved anyone outside my family, but I couldn't imagine love being more powerful than what I felt right now. "You're so beautiful."

She glanced over her shoulder and smiled. "You said that before." I brushed some hair off her sweaty forehead. "Could you really escape with me?"

My fingers froze in their path and my mouth went dry. Could I? "I don't know. It would be risky." I didn't want to talk about this with her. It'd been stupid of me to suggest it in the first place. I took her breast in my hand and began to massage it. The nipple peaked immediately and her lips parted.

She blinked and shook her head. "Of course it's risky. But is it possible?" She left my hand alone to work at her breast.

Even though we'd just fucked, with me trying to distract her, my cock decided to take notice. The game was a double-edged sword. "Maybe." I ran my tongue along her neck and kissed the curve where her neck met her shoulder.

Before I could make it far, she spun, grabbed both my hands, pushed me onto my back, and straddled me. "Enough, Hugo." Her eyes were a cobalt fire. She held both my arms next to my head and leaned over me, her breasts hanging over my body. God, I wanted to fuck her again.

"Yes, Raella?" I pressed my hips up against her.

She frowned. "I'm trying to talk to you."

"So, talk." I chuckled. The look on her face made her seem like a child who opened a birthday present and it wasn't what she asked for.

"Stop trying to distract me with sex." She pushed out her lower lip, then released my arms to cross hers over her delectable breasts.

Rolling my eyes, I said, "Fine. What were we talking about?"

She shifted her hips as if trying to get more comfortable, but the movement sparked a fire in my cock and the flash in her eyes told me she knew exactly what she'd done. I narrowed my eyes. She bit down on one of her fingers. What a little tease. I had no clue she had it in her.

"Tell me we can escape together, Hugo." Her voice sounded hopeful.

My chest constricted. I gripped her hips. "It was a mistake to suggest it." I dropped my gaze, unable to see the disappointment slice across her face. "My mother's sick and my brother's already shirking on his duties to the cartel. If we both turn up missing . . . " My chest constricted as my breath caught in my throat.

"He'll kill them," she finished for me.

I met her bright blue eyes and gave her a slight nod. Her nude body crashed against mine and she wrapped her thin arms around me. We hugged for what seemed like ages before she let me go, turning to tuck her backside against me and resume the position we'd been in before. Even though an escape wasn't in the cards, I still couldn't let El Ratón sell her.

She'd leave this house over my dead body.

25

Tulipán

The next morning came quickly. I woke with a warm, heavy arm draped over my shoulder, something hard pressed against my back, and a soreness between my legs. It only took a moment for me to remember Hugo and everything that had happened between us. No man had ever made me feel that sexually satisfied before. My two sexual partners had been more focused on what they needed, never stopping to do anything for me. Especially Brian.

My pussy began to tingle. I wedged my arm between my body and Hugo's and gripped his early morning hard-on. I'd seen a lot of penises over the years as a nurse and Hugo's definitely ranked on the larger side of the spectrum. I stroked my hand along his length, then rubbed the bead of precum over the tip.

Hugo whispered next to my ear, "Good morning, Raella." He licked the shell of my ear, sending chills dancing along my backside.

"Hmm," I hummed, then slipped his cock between my legs, pressing the tip against my already wet opening.

"Needy." He pinched my nipple, then gripped my hips and tilted them back to get a better angle for himself.

This was so new. At home, anytime I'd wanted sex or made an

advance, Brian would snap and get mad. If it wasn't his idea, then we didn't have sex. I'd refused his advances for the last five years. Hugo didn't seem bothered that I'd initiated, and that power set my body on fire.

"I need you, Hugo." I pressed my hips back, then grabbed Hugo's ass and pulled him forward until he was buried deep. I rolled my hips. Shockwaves of pleasure shot straight through me as his cock struck just the right spot.

"*Dios*," he cursed. I grinned, rolling my hips again.

Hugo grabbed my hips in an almost bruising grip, pulled his cock out, then held me in place as he slammed back in, again and again. Obviously, he was done letting me control the moment, and I was completely fine with that as my orgasm began to build.

With each thrust of his hips, his cock struck deeper and deeper inside me. The tension coiled higher and higher, like a bomb on countdown. Sweat gathered on my forehead. I was right on the precipice, about to fall into bliss, when someone gasped and a door slammed.

Hugo pulled out of me so fast I felt empty and abandoned, that coil wound so tight with nowhere to go. He tossed the sheet that had fallen off at some point over our naked bodies.

"What are you two doing?" Abuela's incredulous voice filled the silence.

I blinked a few times, trying to clear my sex-addled brain. I ran a hand down my face to find Abuela, jaw hanging open, standing at the foot of the bed. She held my normal breakfast tray and her cleaning bag.

Real life slammed back like a ten-ton truck to my chest. This wasn't some man after my heart. He was one of my captors, who I was impossibly attracted to and had decided to fuck despite it probably being a terrible idea. I covered my breasts with the sheet and twisted to stare, wide-eyed at both of them.

Segundo took in my look and sighed. "El Ratón knows," he said like he just got caught with his hand in the cookie jar. My cookie jar to be exact.

Abuela's creamy, wrinkled face was pale. She didn't appear

Taken, not Destroyed

convinced by Segundo's admission. She left without another word, taking my breakfast with her. Hugo exhaled loudly and threw his arm over his face.

"What are we supposed to do?" My limbs twitched with the urge to run.

He shrugged.

The intimacy was confusing my priorities. I liked it too much, the way he made my body feel with his fingers, mouth, and cock. I could get used to spending my nights in his arms. That was a really bad place for my mind to be, when I needed to focus on my escape.

I threw the covers back and hopped out of bed. "I need to shower."

He grabbed my hand. I stopped and looked down at his bright hazel eyes. He looked like a god lying naked in the bed with a sheet only covering his lower half. The tattoos gave him an edge of danger that spiked my naughty side. El Ratón had been right; I wasn't totally innocent in the things I liked, which he'd proved to me despite my desire to hate everything he did. A shiver rolled down my spine as I cocked my head.

"You *are* mine, Raella." His eyes burned through me.

I pressed my lips together and tried to pull away, but he tightened his hold. What did he want? I'd given him so much already. I bit at my lower lip. "What do you want?"

This might've gone too far. I'd fucked him last night and again this morning. I wanted to stay with him. He made me feel so good. My heart was going to break if I left. Not if, *when* I left. I couldn't stay here no matter how much I wanted to stay with Hugo. My eyes burned. If I broke out into tears, he'd want to know why. I couldn't cry or even allow myself to feel any of this.

After a minute of silence, Hugo seemed to realize I wouldn't, or couldn't, give him whatever answer he wanted, so he released my hand. The look on his face almost cut me in two, but I didn't have it in me to make him feel better when I was practically coming apart at the seams.

"My room's close," he said. "I'll shower too, then we can spend time together. Talk some more."

I nodded. Choking back tears that threatened to fall, I practically ran into the bathroom, relieved to get a little alone time. I refused to break down into tears. If I let them come, they wouldn't stop.

After my shower, I stepped out and wrapped myself in the white, fluffy towel that always hung on the hook nearby. Abuela spoiled me that way. On some strange level, they took care of me like a guest in a castle, not a trapped victim of circumstance. It fucked with one's mind to have certain luxuries, like good food and a shower, yet be denied the freedom to step outside your own door.

"Tulipán?" Camila's familiar voice called from beyond the bathroom door.

I wrapped the towel tighter. "Just a minute," I answered, then rushed into the walk-in closet that still held only a few clean outfits. At least someone stocked it with underwear now. I pulled on a pair of clean shorts and a top, then rushed into the bedroom.

Camila stood near the French doors with a tray of fresh food in her arms. She wore a bright orange sundress, her hair up in a bun at the crown of her head. When she caught sight of me, she lifted the tray. "Hungry?"

I cocked my head, then headed over and took what she offered. I sat on the edge of the bed and started wrapping the chicken and black bean tortillas with my fingers. "Yes. Thank you." I lifted my gaze to her. She stared at me with a sly grin. "What?" I asked through a full mouth.

"I hear Segundo stayed with you last night." She crossed her bangled arms and cocked a hip.

I raised my brow and swallowed the thick lump of food in my mouth. Was she serious? I felt like a teenager being scolded by my mother right now. "And?"

She perched on the bed next to me and turned so her knees brushed mine. "This isn't smart. The two of you."

I dropped my gaze to the partially eaten tray of food and my appetite vanished. Hadn't I just had these same feelings? But to hear them out loud, from someone else, made it so much worse. "It's just sex."

Taken, not Destroyed

Camila glared at me out the tops of her pure-brown eyes and called me on my shit. "It's never just sex, especially with a man like Segundo."

I set the tray on the ground. The scent of food twisted my stomach. "What do you know?" My insides twisted and churned. I'd slept with this man who I hardly knew. I wanted to say I didn't have feelings for him, but it would be a lie. I felt something. Who knew if it was real or just a product of this fucked up situation.

"I know he doesn't just go around fucking women," she said. "He had one woman in his town for many years. The same woman." She tilted her head, raising her sculpted eyebrows.

Hugo wasn't a player, nor was it likely he fucked me just for fun. He'd essentially admitted that in everything he'd said. He'd even considered running away with me. Even though it wasn't possible, he considered it. That meant something. Acid burned in the back of my throat, and I covered my lips.

"He truly wants to keep me." The weight of that admission hit me like a Mack truck. He'd never kept that a secret, but it hadn't hit me until now. I rubbed my head as a wave of dizziness crashed into it.

"*Sí, mi amiga*. Do you want to keep him?"

My jaw dropped, eyes popping open. "No . . . I mean, the sex is great, but no." I shook my head. Even though I'd considered that too, I didn't want her to know. She might renege on our deal.

She pressed her bright red lips into a thin line. "He's a strong leader. He intends to keep you. He could probably protect you."

I reached for my cross and ended up picking at the neckline of my shirt. These two men, they had this strange need to possess me. I'd already come to terms with it. They'd done what they could to ruin me, but I wouldn't let them destroy me. I looked away from her intense stare, unable to respond.

"Now you understand." She played with the ends of my hair. After a brief silence, she said, "Don't forget our plans."

My eyes widened. I turned to her and shook my head quickly. "Never."

Maybe she just wanted to make sure I wasn't getting caught up.

Even though I was definitely getting caught up in Hugo and the sex, I would never forget about her offer. Camila straightened, then clicked her fingernails together.

She studied my face, as if she could see through the skin and bone all the way through to the secrets that lay beyond. The silence grew thick around us. My chest constricted. Was she going to back out? She couldn't! My only route of escape couldn't vanish.

As my heart rate increased, I grasped her hands in a vice-like grip. "I won't let anything, not anything, especially not a man, get in the way of my escape." I straightened my shoulders and puffed up my chest. "I promise, Camila. I'm getting out of this place when you say go."

She blew out a slow breath through pursed lips, then nodded. "Good. It's all set."

I pressed my hands to my cheeks. "It is?"

Her face morphed into the brightest smile I'd seen yet. "You know there's a party in two days, on Saturday?"

"A party on Saturday?" I frowned. Days were a blur. I thought maybe Hugo had mentioned a party. "I guess." I shrugged.

She waved her hand at me. "The day doesn't matter. It's in two days. You'll tell El Ratón you're ill at ten o'clock."

"Ten o'clock," I repeated and nodded. Shit! I wished I could've taken notes.

"Come back here and wait another hour," she continued as if this wasn't completely blowing my mind. "Then go out your balcony doors."

"Wait." I put up my hand. "I don't have a clock, or a watch, or anything to keep time."

Her eyes darted around my room as if she'd never fully absorbed how sparsely it was furnished. She shrugged. "Guess. They'll wait for you." She winked. "I promise."

Sighing, I gestured for her to continue.

"I'll have a pack out there with necessary items for you." She inclined her head toward the balcony. I itched to go look for the pack but kept myself frozen to the spot next to her. I couldn't blow this plan before it started. "Until Saturday at ten, you need to play along with El Ratón and Segundo."

I leaned forward, my breath caught in my chest. "Excuse me?" I squeaked.

"Whatever they ask or want you to do. Do it."

Pressing my cool hand to my sweaty forehead, I nodded. "I can do that." At least I could with Hugo. I wasn't so sure about El Ratón.

"You can," she encouraged. "I know the man who wants to buy you." She stood and ran her hands over the front of her silky dress, then combed her fingers through my hair, bringing her hand around to rest her soft palm on my cheek. "You are strong."

A small smile touched my lips as I stared up at this woman who'd offered to be my salvation. Our eyes met in silence, while her hand rested on the side of my face. I swore for a brief second she was going to lean over and kiss me. But then she left without a word, her bare feet slapping on the marble.

The blood raced through my veins like a greyhound on its course. Camila pushed me to leave, and Hugo pulled me to stay. What did my heart truly want?

26

Segundo

I watched as Camila walked past my door before I went back to Raella's room. The guard had told me she was in there, so I'd decided to let them have some girl time while I got some work done. Which turned out to be the best plan as I found some suspicious activity on one of our accounts that might get me in trouble with El Ratón.

I stepped into Raella's room to find her perched on the edge of her bed, gazing out the window. It seemed like she wasn't really focusing on anything. Something had happened when Abuela walked in on us this morning. I thought some time alone would've helped. My gut clenched.

"Good afternoon," I greeted, then moved around to join her on the bed. I couldn't let him sell her, no matter what, but that required her to cooperate. I thought she'd accepted the situation. I didn't have more time to give her.

She glanced my way. Her lips tipped up and her tongue darted between them. "Segundo."

My cartel name on her lips rankled my nerves. Deep down, I knew it was better that we use those names, but it set my soul on fire to hear my true name on her tongue, especially when I made her come. I threaded my fingers in her silken hair. "Raella."

Her eyes softened as she reached out and slipped her hands beneath my shirt. Her cool fingers on my skin ignited a fire below my beltline. My lips parted on a groan. "Hugo," she whispered as her delicate fingers trailed up my stomach, then pinched my nipples.

Every ounce of blood in my head rushed to my cock. Raella leaned up and grazed her lips against mine. My vision blurred. *Fucking hell!* This woman was going to ruin me. My heart rate spiked as I grabbed her upper arms, about to spin and place her on her back.

She dug her nails into my forearms. "No."

My body went rigid.

Raella slipped my shirt off, then guided me onto my back. I watched as the sun shone in through the window, ringing her head and making her look like an angel as she straddled my lap. My chest tightened. Her blue eyes raked over my body as she bit her lower lip. I threaded my fingers together behind my head.

She gave me a sheepish smile, then unbuttoned my jeans and worked them down, along with my boxers. When her head popped back up, she eyed my cock, while biting the inside of her cheek. It seemed like she was nervous but determined. I wasn't about to stop her.

She gripped my cock at the base and it throbbed. I thrust my hips forward. Her hands were cold. The touch wasn't enough. Too soft. She slipped her hand up my shaft, then back down. I tightened my hands beneath my head as I thrust my hips again.

More. Harder.

She stroked, then rubbed her thumb across the tip in the bead of precum. Sparks of electricity shot down through to my balls. My muscles contracted. *Squeeze harder,* I wanted to tell her. My arms tensed and I squeezed my eyes closed. This was going to kill me.

Then something warm, wet, and textured ran from the base to the tip. My eyes shot open just as she wrapped her hot mouth around my cock and took me inside. *Oh fuck!* I thrust up until I struck the back of her throat. She swallowed.

I couldn't take it anymore. I slipped both hands into her hair, holding her head as I thrust in and out of her delectable mouth. She moaned and my cock swelled. She pulled back. I almost didn't let her. I was wound tight, about to explode, but I released her head.

"Fuck me, Hugo," she said, a line of spittle dripping down her chin.

I couldn't move fast enough. I sat up, almost ripped her shirt off and shoved her shorts down. I pulled her on top, then thrust my ready to erupt cock straight into her dripping cunt. She dropped her head back and swore.

I dug my fingers into her hips and guided her to rotate them with every thrust. That coil inside me twisted, tighter and tighter. "Good girl," I said as she moaned and cursed. "Come on my cock."

She leaned forward and dug her nails into my chest just as I felt her pussy clench around my rock-hard cock. "Holy fuck!"

I slammed up into her and released my load, filling her with my seed. The ecstasy over being allowed inside this woman bore no words, because no words would do it justice. She collapsed on top of me, our sweaty bodies melding into one puddle on top of the sheets. I turned and kissed her temple.

"Will you stay tonight?" Her voice vibrated through both our chests.

I winced. I shouldn't. I needed to investigate that transaction. I wrapped my arms around her, my cock softening inside her warm cunt. The sticky juices were beginning to dribble out onto my leg. "For now."

She lifted her head and looked at me. Her face was flushed. "I'll do whatever you say to keep him from selling me."

My hand froze on the low curve of her back where I'd been caressing her. "What?"

"Whatever you say, Hugo," she clarified, "I'll do it. I don't want him to sell me to someone else."

She kissed me. The kiss started soft, a melding of lips and tongues, but quickly turned into a heated dance, like we wanted to devour each other. I could fuck this woman all night long, but I wasn't a superhero. I pulled back.

"What do you think you'll have to do?" I wasn't even sure yet. But my heart soared to think she trusted me enough to do whatever I thought needed to be done.

I could feel the pounding of her heart against my chest. Her eyes darted around my face. "I'm not sure. But I think if I cooperate, he won't whip me again." Her throat bobbed at the end.

I grabbed her rounded ass and pressed her against my pelvis. Superhero or not, I needed to fuck her again. Hooking a leg around her, I flipped her onto her back and straddled her. "I'll stay as long as I can." I leaned down and teased one nipple with my teeth.

Raella fell asleep after I'd fucked her two more times. I enjoyed the taste of her pussy and skin while I waited for my body to recover. Well into the night, I snuck back to my room to shower and take care of business. By the time the sun's light filtered into my room, I'd managed to sift through all the suspicious activity. It told me one thing. I'd fucked up. Someone had skimmed money from the cartel, and they'd been doing it for way too long.

I pushed back from the desk and rubbed my face. I could probably catch a couple hours of sleep before El Ratón expected me for our morning meeting, but that would likely make me feel worse. Instead, I straightened the files on the desk and logged out of the computer, then made my way down toward the kitchen.

As I approached the kitchen, I could hear Abuela humming. I poured myself a cup of coffee, then leaned against the counter. I watched as she cut fruit and lined the pieces on a tray before her. The display was a beautiful array of colors. The fruit was like her art.

I cleared my throat. "What time do you expect him?"

Abuela startled and spun, acting as if she hadn't heard me clink the coffee cup when I poured the coffee. She placed an arthritic hand over her mouth. "Oh, Segundo, you know how to scare an old lady," she said.

I rolled my eyes. "Stop, *Señora mayor*, you knew I was here."

Her rheumy eyes crinkled at the sides when she smiled. "He'll take breakfast on the patio soon." She continued to work. "Will you join him?"

I tipped my coffee cup and took another sip of the bitter, yet delicious drink. "Yes."

I let my mind wander back to the naked woman in the room next to mine. She'd surprised me yesterday when she wanted to suck my cock. She'd seemed so repulsed when El Ratón tried to get her to do it, I'd thought she had something against it. Her mouth looked so sexy wrapped around my cock. Suddenly there was less room in my jeans.

"*Buenos días*, Segundo." El Ratón's voice and the smell of his cigarette came from behind me. He'd snuck up on me, which was very unusual. I stiffened. That woman distracted me like nothing else in my life. Before her, I would've smelled him a mile away.

"*Buenos días*, El Ratón. Welcome home." I turned and offered him a tight smile. Despite the difficult conversations I needed to have, I meant my words.

"You have business to report," he said as if he knew the answer before the words came out of his mouth. The man never ceased to amaze me on his ability to know things. Whether he just assumed I had something to say or he could read my body language, I'd never know.

"*Sí.*" There was no beating around the bush. He wouldn't tolerate a whole bunch of backstory or excuses.

"*Bien.*" He offered me a cigarette, which I accepted, then led the way out to the stone patio table.

Joining him at the table, I lit the cigarette and took a deep drag. I held the breath in, allowing the nicotine to soak into my system, before exhaling and steeling myself to admit to what I'd found.

"The business owner in San Blas has been skimming money off our imports for at least three years." I gave him the facts and nothing else. "He's been taking more money in the last few months. I caught the discrepancy and followed the trail back."

Biting the inside of my cheek, I took small breaths and met his hard gaze. None of the business owner's actions were my fault. Even though it had taken years for me to discover, the cartel hadn't lost that much income. But El Ratón had high expectations. I never knew how he'd respond to shit like this.

El Ratón ran a hand along his freshly groomed salt-and-pepper beard and pursed his lips. "Send Zero. Tell him to be thorough."

I swallowed and nodded. Zero was one of our most notorious and efficient sicarios. El Ratón didn't kill the man because the cartel needed the money, he killed him on principle. No one stole from or killed an Armas Locas member.

Just then Abuela came and served us plates of piping hot breakfast, along with the tray of fruit she'd been cutting earlier. El Ratón gave her a small, soft smile, the likes I'd only ever seen sent in her direction. We both thanked her for the food, then she tottered off toward the kitchen again.

"Can we speak about Tulipán?" I asked after he'd eaten a little breakfast. Since he'd dropped the previous topic, I could only assume he planned to let me off without a visit to the Black Room. Which allowed my stomach to accept breakfast like the hungry beast it was.

El Ratón lit another cigarette, his dark gaze drilling into my forehead. He placed a slice of mango in his mouth, then licked his fingers. Birds snapped at us in the distance. The ease I'd felt moments ago vanished.

The morning breeze caressed my face, and I blinked slowly. "I've fixed the problem. I ask that you not sell her."

His nostrils flared and lips pulled back in a sneer.

Oh shit! "She's agreed to behave," I blurted, praying he wouldn't pull out a gun and shoot me right there and then.

His eyes bored holes into my skull. Sweat began to pour down my back. "You could direct . . . us . . . " My breath caught in my chest. I wasn't exactly sure what he wanted, but I needed to be with her. The thought of them being alone was a knife in my chest that I couldn't remove. "The two of us . . . whatever you want. She'll behave."

My throat swelled. El Ratón had gone rigid. His cheeks were bright red. He stubbed out his cigarette and blew the smoke my way. I wiped a bead of sweat off my brow before it could drop into my eyes.

We sat in silence, the words dried up in my mouth, while he stared daggers at me. I tried not to shift in my chair or draw too much attention to myself. I looked anywhere else I could, and occasionally glanced at him just to see if he'd speak or if his position had changed. This hadn't been a good idea. I just couldn't let him sell her to someone else.

When he finally spoke, his tone wasn't as harsh as I expected. "Do you feel she's yours?"

I stilled, finally understanding his demeanor. "No, El Ratón. She's yours, as am I." I swallowed. "To command as you please."

He leaned back and propped his ankle on his opposite knee, then gave me a curt nod of dismissal. I shoved the chair back. My feet felt lighter as I turned to leave.

"Segundo," he growled.

I froze at the door and turned to meet those eyes of darkness yet again. "*Sí*, El Ratón?"

"Tonight. The Black Room," he ordered, then waved his hand to send me off.

My stomach dropped through the floor. *Fuck*.

27

Tulipán

When Abuela woke me the next morning with breakfast, Hugo was gone. My body was sore in places I'd never imagined being sore in. The man was insatiable. Camila had said to give them what they wanted. Giving in to Hugo had been easy. The next step was El Ratón. I needed to build up the walls around my psyche to survive that.

I spent the day as I had every other, eating when I was brought food, running through my exercise circuit, then taking a shower after dinner. I stepped out of the shower, toweled off, then pulled on stretch pants and a loose top without a bra underneath. With the party tomorrow, I guessed Hugo had responsibilities and I probably wouldn't see him until then.

I stepped into the bedroom and screamed when I spotted the man in question leaning against the post of my bed. He wore a navy T-shirt with dark-washed jeans. His tattooed arms were crossed over his chest. "Are you ready?"

Pulling my hair up into a ponytail, I frowned. "For?"

He moved faster than I could blink and came to stand six inches in front of me. "Keeping your promise." His hazel eyes shined in the melting daylight as he watched my chest rise and fall heavily.

Tingles rushed around in my pelvis. *How did he do this shit to me?* I pushed at him and turned away. "He wants me n-now?" My cheeks heated.

Hugo pressed up against my back and ran his calloused hands up the front of my shirt. "Now," he whispered against the shell of my ear.

Chills raced down my back and fire ignited in my groin as he reached around and pinched my nipples. I pressed my ass back against his hard-on. "Are you going to fuck me first?" It seemed like a reasonable question, considering.

He dropped his hands and stepped back. "We don't have time." Hugo grasped my hand in his and moved past me.

Ice washed from my head down through my limbs. I tried to maintain a normal gait as I followed a pace behind him through the halls. He led me back to the Black Room. At the morbid looking door, all the small muscles in my body began to shake. My teeth chattered. I pulled my hand out of his and tried really hard not to run the other way. What had I been thinking? Had I not considered El Ratón would bring me back here?

"Why?" My voice was barely a whisper.

Hugo shot me a glance out the side of his eye. He stood rigid with his shoulders straight, chin high. His lips barely moved with his response. "Be a good girl."

He reached out and opened the door of doom. Cold air rushed out and slammed me in the face. I reached for Hugo's hand, but he clasped them behind his back as he stared straight ahead. Segundo was back. I had to remember that. I wiped the sweat from my hands down my pants and gritted my teeth, then followed the cartel's second into the Black Room.

El Ratón sat shirtless in one of the chairs at the center of the spacious room. He watched the two of us approach while sipping on a glass filled with amber liquid. There were two more glasses on the table, both half full. When Segundo and I arrived at the grouping of chairs, El Ratón gestured at the drinks.

My feet froze to the floor. Segundo grabbed the glasses and handed me one. I downed the whole glass in two swallows. The liquid burned a path straight to my stomach. I set the glass back on the table a bit too hard. Both men stared at me. I stared at the ground and chewed on my lip.

The two of them began to have a discussion. Their voices fuzzy, I gazed down at my hands as I fidgeted, interlacing and twiddling my fingers around each other. What had I gotten myself into? I should've asked Segundo for more details. The anticipation was killing me.

"Tulipán," El Ratón's voice beat through my nerves.

My head shot up and I met his endlessly black eyes. "Yes?"

"Clothes off. Both of you," he commanded, then took another sip from his glass. Without missing a beat, Segundo stripped off his shirt. He shot me a glare when I hadn't moved by the time he'd unbuttoned his jeans.

With shaky hands, I pulled my arms into the roomy shirt, then stood huddled there for a moment, basking in the warmth of my own body. El Ratón narrowed his eyes. I pulled my shirt off and tossed it in the pile of Segundo's clothes, followed quickly by my pants and panties.

I tried not to look at him, but my eyes drifted to the man next to me. He was hard even in this situation. Just remembering his cock inside me last night brought warmth and wetness to my pussy. Those feelings were wrong when faced with the evil cartel leader, but I had to hold on to something good.

"Tulipán, lie down. On your back." El Ratón pointed to an open spot on the floor near his chair.

My eyes darted to Segundo, then at the spot on the floor. I wrapped my arms over my breasts and moved on shaking legs. I almost tripped over my own feet. Both of them devoured my body with their eyes. This was so wrong.

When I reached the indicated spot, I dropped to my knees, then lay down on my back. I pulled my legs together and bent my knees up. When I looked back at the others, they were talking in low voices. Segundo glanced from El Ratón to me, then back. His chest rose with a deep inhale, then fell sharply.

He stalked across the black, padded floor and knelt at my feet. He gripped my knees, his hands rougher than normal, then pulled them apart, exposing my nakedness. His eyes hooded as he drank in what he'd been devouring for the past few days.

"Lick her." El Ratón stood at Segundo's shoulder. I about jumped out of my skin; I'd forgotten he was there for a second.

Segundo dropped down and licked me from asshole to clit. Like before, all it took was one touch from him and my whole body was on fire.

"Again," El Ratón ordered, kneeling next to us. "Shove your fingers inside."

Segundo followed his orders without question. He wasn't kind or gentle, but I didn't need it. The fire burned hotter. The coil wound tighter in my core. I ground my pelvis against his face. I lifted my head. "Holy fuck!"

A hand covered my mouth and nose. "Don't speak."

The orgasm I'd about had almost died as I fought to breathe. Segundo paused when El Ratón slammed his cigarette-stained hand on my face. "Don't stop." His voice held no room for argument.

Segundo started his ministrations on my pussy again. El Ratón released my nose, allowing me to take a small breath, then he covered it again. I writhed my hips and shook my head as the pressure in my chest and core built together. My vision began to blur as my pussy contracted and my lungs burned for air.

Fuck! I wanted to scream. I reached out, clawing at El Ratón's arm as the edges of my vision started to go dark. He said something as I climaxed, and my whole body shook uncontrollably. His hand vanished, and I gasped and coughed. The cool air was the best thing I'd ever tasted.

"Put your cock in her mouth. Now."

I heard the order seconds before a hand grabbed my ponytail, lifted me up, and a hard cock was thrust into my slack mouth. Someone pinched my nipple. I groaned, followed shortly by a male groan.

I was still a little dizzy from the lack of oxygen. Someone controlled my head with my ponytail as Segundo fucked my mouth. He

Taken, not Destroyed

drove his cock deep inside, striking the point where I gagged. Tears rolled down my cheeks.

"Stop," El Ratón called out. Like the good soldier Segundo was proving to be, he paused with his cock half in my mouth. "Do you want to fuck her?"

I swallowed. The way he said it, I got the feeling he didn't know what we'd been up to the past couple days. Segundo had said El Ratón knew everything. That he had a way of finding out everything. How could we fuck under his roof without him knowing?

"Yes," Segundo said as if his cock wasn't twitching and throbbing in my mouth.

I circled my tongue around the head. The fucker had kept more secrets than I thought. His jaw flexed, but nothing else changed on his face to show he'd felt what I'd done. I knew I couldn't move, so I kept rolling my tongue around the tip of his cock.

El Ratón downed his drink. "Put your cock in her cunt. Fuck her hard."

Segundo moved like lightning. He pushed me back, mounted me and shoved his raging cock into my sopping pussy. He grunted and met my gaze as he pulled out, then slammed back in. I could almost close my eyes and forget El Ratón watched us, but every few minutes he called out for Segundo not to come.

Segundo would pause and the coil would relax. I began to dry out a bit too. When he slowed in his thrusts, El Ratón ordered him to "Fuck harder and faster." Segundo grimaced as our skin chafed. My pussy burned, and not a good burn. When I thought my entire female parts were going to shrivel up and die, El Ratón ordered Segundo to come.

Segundo grabbed one of my legs and pulled it up, bracing his shaky arms next to my head. His face was covered with sweat that dripped down onto mine. He thrust into me, his angle deeper, harder than before. He grimaced and grunted, then I felt his cock swell and pump as he released into me.

"Oh fuck," Segundo cursed.

Seconds after his orgasm began, I heard the air sing, then the whip landed on Segundo's back in a loud crack. His hazel eyes darkened as he met my gaze. My mouth dropped open. The whip landed a total of three times.

"Get out," El Ratón ordered.

Segundo pulled out, then stood. He offered me a hand, which I reached for. El Ratón smacked Segundo's arm.

"No. You. She stays."

Segundo's eyes widened as he stared down at me curled on the ground with his cum leaking out of my pussy. El Ratón growled when Segundo hesitated. So he left. Naked, with bloody, fresh whip marks on his back, he left, leaving me to face this hellish man alone.

Again.

I turned and started to crawl away from him, working my way to a stand. He grabbed my leg and pulled me face down on the ground. He straddled me, then reached a hand around and gripped the front of my neck. His hand was like a block against my windpipe.

"You belong to me," he growled in my ear. "Not him." He pulled me so my back was flush with his chest. The hair that ran across the top tickled and brought goosebumps to the surface.

I opened my mouth but couldn't speak. I nodded.

He released me, then pushed my chest against the ground, so hard the air left like a deflated balloon. His weight left me for a minute, but I'd learned not to move until told. He came back and straddled me again. His bare skin hot against mine. I dropped my forehead against the ground and squeezed my thighs together.

Oh God, please no.

He slipped his hand between my legs, gathered some of the moisture from Segundo's release, and spread it around, even over my ass. He grabbed my ponytail.

"Never forget, Tulipán." Then he shoved his cock in my ass.

I felt like I was being ripped in half, the burn was so much worse than the silver tail. When he finished, he yanked me to my feet and pulled me to the door by my hair. Pink-tinged cum ran down my legs.

El Ratón looked at the man who stood guard on the other side. "Return her," he ordered, then brushed past us both, leaving me standing with my chin up despite everything that'd just happened.

Taken, not Destroyed

They'd ruined me. But I refused to let them destroy me.

28

Tulipán

The next evening, I stood in front of the floor-length mirror in my bathroom and eyed the dress Abuela had left for me that afternoon. It was shorter than the dresses I usually chose for myself. My body had changed since I'd come here. My legs were thinner, and I'd lost weight through my hip area. I was still curvy, but I'd lost at least two sizes.

The dress had red sequins with a V-neck that dipped halfway to my navel and was so tight my breasts were squashed together. There was a ring of dark purple bruising around my neck to compliment the flashy dress. By now my core and butthole had stopped aching, but I swore I could see the ghost of bruising trailing up my inner thighs. A sign for all to see of the horrors I'd faced last night at the hands of that animal.

"I don't like that dress on you." I jolted and glanced up, catching Segundo's hazel eyes in the mirror. He'd snuck in, which didn't surprise me. I'd been in a daze since waking this morning. I couldn't believe today was the day.

I shrugged my shoulders. "We have no choice in the matter."

Segundo's gaze dropped and his eyes narrowed, but he said nothing. I ran a finger across my neck. His eyes followed. I pressed my lips together and wondered if he'd ask or even comment on what happened to either of us last night. Or would he do exactly as he'd done since I'd arrived—nothing. I gritted my teeth, then pushed my hair back behind my shoulders. I turned toward him.

"We have a party to get to, correct?" I asked, running my hands down my front, as if the dress could possibly be wrinkled.

He nodded, but didn't remove his gaze from my neck. The man had no right to be angry, or feel anything, about the bruises on my neck. What El Ratón had done to my neck wasn't even the worst of it, but I was done with them, both of them. I brushed past him and made my way to the door I couldn't open. I stood stock-still in front of it, waiting with my back to him. My attendance at this party was inevitable, even if I would've preferred to be left alone here to escape while they all partied in ignorance.

Too soon, I felt his presence behind me. The heat from his body sent chills along my spine. Segundo reached around my side and placed his hand on the door. He absolutely did not have to be that close to open the door. He pressed his lips to my ear, his breath hot against my lobe.

"Don't be angry with me." He nipped at my ear, then ran his tongue over the little hurt. "I only do what I must to keep you here . . . with me."

The last two words were said as if he hadn't meant to speak them aloud. I closed my eyes against the sudden heat that roiled in my gut. The man could turn me on with barely a touch, even when I didn't want him to. I fisted my hand at my side as I tried to fight against the need building in my core.

Segundo chuckled, then moved away to open the door.

Once in the hallway, he led me down the front stairs. As we walked along in silence, I remembered I needed to have a reason to leave early from the party. I pressed my hand to my pelvis. It was a stupid thought, but I had to try.

"Segundo?" I tried to make my voice sound pathetic.

He glanced at me but didn't give me his full attention.

"Do you think El Ratón will let me leave early? I . . . " I glanced away, my gut clenching. "I have cramps."

Segundo stopped and turned, a deep crease between his brows. I could tell he didn't believe me for one second. "Abuela said you don't bleed." I thanked God for my IUD, the last thing a forty-year-old woman needed was a pregnancy, but he was right that I no longer got my period. It sucked that I didn't truly have that excuse.

I grabbed his arm, sinking my nails into the flesh. My throat tightening, I tried again. "Please. I . . . I don't want to be here tonight." He had to understand, especially after what I'd gone through for him last night. "Last night was . . . hard."

His face softened for a second, then returned to the mask he wore outside my bedroom. He nodded curtly, then turned to resume our walk. I released his arm. The blood rushed through my ears as I followed a few steps behind him with a prayer on my heart. This was my only hope. If I didn't get out of this party by ten, at the absolute latest, I was doomed to this hell.

We paused outside an open door to a room that, by my calculations, sat beneath the Black Room along the back of the house. He rested his hand on the small of my back and stood uncomfortably close.

"Were you a good girl after I left?" It sounded like he almost choked on the words "good girl."

I stepped away. "Fuck you," I said, then moved into the room.

Once inside, my feet planted as my eyes took in the so-called party. The room was the size of my bedroom and bathroom put together. The wall opposite the door had two arches that were open to the backyard and looked to lead into a garden with dim lighting. People milled about out there with drinks in hand. Inside there were couches covered with naked people in various stages of orgies. Some people were dressed, holding drinks, watching as if they couldn't decide whether to join in or run away.

"What the fuck is this?" I asked, hoping Segundo would hear, because I wasn't sure he had followed me inside.

He gently squeezed my upper arm, then turned my body away from the debauchery. "El Ratón's party."

I covered my mouth and let Segundo guide me to a bar that lined

Taken, not Destroyed

the same wall we'd entered through. He leaned on the bar, nodded at the man behind it. "Two whiskeys."

"*Sí*, Segundo." The man was dressed in a casual T-shirt and when he turned to grab the glasses, I saw the butt of a handgun sticking out of his jeans.

Well fuck.

After I'd downed two glasses of the burning liquid and had a tiny buzz going, I turned back to the ridiculous party with a third glass in hand. I wasn't sure three whiskeys was a good idea before I did whatever Camila had planned for my escape, but I needed to get through this party first. One thing at a time. I put the cool glass against my lips and tipped it up.

"You've been hiding this evening," a husky, male voice said from nearby.

I coughed and spit the alcohol back into the glass at the sound of El Ratón's growling voice. I glanced to the side as Segundo darted away, the wimp. El Ratón stood, wearing a red button-down, half open, exposing his tattooed chest. His posture appeared relaxed, but still held the commanding presence he had every time I met him.

Swallowing hard, I shook my head. "No," I managed to say. "Not hiding. I just don't feel well." I rested my hand on my stomach. His eyes darted to the glass in my hand. My cheeks heated and I hung my head. *Fuck.*

His strong fingers gripped my chin and lifted. I met his dark eyes and his jaw flexed. He glanced over my shoulder. "Segundo, go arrange the deal with Señor Garcia."

I glanced over my shoulder. Segundo had been hovering. I wanted to cry out and thank him for trying, but neither of us could defy El Ratón and, as much as I wanted to hate Segundo for that, I knew it was true. El Ratón grabbed my chin again and yanked my head just as I lost sight of Segundo out on the patio.

I shivered under his touch and bit my lower lip. He leaned in until his body was almost flush with mine. I felt his breath, hot against my ear. My entire body stiffened. It took everything in my power not to run, follow Segundo out those doors, into the night. But my escape was waiting upstairs. I couldn't be stupid now. I locked my knees.

"You see the man with the white tie?" He pulled back slightly and inclined his head.

Widening my eyes, I turned and searched the room. There weren't many people who still had clothes on. I found a bald, heavy-set man, who sat on one of the couches. He wore only a white tie while the only remaining hair God had gifted him covered his entire chest and stomach like an ape. A woman knelt between his legs and looked to be sucking his dick, but I couldn't tell past his belly. He had his fingers in the pussies of two other women, who were both moaning as if they were staring in a porn. My stomach turned. Whiskey and stomach acid threatened to come up.

I turned back to El Ratón and nodded, my jaw clenched.

His lips tipped up. "He offered me ten thousand US dollars for you."

My glass shattered on the floor. I hugged my middle and my lower jaw shook. The sound barely made a dent in the noise around us. I shook my head, glanced at White Tie, then back at El Ratón. He couldn't, not now.

El Ratón slipped his finger under the strap of my dress and pulled it aside until he exposed most of the Armas Locas tattoo and my breast. He stepped in front of me, then trailed his finger down my chest over the tattoo. "You. Belong. To. Me. Don't you, Tulipán?"

My nipples peaked and I wanted to beat my traitorous body for responding to his touch, but it always did what it wanted no matter what my mind thought. "Sí, El Ratón," I said, keeping my gaze on his toes.

I stood there, my whole body shaking, while he traced the lines of my tattoo, occasionally touching my nipple. I kept my head bowed, unable to look anywhere else. If he sold me to that man right now all my plans were shit. I'd never get out of this horrible house or country. Never get back home to see my sister or my kids again. All those other women would be just as fucked as me. We'd all be lost to the chains of evil that started with the Armas Locas cartel.

Taken, not Destroyed

He pinched my nipple. "Segundo will return you to your room." He gripped my chin and forced my head up. I probably had purple marks on my chin to match my neck now. "Never forget who you belong to."

"*S-s-sí*, El Ratón," I said. If he caught me trying to escape, he'd kill me, there was no doubt in my mind. There was too much riding on my escape. Too many people. I couldn't get caught.

Despite the chill in the air, sweat gathered under my arms and between my breasts. He continued to hold my chin; his grip tightened. The scent of cigarettes and alcohol accosted my nose. His eyes darkened for a moment, then he ripped his hand away and turned to stalk across the room.

I glanced down at the broken glass near my feet, the liquid spread between the shards. That glass was doomed for the trash, but not me. I could go on. I'd gather up my pieces and put them back together. And I'd be stronger for it. Like the glass, they'd shattered me, but I'd put myself back together and get the fuck out of here. Tonight.

Segundo arrived at my side. He glanced down at the mess, then looked up at the bartender and shouted at him to come clean it up. Without another word, he took my arm and guided me toward the door. "El Ratón says you don't feel well," he said as if we hadn't spoken about it earlier.

"What time is it?" My heart rate picked up.

Frowning, Segundo paused in the hall outside the party room and pulled his phone out of his pocket. He flashed the screen at me.

9:50

My mouth went dry. Right on time. I reached for his face, then stopped short, glancing at the party. "Will he notice . . . " I swallowed hard. Thinking fast, I had to give him a reason for my question. "If you're gone for . . . " I shrugged and tilted my head.

His eyes widened and he turned, his steps swifter than before. Camila said ten, but she also said her guys would wait. He likely had less time. This was the last time we'd have together.

29

Tulipán

Back at my door, Hugo punched in the code three times before the door unlocked. He pushed me into the pitch-black room, grabbed my arms and spun me, crowding me against the door. He hooked my leg over his hip and wasted no time shoving my panties to the side so his fingers could part my folds.

My jaw dropped open on a moan as I ground my hips against him.

"So wet, *mi tulipán*," he whispered, then slammed his mouth against mine. At the same time, he shoved two fingers deep inside my pussy.

The kiss was all tongue, teeth, and lips. We were desperate for each other. He circled my needy clit, then curled his fingers pulling an orgasm from me. I dropped my head back and cursed. "Hugo."

Even though it was dark, I saw the devilish smile that flashed across his face, moments before he bent down and picked me up. He tossed me on the bed, then stripped off his pants. My eyes feasted on his cock. This was the last time I'd see him, have him inside me. Something inside me broke, and I was glad he couldn't see my face as a single tear escaped down my cheek.

Hugo shoved my dress up and pulled my panties down. He bent over and licked me, then drove inside me in one thrust. I grabbed his solid ass and dug my nails in. My insides ignited as he began to thrust, slowly at first, then faster. It felt like my world was unraveling at the seams as this man fucked me harder and harder.

"Raella," he grunted. "I love fucking you."

I almost stopped breathing when the word "love" left his mouth. He grabbed my leg and pulled it up. My pussy contracted. Sweat gathered on my forehead. Hugo grabbed my ponytail and pulled the band out. As it fell loose, he threaded his fingers in my sweaty hair. I tilted my hips in time with his thrusts.

He leaned in, grabbed my hips, and flipped us so I was on top. "I want to watch you come all over my cock." Then he took hold of my hips, lifted them up and continued to slam into me. Oh, so deep.

"I'm going to . . . " I grabbed his forearms as my core clenched down. "Oh God, Hugo. Fuck!" My entire body spasmed with the orgasm.

He thrusted a couple more times, then roared his release as his cock spilled into me. I fell forward and rested my cheek on his chest while his dick softened inside me. I needed these last few moments with him. He meant something to me, even if it wasn't true love, it was something. He'd been the light in this darkness. Something good for me and, on some level, I was going to miss him.

He cupped my face and pulled me up for a soft kiss. He pulled out, whispering, "I should go back."

I rolled off and pulled my dress down, then watched as Hugo dressed. He paused at the door and glanced back at me. I didn't know what he could see through the darkness. "You're mine," he said, then left the room.

I stared at the closed door until I knew I had to get ready to go. I refused to allow my heart to break for that man. I changed into a black, long-sleeved shirt and black leggings, pulled my hair into a ponytail, then stood in front of the balcony door. I had no way of knowing how long that had taken. It could've been minutes or an hour. I touched the handle, looked behind me, then clasped my hands together.

This was insane. She'd given me a timetable without any way to tell time. *Fuck it.* I reached up and took the door handle in my hand.

This had been locked since the day I'd gotten here. I might've worked myself into a frenzy for nothing. My heart slammed against my chest as I squeezed the handle and turned.

The door opened freely, as if it had decided one day to work like it was supposed to. I slid one foot past the threshold and held my breath, waiting for the shot to fire. When nothing happened, I stepped out.

The air was tepid and fresh. It ran over my skin like a lover's caress. Music sounded to my left. I turned and saw lights from the house behind some tall trees. I could hear voices, and I bit my lip. That was probably the people from El Ratón's party. I swallowed, scanning my surroundings.

The balcony was a half oval and had access from my room and the one next to me. The railing was made of some thick, overly priced stone and fit with the gaudy design of the whole monstrosity of a house. The backpack Camila left for me sat in the corner to my right.

I took a step back, glanced over my shoulder at the room that had been my prison. The party was a complication. Camila knew about the party when she chose now for me to escape, so I couldn't let it deter me. I grabbed the backpack. Inside, I found a pair of sneakers and socks, a rope, a knife, a syringe labeled Fentanyl, two bottles of water, some protein bars, and a box of hair dye.

I held up the hair dye and frowned at the female with black hair on the front. It wasn't my color, but I didn't really have time to argue the point. I shoved it back inside, then dug through the other pockets. In the front pocket there was a note:

Tulip,

Use the rope to get off the balcony. Remember that there will be a guard at the gate. The man from El Mil will be on the path to the left once you are out. He will be in a blue car. He uses my name. Change your hair color once you arrive at the apartment. See you tomorrow.

C

The English wasn't perfect, but I understood all the same. I pulled out the rope. One end had a loop already tied off and there were knots tied at regular intervals all the way to the bottom. I zipped up the backpack and pulled it on, then walked to the edge of the balcony and looked over.

Just below sat a stone table and some chairs with red pads on them. I walked around to the right, closer to the wall. The patio turned into grass, which was higher but farther from the partygoers.

I wrapped the rope around the edge of the stone balcony, then threaded it through the loop already tied on one end. I threw the rest of the rope off the side and pulled tight. When I looked down, the rope stopped quite aways from the ground.

From here, that looked like a neck-breaking jump. How could Camila give me a rope that was way too short? Wasn't this her plan? Didn't she know how far I had to climb? My leg bounced as I glanced at the room, then down the rope toward freedom.

Fuck this!

I stomped back into the prison room, stripped the white flat sheet off and returned to the balcony. I pulled the rope back up, tied the sheet to the bottom and tossed it back over. The sheet landed in a puddle against the green grass. I wanted to celebrate that small victory, but I hadn't even done the hard part.

Stepping up to the ledge, I wiped my sweaty palms on my pants and climbed up onto the railing. It was wide enough I could sit and look over the side, which is what I did. I stared down, trying to figure out how I was going to maneuver my body over the side, and onto this rope. I couldn't fall. There was no surviving a fall. Even if I lived, El Ratón would kill me.

With the rope next to me, I gripped it just above one of the knots and flipped onto my stomach. My legs hung off the edge and my heart thundered in my chest. I took ten quick breaths, slid to the side so the rope was between my legs and found a knot with my feet. Once I felt remotely stable, I began to inch down the rope.

As I made my way down, I tried to use the wall for support, but I couldn't take my hands off the rope long enough to find any comfort in the wall. All it did was rub up against my shoulder each time the rope swung that way. My hands burned and my arms and legs shook.

The wind blew and it tossed me around like a pendulum. My stomach was tied in a million knots and the whiskey was burning a hole in it. I glanced down and the ground wavered. I closed my eyes and rested my sweaty forehead against the rope.

"One. Two. Three," I whispered to slow my rapid breathing. There was no need to hyperventilate and pass out.

Once I'd calmed down, I opened my eyes again and looked at my situation. The knots were gone. I'd come to the point where it was me and the sheet. I loved this sheet. Hugo and I'd just had sex on it, but I wasn't sure it would save me if I couldn't hold on to it. The only thing I could do was brace myself on the wall and walk down it, while holding on for dear life.

When I felt stable with my feet against the wall and the remaining rope between my legs, I began to walk down the wall, moving my hands down the sheet along with my feet. I was so focused on the task that, before I knew it, the stone table was in my peripheral vision. I glanced down, then set my foot on the ground.

My foot sank into the cushy grass. The blades tickled my feet. I dropped to my belly and smelled the dirt. I tried to hug the ground. My heart soared. I'd made it. I was out of that room. Those four yellow walls were gone. I flipped over and stared up at the star-flecked navy sky as the blood rushed behind my ears.

Nothing in my life had ever felt so good as this small taste of freedom. Of being able to step out into the world on my own free will without someone saying no. This. This was what I had to live for. Being my own woman. Being the creator of my life and directing it.

I sat up and dug through the backpack, pulling out the sneakers and socks and tugging them on. I pressed my back against the side of the house and, one last time, peeked around it at the party. I couldn't see anyone, only light and distant sounds of music and voices. I closed my eyes. Kissing my fingers, I tossed it over my shoulder for Hugo, wherever he was in that party.

I edged along the side until I came up to the front corner of the house. The front yard was almost as vast as the back. The pebbled drive that led from the front gate made a circle with a beautiful fountain in the center. Currently the drive was lined on both sides with cars with a small path down the middle just wide enough for a car. There were a few trees and bushes but, for the most part, the yard was an open expanse of grass.

My only saving grace was the small slice of moon and no lights except those from the house. Even out in the open, I'd be hard to see in my dark clothing. There was a dim glow coming from the front of the house, so I dropped to my knees and crawled forward.

As I moved out from behind the house, my arms shook. There were many dark windows and arches in the house. Anyone could've been sitting there watching. El Ratón's security measures could've been top notch for all I knew.

I was completely exposed before I saw that the light came from the porch. Two men stood on the stoop, facing each other. They each had a rifle slung on their backs and were smoking cigarettes. Neither seemed to notice me, but I couldn't stay here. Sweat rolled down my back and sides.

I glanced forward, then back. They hadn't changed position and were still talking with each other. I crouched down, crossed myself, then darted across the lawn toward the line of cars. When I reached them, I dove onto my front and skidded to a stop next to a black SUV.

I heard a shout behind me. *Oh shit!*

I glanced back. Both men stood at the edge of the stoop. They'd been joined by a third. Someone I recognized wholeheartedly. He'd just had his cock buried inside me. Electricity shot through my body. He couldn't catch me. That would be worse than El Ratón. I could handle El Ratón killing me, but not Hugo.

Fuck, fuck, fuck.

With my body plastered to the ground, I looked around for somewhere to go. Under the SUV was too obvious. I slid backward, slipped the backpack off, then squeezed under a sports car just as a gun rattled off a few shots. I turned my face to the side, pulled the backpack in front of me, and closed my eyes. The gravel dug into my body, but none of it mattered. If they found me, I was dead.

More than dead. If that was possible.

God, please. Save me. Watch over me. When I get home, I'll find the others. I won't let them suffer any longer. I swear it.

My eyes burned. Two more bursts of gunfire rattled off as I huddled beneath the sports car, praying they wouldn't find me. That I'd have the chance to escape this nightmare.

30

Tulipán

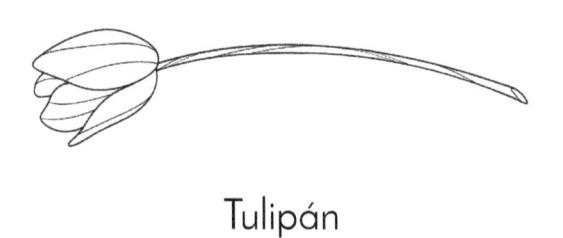

It could've been minutes or hours before I peeked around my backpack. The silence in the yard was loud. It pressed against my ears like I was in a vacuum. There were four small crescents branded into both my palms, which I could barely feel. I pushed the pack aside and glanced around the front tire back toward the house.

The yard was empty, save for a fresh line of divots between here and there. I slid out from beneath the car and froze. There was a divot right next to the passenger front tire. They'd come so close to me. Had he walked right past me? Had he sensed me?

I glanced back the way I'd come. My throat tightening, my breaths coming harder and harder. Was this a mistake? Should I go back? I slapped myself in the forehead.

No! Stop it!

I rubbed my hands over my face. This wasn't the time to get sidetracked. There was no way back. I'd barely made it down. I didn't have the strength to climb back up, even if I wanted to, which I didn't. I pressed up to hands and knees and gritted my teeth as I shoved every doubt out of my mind. There would be no more questioning or backtracking. The only way was forward.

I squeezed between the SUV and sports car, then checked to make sure no one was coming down the lane. Satisfied the coast was clear, I got to my feet, and crouched down, then darted across the lane to the line of cars on the other side. Bullets and eyes were less likely to reach me through two lines of cars.

Once I was hidden behind the second row of cars, I paused with my back against a flashy, yellow Mustang. I wanted to sit and rest again, but I was wasting time. I glanced over my shoulder. The guards were barely visible through the cars. This need to see Hugo again bugged me. It made me want to rip my hair out. Maybe the farther I got from the house, the less I'd feel that way. I shook my head and looked toward the entrance of the grounds. I still had to get past the guard at the gate.

"Get a grip," I chastised myself.

Staying low, I moved as quickly as I could, ignoring the ache in my chest. I'd appreciate the irony in this someday. Maybe. I wanted my freedom, yet I desired to stay with a man who wanted to own me. It was fucked up, on so many levels.

At the end of the line of cars, the front gate came into view. It wasn't anything spectacular like in the movies, just a plain metal gate big enough to admit one car. It didn't even look electronic, though I couldn't be sure.

I pulled off the backpack and laid on my stomach behind the last car. I squinted as hard as I could, but still couldn't see the guard. A gust of wind struck my face, bringing with it the scent of pot. He was there, somewhere.

I dug through the bag and grabbed the Fentanyl syringe. It was a standard syringe and held just over ten milliliters of fluid. I bit the inside of my lip. This was enough to stop a man's breathing. He'd die. I rolled the syringe around in my hand and stared as the liquid sloshed around inside.

My throat tightened and my eyes burned as tears pressed against them. This wasn't what nurses did. They saved people's lives; they didn't end them. Even though I couldn't think of another way to get past a cartel guard who likely had a gun, could I truly kill him? Did I really have that in me?

Footsteps sounded in the gravel, and I glanced up. A man dressed in all black appeared on the other side of the gate. I couldn't see anything specific about him in the darkness other than the fact that he was there, which meant he'd see me if I moved right now. He'd also hear my shoes on the gravel. I took off the shoes and tucked them back in the backpack but left the socks on to protect my feet. Even with the socks on, the jagged rocks would be difficult to move on quickly without pain, but I'd have to endure it.

Just then I heard noise behind me, then saw a beam of light flash across the drive. I glanced back just in time to see a car moving toward me. They likely wouldn't see me here, but I couldn't take any chances. I rolled onto my back and slipped under the car next to me. I craned my neck and watched as the dark figure of the guard opened the gate inward to let the car out.

This was my chance; I couldn't think about it anymore. The gate was open, the guard was distracted. It was now or never.

I rolled out from under the car and tightened my fist around the syringe. I ran as fast and as quietly as I could toward the guard once his back turned. Sharp edges of rock dug into my feet. They screamed bloody murder at me. My hand shook. My steps began to slow, but I gritted my teeth and pushed on. This was my life, and I had to do this if I wanted to survive.

When I reached the guard, he was still looking away, but he must've sensed me because he started to turn my way. I was running so fast, it was hard to slow down. I dug my feet into the gravel, then slid to my butt, scraping my free hand on the ground and tearing the skin.

The guard turned and caught sight of me. His eyes widened as he moved for the gun at his waist.

"Fuck," I blurted. I jumped up and moved for him.

He stepped back and gripped his gun.

I slid to the ground at his feet. His hand wrapped around the gun. I looked right at the curve of his leg. He had a major artery and vein there. I reached up and jabbed the needle in and depressed the flange, emptying the syringe.

He pulled the gun out and managed to point it my way, seconds before it fell slack in his hand and dropped to the gravel at my side. His eyes dulled and he drooped to the side, falling over with a crunch against the gravel.

My mouth hung open as I stared into his vacant eyes. "Oh God, please forgive me."

I checked his pulse. Nothing.

I covered my mouth, holding back the vomit, and looked around, resisting the urge to scream for help. But no one could come. I'd done this so I could get away. I needed to go. But I'd killed him. He was dead. What kind of a person did that make me?

My fingers shook as I closed his eyes and said a prayer. I sat for a minute longer to collect myself, then pulled on the sneakers again. I stood next to him staring at his unmoving body. The pallor of his face was all wrong. Everything about this was all wrong. I grabbed the gun and stuffed it in my bag, then left the guard lying where he'd fallen.

The drive ended at a road that disappeared around a corner to the left. Camila had said to follow the road and someone would meet me in a blue car. The road was surrounded by thick foliage, and there was no visible path into the dense forest area. Hugo had said it was thirty kilometers to the nearest village, but I'd need to go around the property since my room faced the back. I glanced through the gate, back at the place that'd been my prison for who knew how long, then looked back down the road. I could only trust myself.

I backtracked a bit until I found an opening in the tree line, then stepped off the road into the dense, mountainous forest. Seconds after I stepped off the road, headlights flashed across my feet. I was rooted to the ground and my whole body went rigid.

Holy shit!

Had Camila's men driven up here to find me? Or was this one of El Ratón's guys coming to the party? Would they catch me? Tires crunched on gravel as a car moved closer, then slowed to a stop just on the other side of the tree line. My legs ached to run and my stomach churned with acid.

Two car doors slammed, then a deep male voice spoke, "Did you see her?"

"No," a second responded. It was male also, his voice higher, possibly younger than the first.

Their feet crunched across the gravel. "She was here. Go look," the first ordered.

My heart rate spiked. I covered my mouth as I crouched down and looked around desperately for a place to hide. They couldn't find me. Not when I was seconds away from freedom. I'd done everything to get away, even killed someone.

I spotted a dense bush behind me and just to my left. With every muscle in my body tensed, I stepped one foot, then the next. I paused between each step to listen and make sure they hadn't heard. When I reached the bush, I stopped in front of it, put my hands together, and tried to spread the branches to make room for myself.

"Did you hear that?" The young male's voice came through the darkness.

Sweat ran down my face. I froze like a statue and closed my eye as the drop threatened to land in my eye.

"No," Older Guy answered. "She left. Grab the syringe."

Feet crunched across gravel, then a car door slammed. I started to breathe normally, but didn't dare move yet. Then a sharp *whap* cut through the darkness, followed by more footsteps and a car door. I wasn't completely sure, but that might've been a silenced gunshot.

The headlights sliced through the darkness again, then the car retreated back down the road from the way it'd come. I pulled my hands out of the bush. The tops were lined with little bleeding cuts. Squinting, I leaned in and saw the bush had tiny thorns on every branch.

Shaking my head, I pushed through the undergrowth until I found the wall that surrounded El Ratón's fortress. Thirty kilometers couldn't be that far. I had some protein bars, water, and a gun.

I'd survive. I had to.

31

Segundo

I'd gone back to the party after leaving Raella and been in a dream state ever since. I couldn't get her out of my head. She'd gotten so wet for me and come so hard. We'd both been so desperate for each other. Ever since I'd left her, all I wanted to do was go back and sink into her arms.

"Segundo." Trigo, our head guard, stood at my shoulder with a severe look on his face.

Turning my back on the orgy-filled room, I raised a brow. It didn't help that this party was all about sex. I generally bowed out and helped with security, but El Ratón was feeling extra controlling tonight and wanted me here, as if the whipping and the mindfuck last night weren't enough of a punishment.

"What, Trigo?" The short, stocky guard looked distressed, but I wasn't really in the mood to deal with anyone else's issues.

"Someone killed Jugar." His voice was just loud enough to be heard over the music.

My muscles tensed and all thoughts of Tulipán vanished as this new problem presented itself. Someone had killed our front gate guard. I gripped his shirt in my fist and pulled him close. "Who killed him?" I

Taken, not Destroyed

asked through clenched teeth. As head of security, he should know that answer.

He ducked his head. His gaze dropping to his feet. "I don't know. We focused security on the party and the garden." He squirmed as I tightened my grip on his shirt. "We only noticed when Jugar didn't check in on the radio."

"Fuck," I said and released Trigo's shirt. Hurting this man wouldn't fix our current problem. We needed to figure this shit out before the asshole got too far away. No one killed an Armas Locas and lived.

"How?" It didn't matter, but it might give me a clue to who'd done it.

Trigo's eyes darted around the room. "Shot. In the neck."

I raked my fingers through my hair. That was the usual assassination style for the Zapas. Why would they kill our gate guard, then disappear? My gaze darted from the security head to El Ratón, then back. El Ratón was sitting on the couches with El Mil, each had a tumbler of whiskey and a cigarette. Both men had their gazes pinned on a group of naked women writhing around in pleasure at their feet.

Gripping Trigo's upper arm, I turned and strode from the room with him in toe. In the hall, I turned to him. "When did he check in last?"

Trigo pinched the bridge of his nose. "Eleven."

I glanced at my phone and slapped the man upside his head. "It's after one."

"I know," he moaned, shaking his head. "I . . . I stepped out."

My chest constricted. How were we going to figure out who'd done this? They had a huge head start. If it was the Zapas, we'd never find them. They could be in the house. My eyes widened. "Go check on Tulipán's door. Make sure it's locked."

"Yes, sir." Trigo disappeared down the hall. No one could get beyond that door without the code. She was safe inside that room.

I straightened my shoulders, then headed toward the front entrance. Once I knew Raella was safe in her room, the investigation would provide a good distraction from El Ratón's party. I strode up behind the two guards at the front door. They'd had a scare earlier in the evening, but the three of us had investigated and determined it'd just been a rabbit bolting across the front lawn. If one of the Zapas had made it through the front gate, hopefully these two would've seen them.

When I stepped up behind the men, they both went rigid, as if they sensed my presence. Naranja was on the right; he turned his head slightly, then relaxed. "Segundo." His eyes narrowed when they took in my expression. "Did we miss something earlier?"

"Have you seen anything else suspicious?" I demanded.

Both men made eye contact, then frowned. Taking charge of the situation, Naranja said, "No."

"Has anyone left?"

"Just Señor," Naranja responded.

I rubbed my forehead. "No one else?"

"No, Segundo," they each said in turn.

I frowned and stared out the doors into the darkness. Señor was an old man, close to eighty. A legacy in the cartel. He wasn't involved in business anymore. He only came to El Ratón's parties to drink, watch, and sometimes left with a woman. Half the time I was surprised to see him.

I rubbed my chin. "Did he leave alone?"

"*Sí*," Naranja said.

Just then Trigo appeared at the top of the stairs. I tapped my foot as I waited for him to descend. He stopped next to me, breathless. "The door's locked. I checked the rest of the floor also. It's empty."

Warmth filled my chest. I wanted to shout my joy, but knew these men wouldn't understand. She meant nothing to them. "Good," I replied, deadpan. I glanced at the three security men in turn. Where did we go from here? They all looked to me. "Where's the body?"

"I put a new man at the gate." Trigo cleared his throat. "I have two others burying him." He inclined his head toward the backyard.

Growling, I squeezed my eyes shut and pressed my fingers into them. This was going to be a long fucking night, and I hadn't been getting enough sleep lately. I had nothing to go on other than a dead body that Trigo decided to bury. Not that I was a cop or anything. El Ratón was going to fucking kill someone, or multiple someones.

Taken, not Destroyed

I dropped my hands, then met the gazes of each guard in turn. "No one leaves."

"*Sí*, Segundo." Both front door guards straightened and gave me curt nods.

Turning my attention to Trigo, I said, "We have a lot of work to do. But first, we need to break the news to El Ratón."

The man pushed his shoulders back, slid a glance to me, then nodded. El Ratón would likely punish Trigo for his failure. But first, we needed to find out who killed our man and either kill him ourselves or send a sicario after him.

The sun peeked over the horizon as I let the last of the party guests leave. My body ached, I stank, and I just needed to go back to my room for a shower and a few hours of sleep. I glanced at Trigo. I could tell the man had the same thoughts as me. Who the fuck had killed Jugar? And why?

Abuela burst into the nearly empty party room, out of breath and in a complete state of panic. I rushed to her side and took her elbow. "Calm, Abuela. Come sit." I led her to the nearest couch.

As we walked, she stopped and shook her head. "No. Segundo. No." She turned to face me and grabbed my arms with her amazingly strong, arthritic hands.

I looked down at her wrinkled face and wondered what could cause such distress in this kind woman. And after the night I'd just had, I prayed it was something only a woman found stressful.

I pried her hands from my arms, then cupped them between mine. "What distresses you so?"

"She's gone," Abuela shrieked. She shook her hands free, then placed them on my face. "Segundo. Her room . . . it's empty. The sheets . . . " She dropped her hands and turned away.

My jaw dropped and I shook my head in an attempt to register her words. "No." I shook my head faster. "She can't be."

"*Sí.*" She grabbed my hands.

"But he . . . " My mind went blank for a moment while I tried to pull my shit together. I shook her hands off, turning away. Trigo had said her door was locked. But had he gone inside? I dug my fingers through my hair. I couldn't remember. I spun and met Abuela's eyes. "Are you sure?"

She exhaled heavily and her face pinched in a look that tore my heart from my chest.

My world came crashing down. Last night started making sense. The mind-blowing sex, initiated by her. The dead front gate guard. Somehow Raella had found an escape. How she'd gotten her hands on a gun was beyond me, but that was a problem for later. Bile coated the back of my throat.

On swift legs, I ran through the house. I slipped and missed a couple steps before I reached the second-floor landing. Blood rushed through my veins and pounded inside my head. After all the things I'd done to save her, to keep her here and prevent El Ratón from selling her. My heart burned.

After everything I'd risked for her. She'd still escaped. She'd given herself to me, told me she was mine, then ran when I had my back turned. We'd talked about leaving, but that was together. I didn't think she'd go without me. I thought she understood why it had to be like this.

When I reached the door to her room, I pounded the code into the keypad and the light blinked red.

"Fuck." I punched the wall, then took a breath and started over—slower.

The light blinked green, and the door unlocked. I turned the handle and shoved it open so hard it slammed against the wall. My breath came in sharp, heavy gasps as I took in her bed, stripped of its covers and sheets. Someone took a spoon and dug it through my ribs in search of my heart.

"Raella," I yelled. My voice seemed to echo through the empty space.

I ran to the bathroom, flipped on the light. Empty. The spoon pushed farther. The closet was empty too. I rushed back into the main

Taken, not Destroyed

room and spotted the French doors standing wide open. The spoon dug in and carved my heart out. Somehow, she'd gotten them open. I stepped out onto the balcony and scanned it.

My gaze caught on a rope tied around the railing next to the wall. My empty chest contracted, and I gasped for breath. I rushed over and grabbed the rope, pulling it up. The rope came, along with the sheet from her bed. I threw my head back and yelled.

How could she have left me? Why? Why would she go? Who helped her?

"Now we know who killed the guard," El Ratón said from behind me. His voice held no satisfaction, no anger, it was just a statement of fact. This wasn't emotional for him. But it sure as fuck was for me.

"Yes, we do." I squeezed the rope, my nails digging into the heel of my palm so hard I broke the skin. She'd chosen, then rejected me. I'd find her. "Who helped her?"

"Assign Zumbido," he said, then left.

Not only had she left me after everything that'd happened between us, now I had to send a sicario after her. The woman that my heart had claimed as its own. I dropped to my knees and yelled her name into the distance, hoping she'd hear me, wherever she was, and know I was coming for her.

Epilogue

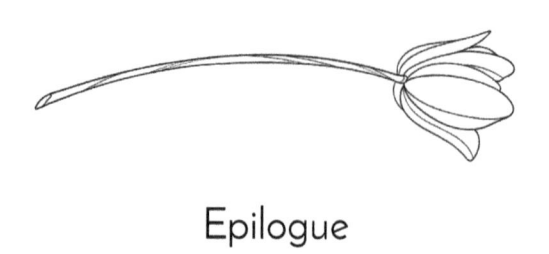

Many days and miles later, an old man dropped me off at a US Consulate in Mazatlán. The woman at the front desk had taken one look at me, heard my explanation, then shown me into this conference room. She'd given me a sandwich and water, then left.

That'd seemed like hours ago. The food and water were long gone. The door was locked from the outside. I was back to being a prisoner, just in a smaller room without a bed or a bathroom. There was only a table and four hard plastic chairs, one of which I sat on. My butt had gone numb quite a while ago. My exhaustion was real, so I folded my arms on the table and rested my head on them.

The forest had been denser than I'd expected. There were bushes that grew below the tree line that had been hard to push through. I had cuts and bruises everywhere. My clothes were torn. I'd tripped over things in the dark, run so hard my heart beat out of my chest, fallen over my own two feet multiple times, and taken a path, then looked back to find that I'd chosen the hard way more times than I could count. I'd stopped long enough to nap when I couldn't keep my eyes open any longer, but never more than a few hours. I feared they would find me; I'd feared it so much that I heard them in the wind.

Taken, not Destroyed

The Armas Locas were everywhere. In the bushes, the trees, behind me, beneath the water. I'd gotten to the point that my mind played tricks on me. When the old man stopped to pick me up, I swore he was Hugo at first. I fingered the space on my neck where my cross used to hang and pinched my eyes closed. He still had it. I'd never get it back.

A man cleared his throat. I tipped my head to the side and cracked one eye open.

"Mrs. Waters says you claim to be an American citizen," the man said, doubt lining each word that came out of his mouth.

Wincing, I straightened and rubbed my neck. "Yes." My voice cracked. "Why do you say claim?"

The bespectacled, blond-haired man narrowed a pair of dull blue eyes at me. "You have no identification. You come in here looking like a pauper with a backpack, a gun, and a few other items." He raised his bushy brows.

I'd forgotten about the gun. I buried my face in my hands. "I'm sorry. I was kidnapped . . . "

"Okay, miss, let's begin with a few basics." He pushed a sheet of paper across the table along with a pen. "Fill this out. I'll see if I can help you." The man brushed his hands down his pin-striped, navy suit and looked down his nose at me, then turned and left the room. The door closed with a snap.

My mouth hung open as I stared at the closed door. He hadn't even showed a lick of emotion when I'd told him I'd been kidnapped. It was like women showed up here after escaping a kidnapping every day. I picked up the pen and glanced down at the piece of paper. It asked for basic information: name, date of birth, address, etc. I filled it out, then pounded on the door.

"Hey! Is anyone out there?" I pounded. "I have to pee, and I'm done filling this out," I yelled. How could they treat someone who'd been through what I'd been through like this? I wiggled the knob, then pounded some more. I didn't want to be locked up again.

The door opened abruptly. I jumped back. The thin, blond man in the navy suit stood there with an armed guard at his back. As if I was some kind of violent threat. The blond held out his hand for the paper, then inclined his head toward the guard. "Officer Maddox will escort you to the bathroom."

After relieving myself, I returned to find Navy Suit in the room with a manila folder resting on the plain table. He stood with his hands clasped behind his back, facing me. "Please have a seat," he said, then gestured toward the chair I'd occupied earlier.

His demeanor seemed different from before, but I couldn't place why. I bit my lower lip and moved slowly toward the offered chair, not taking my eyes off Navy Suit. The food I'd eaten not long ago rolled around in my belly.

"My name is Agent Pike." He opened the folder, removed a piece of paper, which he slid across the table to me. "Please tell me who you are."

Unable to pull my gaze from him, I frowned. Was he joking? "I filled out your form."

He dropped his gaze to the paper, then crossed his arms. My jaw shook. Something was seriously off here.

I pulled the paper closer. It wasn't a normal, thin piece of paper, but thicker like cardstock. There was an official seal in the top right corner. Large fancy letters lined the top that marked it as a death certificate. I opened my mouth.

The room suddenly became hot and really quiet. Why had Agent Pike given me a death certificate? I glanced up. He cocked his head. His arms were still crossed and he tapped two of his fingers against his opposite arm. I swallowed against a thickness in my throat, then looked back at the form.

I read the name. It was my name. Raella Marie Calgary. This death certificate belonged to me.

A cold sweat broke out on my neck and bile coated the back of my throat. Someone was clearly playing a joke on me. It couldn't be real. This couldn't be a real death certificate. I wasn't dead. I pinched my arm, then squeezed my eyes shut.

When I opened them, the name hadn't changed. It was my name. I shook my head. I met Agent Pike's pale blue eyes. "But I'm not dead."

I hadn't lived through that nightmare with El Ratón just to get here and not find salvation. I hadn't survived for days on my own in the mountains with barely anything to eat or drink, only to find out that my family all thought I was dead. That everyone who cared about me, and I cared about, had given up on me because they were told I'd died. If everyone thought I was dead, then they could leave me in this country. They couldn't do that. They were meant to get me out of here and away from the Armas Locas cartel.

"I can see *you're* not dead, miss," Agent Pike said with a very professional, almost dismissive, attitude. "But Raella Marie Calgary has been declared dead by a medical examiner."

My heart shattered and I dropped my head to the table with a *thunk*, then shook it. "No, no, no, no."

My eyes burned. I'd held off crying until this point. I'd lived through so much. Endured everything Hugo and El Ratón had put me through. These people were all I had to get me home and away from that cartel. If I stayed in Mexico, they would surely find me. I couldn't hide anywhere in this country. If either of them found me, they'd either kill me or lock me back in that box. I couldn't go back there. I sniffed, wiped my eyes, and gritted my teeth. I couldn't fall apart.

I sat up straight, fisted my hands and met the agent's pale blue eyes. "You *have* to help me, Agent Pike. You just *have* to believe me when I say that I'm Raella Calgary."

His features softened slightly. He pulled out the chair across from me and sat. "Look, miss . . . "

"Rae, please." I picked up the death certificate. Pain sliced through me as I thought about what my family must be going through thinking I was dead. What had happened to Misti and my kids? "I'm not dead. This isn't me. I mean, it's my name, but it's not . . . " I closed my eyes and crushed the paper against my head. How could I explain this to him?

The chair screeched against the floor. The door opened, men exchanged words, then the chair screeched again. I didn't move. I needed to figure out a way to make this go away. How did a person convince another person that they existed without any real proof?

"Why don't you tell me what happened?" Agent Pike said.

I peeked around the paper. He'd set a bottle of water in front of me. I took a sip of the cool liquid. "I came here with my husband, Brian, on a vacation." Pike nodded. "I went on an excursion . . . "

"Alone?"

I winced at his tone. "Yes. But there were two others with me." I gasped and covered my mouth. "They took us all." I stood up. "Oh God." My heart rate kicked up.

"Miss?" His voice sounded impatient.

I glanced at him with wide eyes. "They tricked you, somehow the Armas Locas tricked you into thinking I was dead."

Agent Pike straightened and tilted his head to the side. "Armas Locas?"

I turned my back on him and clasped my hands near my heart. "Yes. They took us, but they kept me. They sold the others." None of it was right. I shouldn't have to try so hard to get this man to believe me. He should be able to see the trauma I'd been through and want to help. I looked like a disaster walking. He should want to help save those other women too.

I spun to face him, threading my fingers in my hair. "What about the others? I'm here, but they're . . . " I dug my nails in. "Lost."

He pressed his lips into a thin line, then asked, "What others?" His face screwed up. I knew I wasn't making any sense, but my mind was a mess.

Dropping my arms to my sides and fisting my hands, I paced the small room. All the promises I'd made to myself and the women I'd shared that small, dark room with came rushing back. "I wasn't the only one. We have to find them. What if"—I continued to pace since three steps were all it took to cross the room— "what if they're worse off than I was?" I couldn't imagine what worse looked like, but I knew it existed. I'd been kept clean, fed, and been given clothes. Worse definitely existed.

Agent Pike said something, but I couldn't register his words as the enormity of everything that'd happened to me and those other women crashed down around me. My mind raced with all the "what ifs." Each one of those women had a name, a face, a story, loved ones who missed them.

It had to stop. All of it. The stealing of women. The selling of women. All of it. The Armas Locas had to be stopped. I had to find the others. But first, I had to get the fuck out of Mexico.

My feet froze to the ground, and I twisted to meet Agent Pike's pale blue eyes. The way forward solidified in my mind. I couldn't let this man stand in my way.

"Let me make a video call, Agent Pike. I can prove to you I am who I say."

Afterword

Thank you for taking the time to read my book. I appreciate you! Please leave a review. . . they are like spankings, pleasure and pain all rolled into one 😈

www.linktr.ee.com/svonauthor

If you enjoyed Raella's adventure:
Stay tuned for her next one in. . .
Mission of Destruction coming in Spring of 2025

Afterword

Now that Raella is back in the U.S., she has to find the will to keep all the promises she made to herself, to the women who were locked in that horrible room with her and to God, Himself. Even though she's plagued with memories of El Ratón, how he changed her, and Hugo, the only man who showed her true pleasure, she can't let that stop her from pushing forward.

Join Raella in her struggle to find a way to destroy the Armas Locas sex trafficking efforts. How can one woman make a difference in the actions of such a large, powerful organization? What if she has to go back to Mexico, will she survive such a feat? Will she ever find the women who so easily touched her heart?

Can she truly break the chains of evil that still have a grip on her and accept what the past has done to her mentally and physically?

I don't take writing about sex trafficking or ending it lightly. It is truly a horror on the existence of our civilization. United Nations Office on Drugs and Crime (UNODC) considers human trafficking a modern-day form of slavery. This is a REAL thing and a REAL problem. People are victimized daily for money, labor, sex, and other horrific things. Sexual exploitation is the most common form of human trafficking. Most sex trafficking actually takes place close to home and is often parents or relatives trafficking a family member (or loaning them out for sexual acts).

No country is exempt.

Every person is at risk.

We are all targets.

Be aware of the threat. You can help the cause to destroy the evil that lurks. Awareness is the first element in fighting this evil. There are organizations in your community that help fight this crime where you can help as well, either through donations or your time. Operation Underground Railroad is an international organization that I love. They do their part to help worldwide to end the suffering.

OUR link: https://ourrescue.org/

You can visit the UNODC for further education https://www.unodc.org/unodc/en/human-trafficking/human-trafficking.html

Thank you for reading my book and letting me get on my high horse about trafficking.

Please follow me on my socials and join my newsletter to keep up to date with my next release.

www.linktr.ee.com/svonauthor

Author note